Dedicated to Our World
You and Me & Everything
and Everyone we love...

Cover Art by Alecia Jensen ~ aleciajensen.com

IJustKnowLove360°

Jon & Kati

...from the cold

ISBN: 978-0-9892032-2-7

"Some men see things as they are and say, why....
I dream things that never were and say, why not."
~ JFK

"I have a dream."
~ MLK Jr.

"When the power of love overcomes the love of power,
the world will know peace."
~ Jimi

"Imagine"
~ JL

"It's better to know some of the questions
than all of the answers."

~ James Thurber

"Eventually, all things merge into one,
and a river runs through it."

~ Norman McLean

"If you obey all the rules, you miss all the fun."
~ **Katharine Hepburn**

"It's fun to attempt what's considered impossible!"
~ **Walt Disney**

1

Emergency

5:45 a.m., Boulder County, Colorado

Am I dreaming? Yes, it was a dream. "God, I'm glad it wasn't real," Jon whispered to himself. He took deep breaths to slow his racing heart. Rolling to his back, he looked up at the panel of four windows set high into the thick adobe walls. It was verging daybreak. Shades of grey walls were becoming the salmon colored paint of his bedroom. The cool air was strong with the smell of wet sage from a light, predawn spring rain. A few faint, sweet bird songs drifted in through the opened windows.

Jon watched the tree tops silhouetted against the first hint of sky. First light of dawn erased the tension from his waking dream, eased the loneliness he still felt every morning without her next to him. Each moment brought change. The sunrise turned the edges of a cloud to a fiery mixture of blood orange that became the exact color of his room. He felt like he was floating in the sunrise. A slight breeze rang ceramic chimes. With eyes transfixed on the cloud, he let his mind wander into the dark space beyond, visualizing stars, galaxies, and other worlds. I wonder if we'll ever get a chance to really understand what exists way out there, he thought.

Digging in the pillows, he found the remote and started the day moving with piano music by Peter Kater and some songs by his favorite vocal artists. He noticed the message light blinking on his cell phone as he headed to the bathroom. Twenty minutes later, after his morning core exercises and a shower, Jon was sipping a cappuccino and pulling on black Nikes to go running as he touched the message buttons on his phone.

"Jon," came his old girl friend's acerbic voice. "I'm calling because you haven't come to get the rest of your things that you have in my basement, as you agreed. So, I'm putting your stuff out in the street. You might want to get it before it starts raining. Thank you."

Thank you— Jon was thinking about his books getting soggy in the street at his ex-girlfriend's house when his cell hummed in his hand and Ian's name came up. "Hey there big boy," Jon said happily. "You on your way out here?"

"I'm in the air now, actually."

"Are you comin' in that shamrock covered hot air balloon or some new fancy jet?"

"Funny you should say that, Dr. Wolff. The engines we're testing on this jet have almost no toxic emissions. I'll tell you about our design breakthrough when I get there."

"Green jet engines," Jon chuckled, "but then Ireland has some green, huh?"

"Amusing."

"You're amazing, bud. Are you roughing it, or do you have naked women serving you champagne and organic strawberries?"

"Neither, unfortunately. I'm just listening to Josh Groban songs and testing my Italian language skills."

"Aren't you cool? Let me know when you're running for president of the world, and I'll vote for you, man."

"Don't hold your breath," Ian replied. "Presidents are just pawns; you know that buddy. Listen, something serious is happening, but I can't talk about it over this connection."

"Uh oh, the problem too serious to talk about…. Sounds like a wonderful 'gift' you're bringing with you, Ian."

"Believe me, I wish I didn't need to bring this particular one to you. And I also have another, more mundane, problem. My right leg hurts when I play golf. I need you to fix it."

"On the house, I suppose."

"You're the best."

"Complimentary champagne."

"I'm getting into Rocky Mountain Metro about 10:30," Ian said with a smile in his voice. "I'll call you, and we can meet at that new hotel in town for lunch. The St. Julien, is it?"

"Sounds good."

"Jonny, I'm going to make you an offer to come work with me that you can't refuse."

"I'll meet you after my run, and I'll be thinking about how to get ten times the amount you'll offer, Jon said, laughing. Oh, and remember, pawns can capture kings...."

*   *   *   *

Between sips of strong coffee, Keppe crushed the perfect little wild strawberries against the roof of her mouth with her tongue. She loved the cool and damp Paris spring morning. Streaks of sun were cutting through the mist over the city, illuminating a window pane here, a puddle of rain water, there. The soft breeze lifted her hair a little. She felt the charge just from knowing her lover was near, watching her, painting her.

Keppe's thoughts wandered from her Montmartre perch. The breaking sky reminded her of the poem her lover had written for her. She unfolded the note he had penned and read it once again.

Wind-storm brought it,
the swirling haze
of snowflakes white, all alike,
all separate in dazzling
beauty.

Heart-storm found it,
the still, sweet clarity
in your graceful ways, each
unique as every snowflake
falling—

I, Jonathan, claimed it,
the vision, far-seeing through
passion's blaze, teaching
love for Keppe and love
for human-kind, forever and
forever—

Kati rested the pen on her manuscript and rolled to her stomach, stretching with her toes pointed and fingers reaching. She arched her lower back, pushing her pubic bone down hard into the bed, holding the pressure and letting a deep breath out slowly. Then she sat up and looked over what she'd just written. Hmm, the poem sounds a little archaic, she thought. Not what I intended

to write at all. I wonder where that came from? Then
she shrugged. I'll just have to revise it later. I've got to
get going. I want to go for a skate before packing.

Maybe I should drive to Denver today to get my
things and say a final goodbye to everyone at the Trauma
Center. I'll miss the Monday traffic and have more time
to dance tomorrow at the university. I can't believe my
fuckin' dream is comin' true. I'm going to dance in the
San Francisco Ballet…shit!

*   *   *   *

Jon cut off the main trail to run along the path by the
riverside. Layers of wet leaves, a spectrum of greens,
canopied the creek which was illuminated in the low
angle of early light. The crashing sounds from the rush of
the full creek powered by the snow melt were laced with
pungent, wet earth smells. All this pure free energy in the
cool morning air made running feel effortless.

Perfect, he thought, flashing back to some of the
dreaded running workouts he and Ian used to push
through when they were on the Princeton basketball team
together…so many hours on the court in that gym…. I
haven't even touched a basketball in over a month….

Maybe we'll go shoot hoops while we talk today, Jon
thought. It's funny, even though we're as close as
brothers, it seems like Ian has a hidden and almost
inaccessible dark side because of his family's history. I
could've never dreamed of meeting someone, hell,
anyone even really existing like him.

Jon thought back to the summer he'd spent at Ian's family estates in Ireland. Images of their high castles drifted into his mind, and he considered their incredible history of fighting for survival and what they considered right. He'd lost that crazy bet he'd made with Ian and had been compelled to take Ian's family's summer camp "training" which Ian had termed "a family ritual for centuries."

The camp had turned out to be a cram course on survival and combat skill. Their particular brand of radical conditioning under stress had almost killed him, Jon remembered. But because of that training, he now ran through wild terrain like his namesake animal, the wolf.

*   *   *   *

Kati loved to rollerblade on the creek bike path. Her strokes had the authority of a professional skater. She let her fingers fly into some pink blossoms dangling over the trail edge...expecting nothing...then smelled a faint sweetness.... She was going to miss this place. God, what a morning! Listening to her iPod, she was dancing, skating...outright performing this morning, with every movement a graceful expression of beauty.

Her mom had been an ice dancer when Kati was growing up and was now in theatre as a Shakespearean actress. Kati had begun skating and walking at the same time. Then she had progressed into gymnastics, and the gymnastics had morphed into ballet. Ballet had become her passion. But her dad, a San Francisco fire chief, had

insisted she train for a real job. So, she'd become a
trauma nurse and surgical assistant. Most of the trauma
center doctors marveled at her "one-step-ahead thinking."
Now her mind and body were flowing free and clear, like
the water dancing down the rocks in Boulder Creek on
this perfect morning….

*　*　*　*

Slanting sun highlighted the insect life on the surface
of a slow swirling side pool along the main creek. Two
ducks caught relief in the slower water. One was all
shades of brown while the other was feathered in colors.
The multi-colored one had an iridescent green band
around its neck. Was that one a male and the other a
female? Jon wondered. He laughed to himself. After all
the years of biology I don't know duck…but now I want
to find out.

A huge flat of the creek which looked like a slow
moving plate of gel, poured between rock funnels. He
thought of the orchard hole off the rushing Montana
stream where an island formed around a horseshoe bend
behind his grandparents' cabin. Floating across the cold
deep water on the log raft to the small island that
bordered the faster water, Jon and his sister had spent
hours playing in dream worlds on family vacations.

Jon remembered how he'd loved waking up on the
screened cabin porch that fronted the creek which came
down from the Beartooth Range. He held the memory of
getting up early, grabbing a fly rod by the porch door and

heading down the stoned steps to wade in the water and catch trout for grandma's breakfast, dearly in his mind. No wonder he loved running this creek trail so much.... Jon could still hear his sister's voice when she was about five years old. *"Jonny, there's jaguars on this island, so we have to make a hiding place right now. Jonny, start getting rocks."*

To his sister's favorite opening gambit Jon would almost always rejoin, *"How many jaguars are there, Sis?"*

" At least thirty-five," she'd always say. *"The boat's sunk , Jonny. It's at the bottom. Let's dig before the jaguars come...."*

* * * *

In a Swiss castle near the Austrian border, a darkly tanned European man spoke in a soft bass voice to a runner carefully following Dr. Wolff. The European man tracked the progress of his runner and of Dr. Wolff on a paper thin flat screen that was cradled in a frame made to match his ornate antique desk. His operative's voice com link was as clear as if they were talking across the desk face to face, rather than from the Alps to the Colorado Rockies. His operative wore sunglasses that contained various technologies, including a thermal sensor so that he could follow Jon when he was out of sight.

The operative slid his finger along the right ear piece of his sunglasses to fine tune his volume reception and the heat signature reading. "If he stays to his usual route we'll have him in the map zone in about two minutes, so I'll be activating the read in about ninety seconds on your signal, Mars."

The European man was called Marcus by the rich and famous clients who came to the exclusive Swiss spa far below his private domain at the top of the castle. He was known as Mars, however, in the world to which he had been born. A spectacular Swiss alpine view from his desk was barely visible through thick walls of glass that were darkened at the moment. Mars intently watched the systems formatted on his cutting-edge monitor. He hated the queasy feeling in his gut. Mars was used to being confident and in control as he watched his operations unfold exactly as his plans dictated. But this whole OP had been pieced together too quickly and was relying on unperfected open-space technology. He just needed to obtain Dr. Wolff's mind signatures before Ian arrived to protect him. With the signatures, he would have the advantage.

The European man's family had been in this battle with Ian's for over a thousand years, and now he was truly the one who could win with this science and this strategy. Stop worrying. Just get this, he thought, as he listened to his tech begin the countdown for powering up the brain read sequence... six... five... four... three... two... one....

*   *   *   *

Crossing a steel and wood bridge, Jon left the bike

path. He turned onto his usual shortcut along a small bricked street towards a foothills trail. As he headed uphill, the sun warmed his back and made the mountains ahead vibrant. His mind wandered back to the Montana cabin when one morning their donkey, ironically named John, had leaned against the outhouse door pinning Mom in there until she started screaming for help.

Ahead, at the street corner, Jon saw a young mother standing next to her baby stroller. The blond woman was in the process of shrugging off her back pack. She had a golden retriever tethered to the stroller, and her navy dress and heavy clogs made her look like she'd stepped right out of old Holland. She looks almost too… tulips… tulips…. Jon felt his mind lose focus as he entered the invisible field of analytical energy waiting for him.

Two men and a woman operative wore European caps with hidden modifications that protected them from the strong energy they were projecting. However, the golden retriever took the jolt to her brain and with a squealing bark bolted into the street, taking the tethered carriage and child for an unexpected ride towards disaster.

*   *   *   *

Jon's brain was so fogged that it took him a moment to realize what was happening. When the import of what he was seeing hit him, he turned his morning run into a sprint. He flew by the mother who was chasing the carriage with clopping footsteps while frantically yelling at her dog, Sisty, to halt. Jon saw the truck approaching out of the corner of his peripheral vision. The surreal scene he'd never remember was about to fill with screeching tires, barking and screams.

Coming down the steep, short hill street she drove every morning, the business woman couldn't see what was coming towards the intersection because of a high, brick fence surrounding her property. Her left hand held the wheel as she sent a text message with her phone in her right.

As she entered the signal zone, she looked up, mentally disoriented. Seeing a man chasing a baby carriage almost didn't register in her mind…but, when it did, her over-reaction to brake quickly resulted in her new, slick leather soled high heel pump slipping off the corner of the brake and jamming into the gas pedal. With a scream of terror from the unexpected acceleration, the driver jerked her wheel to the right hard enough to flip her SUV.

Just as Jon pushed the carriage, the truck hit him so hard that he was thrown off his feet and into the corner stop sign. The impact ripped open his neck and shoulder. Jon's fading stare caught the SUV license plate with its floral, *RESPECT LIFE,* inscription.

As Kati coasted into Jon's brain read zone, she got a full view of Jon's flying impact with the street sign. At first she was mesmerized by the scene—slowed by the brain read forces in her head, but then she was off like a sprinting hockey skater. Pushing her speed, Kati jumped from the bike path over a low stone fence. She bounded from the sidewalk into the street. She was just on the edge of control. She raced low, with her fingertips a fraction above the ground, desperately trying to reach the man with the blood spurting neck wound.

* * * *

Jon's trailing runner operative calmly described the accident as he transmitted a video to Mars in Switzerland. Mars was keeping the brain recording team in place, collecting data that might still be useful. But now he knew time was short with so many people on the scene. Plus, it looked like Dr. Wolff was dying in the street.

"Terminate operation. Everyone go home," Mars voiced and typed to confirm the order. The three operatives cleared the area. Each would be out of the country in a few hours. The runner headed for his locked mountain bike, while a man and woman closed and locked their custom Zero Halliburton cases loaded with technology developed to control human thought. They drove away in a dark green Mercedes sedan.

Mars leaned back with his eyes closed. He rested his head against the soft leather chair cushion, breathing deeply to calm his tension. Then he started to focus on what his next step should be….

* * * *

Kati swerved slightly, tossing her cell phone in the

carriage next to the mother comforting her child. "Call 911," she yelled. Out of the corner of her eye she saw people running to help the woman trapped in the SUV. The woman with the baby carriage seemed ridiculously slow in picking up the phone. "Get emergency medical here," Kati screamed. "Hurry!" She heard the mother talking to the emergency operator as she compressed Jon's carotid artery and probed to assess the vessel damage. Having slowed the carotid blood loss, Kati began checking the man's pulse and looking for other life threatening injury.

The victim's pulse was weakening. His breath was ragged. Kati was struggling. She wasn't herself. She was babbling. "Hang on, buddy. The baby's okay. You did it. Now you stay alive, you hear me?" She could feel tears running down her cheeks.

Suddenly, it was like clouds of pressure lifted off her as she found the femoral fracture with her free hand. Kati straddled the unconscious man, pushing her knee into his femoral tear. Holding her left hand deep into his neck to stop carotid blood loss, Kati worked with her right hand to stabilize the overall neck and shoulder wound. The sirens were closing in as the victim's pulse staggered. Kati was a great technician, but now the artist in her came to the fore, and she let all her life go to him...something she'd never thought of doing before. She visualized a vibrant yellow energy force flowing from her to the victim.

Then the EMT was running toward her. Blood covered, she looked directly into the EMT's eyes and said, "I'm a trauma specialist. Load us together. It's critical…. Get us to surgery now."

It wasn't far to the hospital, and the tech worked with Kati during the ride. When they rolled into emergency surgery, two male nurses lifted her off Jon as a team of minds and hands went to work. The head emergency surgeon cursed as he realized whose life was in his hands. Jon was a friend and colleague of his. He had often sent his recovering patients to Jon for treatment and rehabilitation.

*   *   *   *

Ian sat gazing out across the billowing cloud tops backed by endless cobalt blue. A pure pristine view, he thought. Feeling a pang of guilt for wanting to bring Jon into his dangerous world, Ian picked up the phone to dial Jon's cell.

The EMT was about to place Jon's phone and keys into a property bag to leave with the hospital when the phone rang. He hesitated, then answered, "Hello, this is Ernest."

"Hello Ernest, my name is Ian. I'm calling Dr. Jon Wolff, but I may have…."

"Excuse me please," Ernest interrupted. "Dr. Wolff has been seriously injured. I am the ambulance EMT and…."

"Ernest," Ian broke in, pushing through the

sickening wave he felt rising from his gut. "I'm Dr. Wolff's best friend and, basically, his family. Please tell me where he is and what you know about his condition."

Ernest told him everything he knew.

* * * *

Ian filled in his pilot and head of security, Nicholas, on the situation regarding Jon. Nicholas was the Swönk family's ("Swönk" being pronounced as "Swan" with the "k" silent) number one guardian. Before Nicholas had left his job as a British Secret Service agent, he had been respectfully known as 006½ among the agency and British establishment insiders who knew of his professional exploits. Ian usually called him St. Nick, as he liked having a 006½ Santa by his side.

Nicholas was busily arranging medical and security resources for Dr. Wolff as Ian placed his next call. "Hello, this is Ian Swönk. I'm calling to speak with your director of medical services or the highest ranking administrator available at this moment, please. This is an emergency and could be a security issue for your facility."

"Please hold, sir, while I link you to the director's personal assistant."

Ian felt his plane descending into Denver as he spoke briefly with Maria, the director's assistant. She put him through to Doctor Joseph, the director. "Thank you for taking my call immediately, Dr. Joseph. My close friend, Dr. Jon Wolff is in your emergency surgical center with critical injuries from an accident that occurred less than an hour ago."

"I've met Jon. I'm sorry to hear of this," replied Joseph.

"I will arrive at Rocky Mountain Metro Airport in about twenty minutes. Please excuse my directness, but I feel it's important for you to understand the overall situation."

"My assistant told me there might be a security risk to our hospital?"

"Dr. Joseph, Jon Wolff is very important to me. I am a wealthy man, and I have the resources to build your whole hospital every week for many years. My company, EET, is involved with scientific and medically associated projects which are so sensitive that the stakes have become dangerous. Jon's injury might not be accidental. I would appreciate it if you would allow us to put the best possible private security and medical resources in place for Jon's care and protection. I'm arriving with someone who will coordinate security for Dr. Wolff, and he will keep you apprised of any signs of concern for your hospital."

"You're asking me to operate outside of my usual protocols," said Dr. Joseph.

"Let me assure you, Dr. Joseph, the benefits of working directly with me will be well worth the risk. I'm on my way to the hospital now to make sure Dr. Wolff gets the best possible care and protection."

"I'll meet with you when you arrive," said Dr. Joseph.

As his plane taxied into a reserved private hanger, Ian called Ireland on a secure link to reach Bjen, his younger sister by exactly one year to the day.

"Hi, little brother." Bjen had called Ian her little brother since she was two years old.

"I've just arrived in Colorado, and Jon has been in an accident. He's in critical condition, Bjen.... I'm headed straight to the hospital." He listened to her breathing.... He could almost feel her thinking.

"Ian, this probably isn't an accident, you know. I'll have CJ look for indicators to see if they're after Jon now. Ian, sometimes I just want to walk away from all this."

"We can't do that."

"I know," Bjen responded. "Love you."

"Love you too."

"Talk to me tonight." Bjen hung up.

* * * *

"Coming in riding trauma victims now, eh? Your sex life must really be weak," the weary intern monotoned behind Kati as she sipped her burned coffee in a hospital staff break room. She looked up at the man who had been a disastrous blind date once and stared at him, tight lipped, as he filled his cup with coffee. He shrugged and walked out of the room.

Kati sat in the purple scrubs she'd been given after her shower in the hospital locker room and thought back through the events of the accident. She knew she'd have a full report to make to the police soon.... Hopefully, the man that she'd worked on would make it.

She heard footsteps coming her way again. She was thinking, "Shit, he's coming back," when she heard a warm, Irish sounding voice.

"Excuse me miss. I want to thank you for saving my best friend's life."

She turned and saw a tall, young gentleman elegantly, but casually dressed. He was wearing one of those beautiful white shirts with bright colored striped accents. Kati's glance caught the amber and metal crested buttons on his off white sweater vest. She watched his handsome face, topped with a wild mop of dark brown hair, as he continued.

"Please, stay seated." He took her hand in both of his.

"I didn't do anything that special...."

Ian took over her sentence, "Oh yes, way beyond special."

Kati felt the hot color rushing up her neck for the first time in.... She couldn't even remember. She cleared her throat. "Do you know how he's doing? I'm sorry. I didn't get your name?"

"Please excuse me. I'm Ian Swönk." Ian squeezed her hand again before finally releasing it. "I guess I'm a little out-of-sorts right now." Kati registered the tiny swans on each of Ian's sweater buttons as Ian was speaking.

"Jon's condition is still critical, and he's unconscious," Ian continued. "But he's alive, thanks to you, Kati. You'll never imagine how much I appreciate everything you've done. Please let me take you to dinner to tell you about Jon. Plus, I would really like to hear about the entire accident from your perspective. Any little detail that could help Jon from this point forward is worth exploring. Don't you agree?"

Questions were forming in a haze in the back of Kati's mind. "Some of the details seem to escape me right now. But I saw what he did to save someone's child who he probably didn't even know. Yes, I could meet with you tonight, but I'm scheduled to move to San Francisco in two days."

"Excellent. I appreciate your making time. Could we meet at 8:30 at the St. Julien? I believe the restaurant is called Jill's."

"I'll be there at 8:30, Ian."

*   *   *   *

Ian got a call back from the message he had left for Barb, Jon's "do everything" office manager. He made sure she knew the situation and was relieved to find out she was prepared to handle every detail of Jon's professional and personal affairs in case of an emergency. "Jon certainly trusts you, Barb," Ian couldn't help but comment when he found she had access to all Jon's accounts—everything.

"We agreed that life is too short not to trust the people you're close to." Barb went silent, and Ian could tell she was about to cry. "I love Jon," she said finally.

"Well listen," Ian said awkwardly. "You keep things floating there while I make sure our buddy comes back stronger than ever. Okay, Barb?"

"Sure thing," she said in a breaking voice.

"Barb, I'm going to text you a number where you can reach me or someone who knows who you are 24 hours a day...any help, money, anything...you call. Okay, Barb?"

"Yep, thank you," she said and disconnected.

All Ian could think was...damn.

*   *   *   *

The rest of Ian's afternoon was spent in discussions with Dr. Joseph, Nicholas, and medical experts from around the world who could evaluate Jon's status and make recommendations. It took only a very short time for Dr. Joseph to become fully aware of Ian's connection and moneyed position in certain areas of health related research...particularly neuroscience and genetics. Within hours, over twenty top doctors and scientists were monitoring every detail of Jon's health data and coordinating with the expert team assembled from the

Denver metro area.

Nicholas had implemented a security strategy mixed with technologies that made Dr. Joseph feel like he was in a science fiction movie written for a British secret service agent. "Jesus," Dr. Joseph thought to himself. Ian, however, had at least maintained constant communication with him, and now Dr. Joseph truly believed that the risks of playing outside the rules would be very rewarding. "Possibly a gift from God in these economic times," he said out loud to himself while driving home. Because of the money, he'd agreed not to talk to anyone about any of this.

Everyone involved with Jon's care and the now sequestered portion of the medical center had been screened, interviewed and instructed in the level of security to be maintained. Nicholas had deployed the little security bees that had made the medical complex and its surrounding region their new watch territory. These life-like flying robots were an example of the creative technological prowess that EET was capable of designing and manufacturing. Nicholas only wished he'd possessed his bees when he was operating unofficially as "006½" for Britain. While a few other governments had developed related forms of surveillance, none of them had come close to the capabilities of Nicholas' bees, which were known simply as Santa's Helpers.

Satisfied with the security, Nicholas moved on to his next task. He arranged for a private jet to be outfitted with all the necessary medical equipment and staff to move Jon anywhere in the world.

*   *   *   *

"Why am I doing all this for you, bud?" Ian sat alone, thinking, in Jon's half darkened room. He was next to Jon's bedside with his head down on his forearms, his eyes closed. A large array of medical monitors and life support equipment made an odd combination of muted sounds that at least indicated that Jon was still alive. Ian began whispering his questions' answer to Jon. "I'm doing this because you've become such a good and important friend over these last ten years, you silly fuck head. This is probably my fault, too. Not probably, it is my fault. I'm sorry, Jon. I know you'd understand... wouldn't you, buddy?" Ian felt his cell phone vibrate. He walked away from Jon's bed to answer.

"Hi, Little Bro," Bjen said in a soft, uplifting tone.

"I'm with Jon. I was about to call you."

"Jon's gonna be fine."

"Oh, well I'm glad to hear that. Hell, I'll get the horses ready and just strap him to the saddle. We'll be across the border before dawn."

"I see you've taken over Jon's approach to humor while he's napping."

"Napping, huh?"

"Listen to what CJ and I have found out. We have something odd going on. Someone here at EET knew about Jon's accident. CJ found key word traces in the thought recordings scan. Moreover, that someone feels we'll have the specific brain typing field developed within weeks now. We just have to figure out who the someone is, and we'll be able to solve our problem."

"It was probably you."

"Very funny. It was on the data time line before you called me. I do think you are acting like Jon because he's out of commission."

"Maybe I'm just wishing for some simple solutions to our complex problems, Bjen, like the ones Jon is always advocating."

"Well, here's something simply outrageous for you brother. Miss Kati Hunter, Jon's savior on the spot.... She's in the tree of original Celtic descendants, as pure as pure can be."

"Somehow I'm not surprised. What made you look for her there, Bjen?"

"I remembered seeing a "Kati" with the 'i' ending there and thought it was an unusual name. And Ian, you know I've also been discovering a growing pattern of connection between our family history and Jon's since you met him at Princeton.

"So when...."

"Kati's grandparents left Ireland for California at the end of World War II."

"Geez, I...."

"This just confirms that we're caught in some ancient game that we don't understand, and someone or some force is playing us like puppets."

"Bjen?"

"What?"

"When I start to say something, would you mind letting me finish my sentence before you crank up another of your own, please?"

"Fine, I'm just a little wound up over all this right now."

"That's understandable. I've been hoping Jon's research and unorthodox approaches to solving problems would help us, but now...."

"Listen, oh sorry, are you finished?"

"No problem, thought I'd just eat one chop and leave the other for your dog."

"Very funny. Jon's transmitting his bad jokes right into your damn brain!"

"I think you're onto something there, Sis, and I hope it's short-lived."

"Bad choice of words there, Ian."

"They're Jon's, remember? I'm going back to the St. Julien to get a room and sleep awhile. I'm meeting Kati Hunter at 8:30, and I've really got to think about all this and decide what direction to go. Let's talk tomorrow, Bjen, and I'll have a plan."

"I'm beginning to feel the stakes of our war are

bigger than the stakes in World War II. And hardly anyone is even aware of what's happening."

"Listen, the glass is half-full, Bjen. Our parents left us a path to follow even though on the surface much of the secret history and science developments of our family are lost to us right now."

"Well, if this story ever gets out it will certainly give the History Channel some new material to add to all the World War II re-runs...."

After Bjen disconnected, Ian sat in Jon's room a few more minutes thinking and watching as doctors and nurses came and went. Finally, Nicholas arrived. He walked to the bedside and looked down at Jon, hooked up and impersonalized by all the winking instruments. "Bjen says he's just napping," Ian said.

"Let's hope so," Nicholas replied.

They took a private elevator down to a secure underground parking garage where a very special small, black London cab was parked. Although the small sedan looked docile, it was a mixture of an Aston-Martin and a Bentley, with a sleek custom designed Rolls Royce grill. The sculpted fenders almost hid the wide, low-profile, bullet-proof racing tires.

Ian grabbed the central rear door handle. It read his handprint and opened smoothly. He slid into the red leather rear seat. Fitted with an engine that could contend at any racetrack, the little cab had an exhaust system that $006\frac{1}{2}$, St. Nick could regulate for power and sound. They rolled away from the hospital silently.

"There's no sign of any threatening activity, Ian" Nicholas said. "Do you feel we'll be staying here long?"

"No, as soon as Jon can be moved we'll take him home on the medical transport. I'm going to have CJ modify the neuroscience research lab facility to do everything we can to insure a full recovery."

"That makes sense," Nicholas remarked. He pulled into the underground St. Julien garage and let Ian off with his luggage at an elevator that opened near the reception desk above. "I'll be looking forward to hearing about your communication with Miss Hunter."

Ian stopped at the front desk to check in and headed up to the top floor suite that Nicholas had called ahead to reserve. He walked out on his balcony to gaze at the beautiful mountain view before giving in to exhaustion and laying down for a nap.

*   *   *   *

Mars stood still under the full moon. A thin layer of late spring snow had blanketed the alpine basin shortly before midnight, but as 2:00 a.m. approached, the storm clouds left, leaving a sky so bright with moonlight that the landscape sparkled as if a mirror to the stars above. He wore a full-length, black sable mink hooded cloak for warmth as he awaited a call from his leader, a leader that controlled Mars... a leader he'd never met. Mars took pleasure from the beauty surrounding him, but he felt no joy from it. He felt no joy in life...just pleasure, problems, and pressure.

Walking slowly to the edge of the castle tower courtyard, he looked down to the river running along the base of the ridge his complex had been built on over eight hundred years ago. From this distance, the river was a silent dark artery with white foaming tears, but in his mind Mars could hear the rushing sounds that obliterated talk. Eventually, the slight beep came…. Mars and his leader began to discuss the situation in Colorado.

"I reviewed your report on the Colorado OP to compromise Jon Wolff. So, the strong signal strength led to all the mayhem?" the Leader queried.

"Yes, sir."

"Is Dr. Wolff dead?"

"It's quite possible, but he was taken to the hospital trauma center. Swönk is with him now, and, as might be expected, Wolff's case information is covered up."

"Does our informant have any details regarding any of this activity?"

"No, but due to the thought technology search by EET among their company personnel and our actions concerning Dr. Wolff, I feel we should lay low until we sort through the dilemmas we're facing."

"We're facing a lot of 'dilemmas,' Mars," the Leader said sarcastically. "But with the critical status of Earth life systems, over-population, and destructive radicals, the leader group wants a systematic and orderly approach to gain control as soon as possible."

"Sir, the Swönk family diaries we've captured, along with what we know from our insider and our observation, confirms that getting the EET technology resources and controlling them will be the fastest path for the leaders' domination."

"We want you to confirm Dr. Wolff's condition. If he's alive, get a clear mind map, discreetly. Expedite the tests you are performing on subjects to direct behavior control from external transmission. Get us a report in thirty days."

"It will be done."

"Goodbye, Mars."

Mars shivered and walked back inside the castle. The stars and their mirror in the snow were forgotten.

*   *   *   *

Walking silently out of the elevator in the soft deerskin moccasins Jon had gotten him in Wyoming, Ian found his way to the dinner table. It was situated next to a huge stone monolith in a central open square filled with multicolored glass sculptures. Kati was already there, sipping a drink. She was wearing a sleeveless floral dress that accentuated the color of her eyes. Her reddish blond hair stirred a little in the slight breeze.

"Looks like something is growing in your drink there, Ma'am," Ian said.

Kati smiled. "This is Canyon Mint Mojito number three."

"It's been a long day." Ian looked around. "There's some beautiful stone and glass here."

"The stone is honey onyx."

"You a stone expert?"

"Just asked the guy in the coat."

"Looks like Venetian glass."

"You a glass expert?"

"Yes, would you need another mojito?"

"Yes, please, these go down easy."

Ian ordered two more mojitos. The food started coming, beginning with a delicious beet salad…split for two. "Is this family night or something?"

"I've ordered everything," Kati said. "Figured you've made enough decisions today."

Ian laughed inside but kept his facial expression neutral. "I guess we've both got an Irish heritage."

"You do background checks on everyone you have dinner with?"

"Only if they're going to order everything before I even get there." They laughed hard. Out loud. Even made all the restaurant staff feel happy. Kati looked lovely in her laughter.

Kati excused herself for the bathroom. Ian ordered mojito number two, then opened a small packet with a sterile cloth to wipe Kati's glass rim. He put the cloth in a plastic bag and sequestered it in his pocket.

IJustKnowLove360°…from the cold

When Kati got back from the women's room, she exclaimed, "Wow! The bathrooms here are fabulous."

"Nice, what was your favorite part?"

Kati hesitated and then remarked, "The orchids… snow white with tiny central specks of bright red and yellow."

"I'll have to go sometime. This prime rib is delicious…. Good choice."

Kati smiled with her eyes at Ian. She took a sip of water. "Called the ICU to check on Dr. Wolff. There's no record of him being there, being admitted, receiving any care… nothing."

"Jon's always had a strange sense of humor."

"Very funny. What's going on?"

"What did you say to the hospital?"

"I told 'em I'd bring in some of his blood from under my finger nails and see if they could find someone who matched."

"And they said?"

"That they'd investigate the situation."

"You said?

"Tell Dr. Wolff not to be late for our date tonight!"

"You can call him, Jon… since you've saved his life …not to mention being a likely member of my family tree."

"You make fascinating small talk Mr. Swönk, or are

you a doctor, too?"

"Just Ian, and no, I never talk about the weather…even in a typhoon."

"Very interesting… and your favorite beer?"

"Black'n'tan…Guinness, of course."

They shared a laugh again. "So," Kati said, "are you going to tell me what's going on here?"

"First of all, let me apologize for you being unable to check on Jon after all you've done, Kati. There is a possibility that Jon's security is at risk, so we thought it was best to make his presence at the Med Center as invisible as possible. I have the resources to insure Jon gets the best possible care."

"How can a random accident like this be linked with some kind of security risk? It is odd though…."

"What?"

"I was feeling great rollerblading on the bike path until I came into the area where Jon was chasing the baby carriage. I've only had a migraine type headache once…but all of a sudden it felt like that…a sharp strike of pain in my head, followed by pressure and difficulty in thinking clearly. I had to force myself to focus. Everything seemed unnatural until the head pressure just disappeared…."

"When did the pain let-up?"

"While I was working on Jon's injuries in the street."

"The accident report said a dog took off pulling a

baby carriage?"

"Yes, and the dog's reaction was almost spontaneous with my head pain, come to think of it."

"How's the head after all those mojitos?"

"So funny."

"Well, I think it's probably good you've downed at least four mojitos before you listen to what I've got to tell you. This should not be repeated to anyone. Can I rely on you to keep this quiet?"

"Maybe after one more mojito?"

"I'm very serious."

"Fine. I can keep a secret, if it's a really big one."

Ian was feeling a loss of control around this woman, but his instincts told him he could trust her. "Kati, I'm almost sure Jon's injury wasn't a pure accident and the fact that *you*, someone related to our family, were there…wasn't a random occurrence." Kati wanted to say something but nothing came.

"My family heritage," Ian continued, "goes back to the earliest Celtic records we possess, Kati. My sister, Bjen, recognized your name from our records and found your family's link when I told her how you saved Jon today."

"Well, we're certainly past the small talk, weatherman…." Kati decided to shelve the idea that she might be a very distant relative of Ian's for later consideration. Instead, she asked the next question that came to mind. "But why was Jon's accident, not an accident?"

"I believe a group of people exposed the area where you intersected Jon's run to some forms of energy that adversely affected your brain function, along with everyone else's in the same area."

"Including the dog's brain?"

"Yes, I think so."

"Then this is a police matter," Kati said firmly.

"You know, I truly wish it was, Kati."

"Well, why isn't it? And why was someone exposing Jon to some kind of energy field?" Kati was beginning to feel frustrated and, as much as she liked Ian from her first impressions, she was beginning to wonder if he could be trusted.

"The issues and factions of people involved here have some grey borders. However, to be blunt...there are people out there who are developing the ability to control human thinking, and to do that, they need a certain type of brain map."

"And you and Jon are involved in the neuroscience of brain mapping and mind control? Jesus freakin' Christ!"

"Yes," Ian said, simply.

"And, are you just as bad as the other side, so to speak?"

"No, my motive is to protect people from losing their freedom...and from losing their freedom to think freely."

Kati's was making flash connections, rejecting them, and then making other connections.... "Why don't you think my involvement here is just random?" she asked finally.

"There are factors I can't explain at this time. But, I'm pretty sure your being there for Jon wasn't random. And I know this sounds outrageous, but from all the medical data on record now...Jon should have died.... Your presence there saved him, and I don't just mean the amazing first aid you performed."

Let your life go to him, she thought again as she felt tingles running up to her head then out to her finger tips.... She had a blank look on her face.

"What's wrong?"

"Nothing," Kati said. She couldn't articulate what she was feeling to Ian, and she wasn't sure yet that she even wanted to.

They talked in the hotel lobby until midnight and then made plans to meet for breakfast in the morning.

*   *   *   *

The old Chautauqua Dining Hall was a lovely spot for breakfast. Built in 1898 to host the cultural circuit lectures of the Chautauqua movement, the hall was an airy tribute to the grace of another time. Kati was already at a table on the porch, sipping orange juice and enjoying the view of the range of mountains heading north, when Ian arrived. Legs crossed in jeans with faded swirling designs, her foot was dancing in an old worn-out hiking boot.

"I hope you got some sleep," Ian said as he pulled up a chair and sat down.

"I did, but I feel like I must have re-lived the accident again."

"Is there anything else about Jon's injury scene that has occurred to you?"

"No, I told you everything last night. I feel like I just stepped out of my life into another world. Plus, leaving Colorado to dance in San Francisco…. It's a lot of change at once." She paused for a moment, watching the shadow of a cloud sweep over the mountains. Then she refocused on Ian. "You promised to tell me more about how you and Jon met at Princeton…and more about your Celtic family history."

A waitress arrived with plates of huevos rancheros and a large bowl of cut fruit and berries. Ian poured Kati and himself a cup of coffee from the table pot. "Guess I'll have to arrive ahead of you if I'm ever going to get to order," he said.

"I don't mind ordering as long as you pay. Normally I wouldn't be so brash, but you seem rather long on change, Mr. Swönk."

"It's my pleasure, Miss Hunter."

"Well, perfect then." They both laughed, and for a moment the dark event which had brought them together seemed to recede. They were just a man and a woman enjoying each other's company.

"So," Ian said, "You're planning to leave on Wednesday for San Francisco?"

"Yes, early, I'm driving. I need to start at the ballet center on Monday."

Ian saw her sparkle. "You must be very excited."

"Oh yes! It's my dream…. But Ian, when and how did you meet Jon?"

"Jon was in pre-med at Princeton when I came from Ireland to study some topics of neuroscience and genetics. I was hoping to develop a study for EET there. A professor in the neuroscience department introduced me to Jon, and we all became friends. Jon was in the Princeton basketball program. Our friend, Professor Einstoon, was a huge fan of the game. Pretty soon I started getting hooked on the game too, so much so, that I decided to try and make the team."

Kati maintained a straight face and said, "I don't suppose this 'professor' had wild hair and tried to explain everything in the universe with a simple equation, did he?" Ian just smiled.

"So what attracted you to basketball?"

"In retrospect, there were a number of reasons, but initially I was attracted to the team aspects…the cooperative effort to perform well. I grew up participating in mostly individual sports…gymnastics, running, tennis, golf and so on. My family background and demands kept me from what you might call a normal childhood."

"You don't seem too bizarre," Kati commented.

"Well, thanks. Anyway, Jon loved the game and was always talking about the philosophy and strategy of the Princeton team."

"I've studied lots of literature and philosophy...but not basketball philosophy." Kati smiled. "So, you'd never played before, and then you were trying to make a college team?"

"Right."

"Did you make the team?"

"Yes, I bet Jon he could teach me the game in one year and that I could qualify to join the team."

"Wow...and Jon bet you couldn't do it!"

"That's correct."

"And you trusted Jon would try his best to teach you the game even though he was betting against you? Shit, that's a little amazing.... Did he enjoy the challenge?"

"We both loved it. And I had to enroll in Princeton as a freshman to be eligible, which was something I hadn't planned on when I arrived to work with the EET project."

"Were you only eighteen, then?"

"Yes."

"You grew up fast. What was the Princeton basketball team strategy? Did you have a good team?"

"Well, we didn't have the level of success the Princeton team did when Senator Bill Bradley played, but we won our league championship twice and made it into the NCAA tournament round of sixteen teams once."

"Awesome."

Ian laughed as he warmed to the topic. "We played as an unselfish team and ran offense with continuous ball movement, a system of setting hard screens or picks. We played tenacious team defense and had great fitness. Hell, once we worked for lay-ups on every possession and were up by thirty points by the end of the third quarter."

"Well, damn," Kati laughed. "I wanna get out my pompoms."

"And where did you study, Miss Smarty?"

"I want to hear how your family became so rich, Mr. Swönk." Ian was expressionless and quiet for a moment. Kati wondered if she'd overstepped.

"It's okay. My parents stashed away tons of pizza coupons, so we were able to buy and re-sell pizza at a great profit."

"No wonder you had a brief childhood—delivering all that Irish pizza."

"Exactly," Ian smiled.

"Sounds almost like that Irish family who imported booze during prohibition."

"There ya' go."

"You're talkin' like a Texan, Mr. Irish."

"Jon's a Texan. I get it there, I imagine."

Kati changed her tone, thinking about Jon lying in a hospital bed. "How's Jon doing?"

"He's still unconscious but his vital signs have improved."

"Improvement…good. You know, Ian, you're good at making someone feel comfortable and like you've known them for years…not one day."

"I think I've learned a lot about people from Jon."

"Oh, really? Well, you'll have to introduce us, I hope. Where are his parents?"

"Jon's parents and sister were killed in a freak storm while boating off the coast of New Zealand."

"I'm so sorry."

"And my parents were murdered which is probably another reason why Jon and I are so close…but it goes way beyond that."

Kati's eyes were moist. "You make me feel lucky to have my parents and brothers all alive right now."

"Well, love 'em up 'cause this life we're in seems pretty short sometimes."

Ian left a hundred dollar bill on the table, and they walked out the back of the old dining porch towards the foothills trail. They passed the barn-like wooden Chautauqua Auditorium that was built around 1900. An orchestra was practicing. "Jon brought me here for a concert a couple of years ago," Ian said. "It's a wonderful old hall."

"Who did you see?"

"A pianist named Peter Kater." Just as Ian finished speaking, the whomp, whomp, whomp of a helicopter came directly over them from behind a foothill. Ian stopped to look up. He studied the machine intently. It flew on, and the fading horns and strings of the orchestra became audible again.

They took the path marked, "To Enchanted Mesa Trail," and Kati finally broke the silence. "I was listening to Peter Kater while I was skating on the bike path yesterday.

"That's an interesting coincidence. So you like his music?"

"I love it. I grew up playing the accordion, organ, and piano…all the keyboards. The piano has been the instrument of choice in our family going all the way back to my great grandmother's dance studio in Dublin….You seemed pretty interested in that helicopter, Ian."

"I've always loved them since I was little. A division of my family's company designs prototypes now."

"So, do you have some favorite new secret helicopter, Mr. Swönk?"

"Yes, it's called the Hummingbird."

"And?"

"It's almost as silent as a hummingbird."

"Whoa! Are you serious…how?"

"I'll have to give you a ride sometime and show you how it works."

"A rain check, then."

Ian saw the hurt look in her eyes "Hey," he said lightly. "I've never met anyone I felt more like telling every secret I know to as much as you, Kati. But, let's just keep building our trust, okay?"

"I understand."

Ian watched the bee fly silently in behind Kati's head and hover there before leaving. He wondered if it was a 006½ jesting message. The bees seemed fine around Kati. They had her photo and cellular data loaded into their memory systems. If he'd only been protecting Jon, like he was protecting Kati now….

They came up onto the mesa that provided an expansive view of the Flatiron Mountains jutting skyward. It was a dramatic sight.

Taking a small side trail, they found a large, flat boulder and sat down in some shade. It was nearing noon, and the high altitude sun was so intense they could smell the dry aroma rising from the sage, grass and wild flowers. Two large hawks were circling effortlessly in the thermals above them, with wings fully extended.

"Are you avoiding telling me about your family history and how I fit into this "Celtic tree of descendants," as you call it?"

"Not really, it's just that our conversation tends to jump all over the place. But this rock…this site, seems to be a fine place to talk about the past. I can only imagine all the people who have stopped here to sit, to talk, to revel in this spectacular view." He leaned back on his hands. Even in the midday heat, the shade felt cool in the westerly breeze.

"My ancestors began their existence in Ireland, Kati. We, me and my sister, Bjen, are the last survivors of the Swönk family."

"Jesus, the way you put that."

"It's just the facts. So, to make a long, long story a little shorter, we have a history of friends and enemies, not only in the European region, but globally. And for over a thousand years my family has been involved with developments in science and in thinking that was ahead of their time…even ahead of our time now."

"Can you levitate?" Kati asked in mock credulity.

"Be nice, Kati."

"Go on, please." Kati noticed a couple of bees just hovering near them like they were almost watching… listening.

"So, my family has amassed a substantial fortune through science and business. More importantly, we've always been developing strategies to enhance life here on Earth and well, maybe even beyond. A large portion of our family records and scientific discoveries, however, were lost during a series of conflicts. The faction of people dedicated to destroying our family and what we stand for, is relentless."

"Ian, am I in danger just being here, now...or from being at the accident site yesterday?"

"At this moment, no one but me, my sister, and my inner circle of security know your link to any of this... and we'll keep it that way, Kati."

Kati observed that the first two bees had moved, but they were still circling. "Considering Jon's current condition, your words aren't totally reassuring," Kati remarked. "Ian, are all these bees flying around us your friends, or what?"

"You're safe, Kati. And yes, the bees are my little friends...yours too." Ian held his finger up, and a bee came to land on his fingertip. Then he realized Kati had been kidding. Now, her face was full of the amazement of a child who has just seen Santa Claus for the first time.

"I made a mistake by not putting protection around Jon. I'm sick about it, and that mistake won't happen again."

Kati was barely listening. She was holding her fingers up, but no bees were coming to them. Ian smiled. "You're not cleared for parlor tricks yet, sorry. The bees are robots, Kati, and they are an incredible tool for surveillance and, if need be, protective action."

"They look totally real."

"That's the idea."

"Do you take them on all your dates?"

"Is this a date?"

"A family date from what you're trying to tell me, I think. Actually, I'm feeling like I'm in a science fiction movie, Ian—mind control, hummingbird helicopters, and now these robotic bees—gawd, am I dreaming?"

"There are dimensions to life and our existence that most people never explore, Kati…or even think about. I feel I was born into the future sometimes. However, it's funny how so many answers are lost in our past."

Ian and Kati hiked through pine trees up to the base of one of the ancient flatiron rock formations that had been lifted up with the birth of the Rocky Mountain range. Judging from the pace she set and the bounce in her step, Ian figured Kati could hike right out to San Francisco without breaking a sweat.

Finally, Kati broke the silence. "So, tell me, if your sister found me on your family tree, how far back is the connection…branch, or whatever you call it?"

"At the very origin," Ian replied in a somber tone, "the relation probably started in one of our pre-historic caves."

Kati felt laughter bubbling up. She tried to contain it, but couldn't. She started laughing so hard she could hardly stand up. Ian started laughing just from watching her. Trying to speak through the uncontrolled hysterics, she forced out, "You mean I've known you for one day, and you've traced my ancestry back to a damn cave in

Ireland? I need to see this cave. Maybe my great cave grandma left some hand painted stoneware for me as a keepsake!"

Ian's laughter escalated, and he bent over holding his stomach.

"Were the Flintstones in our neighborhood?" Kati gasped.

After a while they got their breathing back. "I'm serious, you know," Ian said.

"I know," Kati replied. "That's why I lost it."

*   *   *   *

As Kati and Ian neared the Chautauqua development, their trail overlooked a parallel path in a small ravine filled with deciduous trees and a small creek. Half-a-dozen children were at play using sticks for their mock sword fighting while running and jumping around the creek. The view through the trees made the scene almost realistic, save for the children's voices laced with fun.

Kati thought of her mom's Shakespearean dramas, while Ian imagined children growing up to fight with real swords in earlier times. The tinkling music-box sounds of an ice cream truck drifted up from a street below. "That orchestra sounds a little different than before," Ian said.

"I can see you're a connoisseur," Kati teased.

"I like fine ice cream, alright. I'll have to make you some of my special homemade Irish ice cream one day."

"After my Irish pizza?"

"Certainly."

"And just what is Jon's role in this intriguing world of yours, Ian?"

"Foremost, he's my true friend, Kati. I've been trying to get him to work with EET since he finished Med School, but he wanted his own private practice here in Colorado. Jon's very good at finding solutions to health problems and well, let's just say I appreciate his view point on issues."

"So, he's got a good life philosophy…a good heart."

"Kati, I want you to stay a few more days before you leave, please," Ian said abruptly. They reached the tree lined parking area and came to Ian's black "London Cab."

"Wow," said Kati, deferring her answer to Ian's request. "I can't imagine whose car this is. This thing is beautiful." She looked at Ian, noting his expression. "You brought this along with you? Shit!"

"It fits in the jet," Ian said sheepishly.

Kati was looking down the row of cars. "I parked right along here. My car's gone!"

"I think that red one's yours, Kati."

Kati's lips pushed forward in a whistle as she looked at the new, candy apple Prius' temporary plates, remembering a wish she'd voiced last night when they'd been talking in the lobby.

"Where's my real car?"

"I'm sure Nicholas has parked it safely. Kati, we want you to have this gift.... It's just a token of thanks for what you've done for our friend." Kati's eyes were glistening. She'd never had a brand new car before.

Ian got the Prius' keys from his cab and put them into Kati's hand, "St. Nick put all your things into the Prius boot, 'er trunk, as you say. Go dance and we'll talk afterward."

"Come with me," Kati said impulsively. "I want you to come watch my dance workout."

Ian thought he should get back to the hospital. He compromised. "I'll come watch you, and then we'll go to Jon's room...okay?"

"Deal," Kati said, opening the door to her new car.

*   *   *   *

Ian sat with his spine against a tiled wall. The high polish of the studio's wooden floor made him think of the Princeton basketball gym. Mentally, he heard the squeak of sneakers across the court and the rhythmic bounce of the basketball.

His phone hummed. It was Bjen. "Kati could be the key," she said without preamble.

"I'm at her dance workout."

"Boys will be boys."

"She asked me to come," Ian protested.

"Did she love the car?"

"I'd say so. We're going to the hospital after her

dance routine. I want her to do some imagery around Jon before she leaves for San Francisco. Then I plan to bring him back to the neuroscience center."

"Fine, I agree…and I'd like to speak with her before she leaves."

"We'll have a little talk party."

"Very funny, Ian." She hung up.

Kati didn't acknowledge Ian's presence after she entered the gym. She just went to work. She went through movements at the barre. Then she flowed through a series of jumps and dance pieces that encompassed the core elements of ballet. Some of the language of ballet flashed through Ian's mind as she performed. He could see that Kati was a special ballerina. He could *feel* the excellence. The quick glances from the other dancers confirmed that they could too.

Kati finished her routine and walked over to Ian. Ian smiled up at her. "Those were some nice pliés. I'd give you some tips, but I'm sure you'll get them in San Francisco."

"Dance is a journey towards perfection."

"Advanced philosophy?"

"Yee, ha!"

"Funny," Ian chuckled. "That's what I was thinking too."

*　*　*　*

Ian and Kati sat on a dark leather couch in the corner

of Jon's room, watching as a male nurse administered electromagnetic pulse therapy to the region of Jon's fractured femur. Coils wrapped his leg for induction of additional current into the leg injury. This would speed up the soft tissue and bone healing. A stately oriental woman carrying an elegant leather case walked into the room. She sat on an ottoman situated next to Kati and Ian.

Kati could feel a peaceful strength emanating from her. The woman reached out and overlapped Ian's left hand with her right in a firm clasp. "I'm here to do everything I can for Dr. Jon," she said.

"Thank you so much, Zchen, for coming so quickly." Ian introduced Kati and Zchen.

Zchen was a master of acupuncture, massage, and much more. She had left Kyoto, Japan for Colorado immediately after 006½ - St. Nick had phoned her. Her bag was filled with an array of aromatherapy vials, needles, and small laser devices. Ian knew that her most important tools, however, were her fingertips.

As the therapy for Jon's leg continued, Kati, Ian, and Zchen reviewed the accident, Kati's experience, and Jon's records. Zchen turned to Kati. "So, when you thought you were losing Jon, you thought of sending your life force into him?"

"Yes."

Zchen smiled and patted Kati on the shoulder. "Well, Miss Kati ballerina, you'd better consider not leaving health care all together, I think."

Kati swallowed hard. She felt odd…like she was going to a home she'd never visited before. Her look touched Zchen's heart.

The nurse finished. Zchen went to work, starting with a kiss on Jon's forehead. Kati glanced at Ian. She saw the little brown bee sitting on the back of the couch behind Ian. Chameleons, too, I see, thought Kati. Oddly, much later, Kati would remember this moment as her turning point…when her real life began.

After almost thirty minutes of watching Zchen, Ian whispered to Kati, "You're up next."

"What do you want me to do?" Kati asked with some trepidation.

"I want you to put a hand on each side of Jon's head and visualize all the power of creation coming through you to heal him and make him strong…like when he was playing basketball at Princeton…like when he was running to save that child."

"Ok," Kati said, and for some reason she had no doubts. She went to Jon feeling like she was floating in energy. She kissed him between the eyes. With Jon's head in her hands, she leaned over the bed, placed her forehead against his and began humming, chanting and singing a melody she'd never heard before. Time disappeared as her mind followed a path brought on from the experience of the last two days. She traveled beyond her rational thinking. She drifted in a trance-like state, and her visions finally led her into a passageway under an impenetrable archway of dense foliage, thick with spike-like thorns. She was looking for Jon…. He'd just been at her side. Shafts of light filtered through, catching tiny white blossoms….

Kati opened her eyes, coming back from a now lost world. Her senses started returning. She had to think about where her feet were to be sure they were touching the ground. It seemed as if she was finding her way back into her body… back from a very real dream. The room was almost dark, and Ian had silenced the monitors before he'd left her alone with Jon.

Without thinking about it much, Kati walked over to the room's storage closet and pulled out two pillows and a blanket. Being there with Jon felt right to her as she fell into an exhausted sleep on the couch.

*   *   *   *

Eight hours after Mars had disconnected from his discussion with the leader, his backup assets in Colorado had found what they wanted and cleared their plans with Mars. The information they'd recovered by hacking into ambulance and hospital computer systems had assured the European operatives that Jon Wolff was alive in the Boulder hospital trauma center. They'd even watched as all the record data related to the injury case had been erased.

"Ian Swönk's ability to take over a situation always impresses me," Mars commented. He was talking on his cell with his lead operative in Colorado. After some discussion with his operative, Mars directed his technical experts to create a computer system malfunction for the hospital. The experts then intercepted the repair service request. This created their entry strategy to take in cases of specialized electronic equipment.

Surveillance of the computer services company that managed all systems repair for the hospital had given Mars' intruders all the protocol details they needed for a quick and easy entry. So at 5:45 p.m. mountain time, wearing the slightly worn security badges they'd just finished fabricating, the two operatives entered the hospital on their emergency repair request.

* * * *

006½ was wandering around the borders of Dr. Wolff's secured area. Ian had left the med center after he and Nicholas had peeked in Jon's room and found Kati asleep on the couch. They'd decided to let her sleep until Jon's next doctor's visitation in about two hours.

006½ 's light grey silk and linen sport coat held two small Blackberry-like units that connected him to all his sources, bees and world. Tortoise shell glasses gave him a continuous visual link to his watching bee network that only his eyes could see. At the base of his spine, concealed under the loose fitting unstructured jacket, snuggled a holstered weapon made of active stealth materials that were virtually invisible to detection systems. St. Nick's gun contained an arsenal of ammunition options designed for split second choices.

* * * *

Ian, Bjen, and CJ had just connected on a conference call. CJ was the Swönks' chief technical go-to. "CJ," Bjen said, "tell Ian about your discovery."

"Well, I was going over the installations for Jon's room in the old tower of the neuroscience building. I had the new portable TDS (thought detection system) that needed to be calibrated to some of Jon's new gear. The fresh stuff I'd added worked a little beyond expectations you might say."

Ian could hear an unusual enthusiasm in CJ's voice. "And?" he prompted.

"I got a tiny signal from the old stone wall facing the sea."

"A thought signal!"

"Yep!"

"Have you been able to reconstruct the language?"

"Yes, I think it's a voice trace from a very old conversation that actually coded into the rock somehow."

"If walls could talk, huh?"

"Ian, think what this means," Bjen interposed. "We can search for details to all our lost family data."

Ian's emergency page signal from 006½ sounded. "I'll call you back," he said quickly. "Bye for now, you two."

* * * *

Mars' operatives had split up and were checking each computer station in the med center. Alias Jacob received instructions from a floor manager that stations in a "closed zone" of the hospital would have to be repaired later. The operative looked at the floor manager's careworn face and donned his most reassuring manner. "Oh, no problem ma'am," he said. "We'll call to reschedule at a convenient time for your facility. Here's my card. Please notify me personally when your restricted area is open again. I hope it's not a dangerous infection or anything like that."

"Thank you." The nurse took his card, glanced at it, and then led Jacob back to her station next to the restricted elevator. "You can work here for now," she said. "All the computer screens are rolling. Can't make any sense of them."

With the technician working on her system, the nurse took the opportunity to leave for the women's restroom. She grabbed her purse.

Jacob glanced at her name tag. "Excuse me, Doris, but will you be right back? I would like to show you the function I'm installing to fix our little problem here. It's really invisible to your work system, but it might be good for you to know about it anyway."

"Sure," Doris said. "I'll be back in ten or fifteen minutes, okay?"

"That's perfect, thanks." When Doris was out of sight, Jacob opened the security link they'd hacked into.

He placed a video image of the area into the system to erase his presence from hospital security.

A surgeon in scrubs came down the hallway headed in Jacob's desired direction. He glanced over at the technician. "Excuse me, doctor," Jacob called. "Could I just ask you a quick question about this medical document format on screen here?"

As the surgeon stepped into the station, Jacob raised his weapon. "If you move or make a sound, you're dead," he informed the surgeon. "Nod your head if you understand, or you're dead right now."

Nodding his head to affirm cooperation, the surgeon lifted his right heel from the floor slightly, thinking one thousand one…one thousand two….

The second operative arrived to finish the computer repair. Jacob gestured with his weapon. "We're going to the elevator and Dr. Wolff's room. Walk now, I'm right behind you. Follow my instructions precisely or your head will disappear. I'm a professional, so make no mistakes." Jacob and the surgeon left and entered the elevator.

*   *   *   *

Doris walked up to her work station. The new operative turned to her and said pleasantly, "Hello, I'm Hal. Jacob had another call, so I'll finish up here fixing your system." Behind Hal and Doris a row of Nicholas' bees sat atop the picture frame…watching.

Kati was sitting on the couch in Jon's room alone,

having just awakened. She took out a water bottle from her pack. She felt a little dazed from her deep nap.

The surgeon's signal-producing inner sole of his shoe was one of many that had been placed in the shoes of each person on Jon's case as a simple way to alert 006½ discretely of a possible security breech. Nicholas had been watching as the repairman neared Jon's area. The doctor had been early, and now Nicholas had a hostage to consider.

Ian came into Jon's room through a wall panel door flush with the storage cabinet, slightly startling Kati. "Please stay calm," Ian said, "and quietly go through the panel into the next room."

Ian and St. Nick wanted the intruders alive and available to question. St. Nick had a visual on both men on his left eye screen, and the bee sting index was set just below lethal. Bees were hiding in the elevator ceiling grate, and bees were flying in the hall, cycling above the elevator opening.

The elevator door opened. Jacob pressed the door hold-open button. Waiting with his vaporizing weapon trained on the doctor's head, he carefully picked up his metal case of technology in his left hand. Nicholas watched the surgeon step through the threshold of the door followed by his target's aimed weapon hand.

The bees landed on Jacob's eyes at the very moment 006½ 's discharged round severed his forearm. The arm dropped to the floor still holding the custom gun. Jacob's mouth, ears and throat teamed with bees injecting their dosage of venom. More bees covered the operative's weapon and case, secreting a thick viscous fluid that would become a hardened, impervious barrier in seconds.

The doctor stood still, just watching. Nicholas gave him one, quick, assessing look. "Are you able to put this aside and continue?" he asked.

"Yes," Dr. Ewing, the surgeon, responded calmly.

"Then please proceed to Dr. Wolff's room."

Dr. Ewing walked away, thinking, "Gawd, I want that man on my team every time."

It wasn't until Nicholas bent over to tie off the victim's arm wound, that he realized he was dead. 006½ released all the bees into high alert status freeing the operatives' bodies. As he took Jacob's body into an adjacent secure room, he knew his accomplice was already unconscious from stings on the floor below. But now Nicholas expected the worst....

* * * *

"So is this another happy go lucky day in your boring life, Ian?" Kati burst out. "God fucking damn it to hell! I don't know if I can take this shit. What if they'd made it into Jon's room?"

Ian responded quietly, "Kati, I'm sorry this happened while you were here in Jon's room. Believe me; I think you're safer here with our security, than crossing a street out there in the real world." Ian was afraid of losing Kati right now.

Kati snorted, saying nothing.

"Remember, Kati, no one knows you're here, and when you leave for San Francisco you're safe, okay?"

Kati certainly had a look on her face Ian hadn't seen before. Ian tried again. "Kati, please take this phone. #1 is speed dial for me, #2 my sister, Bjen, #3 for St. Nick." Kati still said nothing.

Ian walked her to the red Prius. "Please drive straight to the St. Julien front door entry. I'll have Jeannie, the concierge, meet you and take you straight to a suite. She'll stay the night to see that you get whatever you want delivered to your room…but stay in there until we talk again, okay?"

Kati just looked at him and got in the car.

*   *   *   *

"Well, it seems Dr. Wolff must enjoy all the excitement. He's responding better on every test. I'm more hopeful than before," Dr. Ewing reported to Ian back in Jon's room. Every member of the hospital staff that was associated with Jon's area had been thoroughly briefed on the risks, rewards, and the factors of national security that were at stake. Dr. Joseph just wasn't sure at all which nation's security was at stake, but, oh well. Each of the staff was receiving five times their usual income, plus a minimum 10k bonus when Jon left "for a job well done." They all knew what measures were being taken to protect them and Dr. Wolff.

Ian smiled. "I'm afraid you might deserve an increased bonus, Dr. Ewing."

"I'll probably put a little extra honey in my tea tomorrow morning alright," Ewing laughed.

* * * *

When Kati turned into the St. Julien circular drive, Jeannie was there to open her car door. "Greetings, Kati. Welcome to the St. Julien. I'm here to make your stay as lovely as possible."

"Thank you," Kati said.

"I want you to ask for whatever you need, okay?"

"Okay, thank you." The valet took the Prius underground as they walked in and went straight up to Kati's top floor suite.

"I understand you are about to become a ballerina with the San Francisco Ballet," Jeannie ventured.

"That's the plan," Kati said. She knew she was being short with the concierge, but she was so upset, that was all she could manage.

"Just so you know, we have a private security team here functioning just for you…on the grounds, in the hotel, on your floor, on our roof. Also, there is a guard on each block surrounding our hotel. Somebody wants you to rest well, so it seems."

Kati felt like crying, "So it seems."

Jeannie showed Kati her room amenities…thick terry cloth robes, clothes from the spa, roses, fruit, chilled waters, champagne...everything.

Kati squeezed a fresh lime wedge into ice cold water from Norway and drank it all with continuous gulps. She took a dozen different soaps, gels, and smells into the shower. Twenty minutes later and wrapped in white terry cloth, she tossed back the covers and threw herself on the king-sized bed with the phone Ian had given her. Kati didn't look for bees. She knew they were there. She pressed #2....

"Kati?"

"Bjen?"

They talked...all night long.

*   *   *   *

A leprechaun arrived at the hospital with a large black lab case on rollers for Ian. That's what Ian's jet travel team called themselves...lucky leprechauns. Each wore an emerald and gold four leaf clover pin with the swan insignia carved into the gem's surface. They'd all been in on the design, providing the little special touches that made a big difference.

This particular leprechaun was tall, blond and slim. She gave Ian a long, comforting hug.

"Thank you, Linda, for getting here so quickly," Ian said.

Linda knew what the case contained, so she got right to the point. "Jon's transport is ready to go, Ian. I've been there since it arrived."

"It won't be long now."

"I can't help but worry about you."

"Everything's okay, babe."

"Really?"

"Yes, lovely Linda leprechaun."

Linda smiled. "I'll get out of your hair."

"Let's talk soon."

"Believe it." Linda flashed him a smile and walked toward the exit. Ian turned to look after her before pushing his lab kit towards an oversized elevator leading to a special underground pavilion.

*   *   *   *

Nicholas had prepped the dead bodies on the stainless steel drain tables for Ian with a little help from Dr. Joseph. Dr. Joseph, now that he had had time to process everything, was sweating bullets. But they were small bullets at least, 006½ thought with a smile.

Regardless of what had gone down that day, Nicholas and the whole Swönk organization took death seriously, and their purpose was to enhance life and stop needless death. The relentless life-respecting efforts by the Swönks throughout history was the main reason Nicholas had come to be their guardian.

Losing the operatives was unfortunate because of the loss of life and information which could prevent a little of the mayhem in the world. But Nicholas hoped the postmortem evaluations would at least give them something.

*   *   *   *

Ian could think of a few things he might rather be doing right now, "but hey, buck up ol' boy," he told himself. "Make some good happen from all this shit-headed killing game." He had his science suit on. He felt a little like he was in Crichton's "Andromeda Strain"—all by himself down in the bowels of the hospital's morgue. "I wish Jon was up and at 'em to help with this…of course, then we wouldn't be here. Here we go… 'all booze and no clothes' as Jon's granddad used to say."

Ian had been in various human anatomy labs in his studies and research, but still he was thankful for the lab kit computer voice prompt system of instructions downloaded by his science team in Ireland for this specific situation. CJ had suggested that they get tissue samples separated immediately in order to have the best chance to understand the death activation system their adversaries were using to terminate compromised operatives.

Ian removed vials of body fluid from each directed site and saved the samples in electronically coded containers. These he placed in portable cold storage units. His drilling, sawing, cutting and chemical concocting went on through the night.

After 5:00 a.m. and a half-a-dozen calls to CJ, Ian realized he should have played some good music during the autopsy…. Sometime in the wee hours of the morning he couldn't help but remember some of the silly behavior in human dissection that went on at Princeton... a few spare penises left in urinals...good beer drinking stories.

*   *   *   *

Stop putting my clothes on sir...take them off for me. Kati awoke halfway from her dream, instantly wanting to hold on and not lose her unexpected lover in the fire light of the ancient grey stone room. She wouldn't open her eyes, but her hands became the man she'd trusted for so long now—until her orgasm took her back into the dark mindless sleep she wanted so much.

*   *   *   *

Ian sat on the edge of his bed at the St. Julien finishing the mushroom omelet and fresh orange juice. No coffee, he wanted to sleep now.

Bjen rang his phone. "Hi there."

"Hello."

"You must be beat."

"I'm skipping my morning pushups today."

"I hate to say this, but, she's asleep now...and I promised her you'd get her boxes out of her apartment and shipped to San Francisco for her."

"Oh really? By when?"

"Before noon."

"Today." There was a world of weariness in the word.

"I'm sorry, Ian, but this needs to be done for her. I've got all the information. The keys are at the concierge desk with Jeannie."

"Well hell, I see you've done all the heavy work already."

"Please and thank you, Ian."

"I'll get it done but don't organize any afternoon activities for me, okay?" But Bjen was already gone.

* * * *

Ian knew that he could probably hire someone to ship Kati's boxes, or delegate a leprechaun to do the work, but somehow that didn't seem right. No, he'd do this job himself. Ian didn't know anyone in Colorado with a vehicle suitable for moving things, so he decided to try Doctor Joseph. He'd gotten along with him fairly well at the hospital. After some preliminaries on the phone, he asked, "Do you have a pickup truck I could borrow?"

The line was dead silent for a moment, and then Dr. Joseph said, "You've got to be kidding."

Ian hesitated, then laughed.

"You want to use my vehicle to go out dumping dead bodies.... Man, what are you thinking?"

"Doctor, please, I need a truck to move some boxes for Miss Hunter."

"Really?"

"She's been through a lot. I'm doing this favor for her."

"I've got a 1960 International pickup...as a collector's vehicle. You can use it."

"Good condition?"

"36,000 miles...refurbished like new."

"Hey! Dr. J! Thanks!"

"It will be in my drive with the keys in it. I'll text you my address."

*   *   *   *

Ian took off from the hotel in the red Prius with a double cappuccino in his hand, watching to see if anyone was tailing Kati's car. After glancing at his GPS map, he realized he knew the street in north Boulder where Dr. Joseph lived. Turning onto Juniper, he found the address and pulled up a long drive next to the fifty year old turquoise beauty.

Ian walked around the truck admiring its solid, box-like construction and realized how much better he felt just being out in the fresh spring morning air. He decided to take a walk down the narrow, tree-lined street since he'd spent the entire night underground. Smiling to himself, he wondered if Bjen had planned this moment for him and maybe even Kati.... The way Bjen worked things out sometimes was just amazing.

He had access to everything fancy the world had to offer and still, the most special things were the big hug he'd gotten from Linda last night, this walk away from the craziness, helping a new friend with her boxes, and hopefully, getting his old friend back—who he missed like hell. So many people seemed trapped trying to survive...struggling to make more money, meet demands and cope with the stresses that stole away their precious moments of life...while he was born into riches with access to almost anything on Earth. It was his inherited family quest that took so many of his special moments away. Maybe the rich who didn't care about anything but their next party had the answer; however, they were some of the unhappiest people he knew. He was looking forward to discussing this life perspective with Jon again, and he had a feeling Kati would be there as well.... He turned back up the path to get the truck and move Kati's boxes.

*   *   *   *

Ian fell in love with the 1960 pickup truck and thought it was crazy that the plates were numbered 006. After loading Kati's boxes and getting them shipped, he put a call through to Dr. Joseph. "Mission accomplished. Thanks Dr. Joseph."

"You're welcome."

"I'd like to purchase your pickup."

"Hell, I just got it."

"Give me a price that you can't refuse. Then double it."

"Fine, it's yours. May I ask why you want this particular truck?"

"I want it for Jon." There was silence on the line for a moment. Then Ian heard Doctor Joseph clear his throat.

"Then take the keys," he said, "and I'll sign the title to you and leave the papers in the front seat."

"How much?"

"Consider it a gift."

"Why?"

"Because you opened my mind to things I'd given up on a long time ago."

"Where did you get the truck?"

"West Texas...small town called Canyon."

"You're kidding."

*   *   *   *

"Welcome...welcome, Madame." Marcus greeted the beautiful French First Lady who was already more relaxed than he in this spectacular Swiss alp setting. All arrivals came up the secure road which, after bridging the wide, raging river, led into a tunnel built with the latest high tech systems. The tunnel was decorated as an ancient dungeon, replete with flickering torches. Guests felt as if they were traveling back in time, before bursting out onto the scenic byway which climbed to the castle entrance.

The old castle's huge first-level spa had been recently renovated with a very modern, but country French design which Michelle, the French woman, loved. Arching walls of mixed stone and wood were integrated with chandeliers of cut, glass crystals and colored gemstones. The spa was spacious, yet it felt cozy. And the view was magnificent. The spa's sun-beam crested windows offered a picturesque panorama of mountains, waterfalls, and pines.

The French woman was there to indulge in every spa treatment and to write new music. Feeling more free and creative with her security entourage gone, Michelle wondered if she could arrange a glacial heli-ski trip if time permitted. Having almost qualified for the Olympic team in her heyday, her mind was filled with all sorts of sporting activities that she could schedule in the mountains around the spa.

She'd been given the most spectacular view room in the spa, as promised. The huge square bed was tossed with a plethora of cotton and silk pillows. Above the bed, a giant glass chandelier matching the bed's dimensions was filled with more than a visible lighting spectrum. She washed up in the luxurious bathroom and then, feeling suddenly tired, decided to take a nap.

Michelle's mapping started five minutes into her nap. Two straight failures had left Mars' face devoid of emotion as he watched the French First Lady's brain on his screen. The image took some of the sting away while Mars planned to trigger her desire for the French President to join her at the spa.

*   *   *   *

Ian's wakeup call ironically came from Bjen. He had been somewhere on the Irish coast walking through a thick, wet mist. Now, he was naked, half wrapped in a sheet.

"I hope you're well rested, Little Brother."

"Much better, thank you," Ian croaked.

"Might want to call Nicholas. We think it's time to saddle up and get Jon the *hell out of Dodge.*"

The shower spray felt like holy water of life to Ian as he wondered how Jon was doing.

* * * *

While Ian was sleeping, Kati had returned to the hospital. Kati and Zchen and had kept up intervals of therapy between all the other surgeons and specialists. Zchen was impressed with the way Kati openly accepted her suggestions, and she thought that Kati had an innate sense of healing and music.

Some of the medical team was joining Jon's flight to Ireland, and Zchen was re-arranging her schedule so she could go.

* * * *

Ian called Nicholas on his way to the hospital. "I got a new old truck," he announced.

"Well, well, moving boxes and shopping for trucks," Nicholas said cheerfully. "You really like to pack it all in during a trip."

"You'd make a great travel agent," Ian rejoined.

"Very funny. We've got all the transitional medical support ready to helicopter Jon to the jet. And, I've got The 'Neuro' Group from London meeting us at home."

"You're the best."

"Whatever it takes, Mr. Swönk."

"I want you to take a break when we get home."

"When the time is right, thanks."

Ian rang Kati's room and left a message asking if they could meet before she left for San Francisco. Next he called Dr. Joseph, but reached his assistant, Anna Marie, instead. She told Ian that Dr. Joseph was about to travel, too. "Man, sales tax revenue is goin' down fast around here," thought Ian. Dr. Joseph would wait at the hospital for Ian, and then give him a ride to his house to pick up his pickup. Best of all, Anna Marie reported, Zchen had relayed a message that Jon was moving and making sounds...especially when Kati did her singing and chanting.

* * * *

Ian found Dr. Joseph in his hospital office, packing file folders in a brief case. The doctor looked up when Ian came in. "I have a conference in Honolulu."

"Nice getaway."

"Understand that you'll be gone before I return."

"Unless something weird happens."

Doctor Joseph smiled wryly. "I can't imagine anything unusual could happen around your gang."

Doctor Joseph was anxious about catching his plane, so they left the hospital immediately. Pulling in his drive next to the turquoise truck, the doctor noticed Ian taking some cards from his shirt pocket.

"I thought I'd personally give you some 'thank you' cards," Ian said.

"Cards?"

"Sure, I wanted to save the postage costs. This dark green card with the magnetic stripe and its copy can access an account from a Zurich bank. Here's the business card of a private bank officer who will explain the details of my concept to help your facility and health care in this community...and you personally."

Doctor Joseph started to protest. Ian held up his hand. "Please accept it, Dr. Joseph. You have taken a risk to accommodate our needs, and I'll never forget that."

"Well, hey, keep the truck as long as you want." Ian started laughing.

Dr. Joseph was standing at the pickup open window while Ian cranked the engine. Ian started to wave to him and noticed the truck papers in the seat.

"By the way, I'm sorry, but I've never gotten your first name?"

"Joseph."

"You're a Joseph Joseph?"

"Yes, and my wife's name is Josephine."

"Well, thanks for sharing that Joseph Joseph....what

is your favorite song?"

"Hey Joe."

"Favorite drink?"

"Strong cup of jo."

"Favorite toy soldier?"

"G. I. Joe."

"Favorite sandwich?"

"Sloppy Joe."

"Born in Missouri?"

"Yep, in Saint Jo."

"Get outa here…. Any nicknames you've hated as a kid?"

Dr. Joseph hesitated, then grinned. "Jo Jo the dog faced boy…."

As Ian drove off, Joseph looked at his green cards with a white swan surrounded by the outline of a four leaf clover in the lower right hand corner of each.

*   *   *   *

"Do you want that last beignet?" inquired Kati.

"No, you do."

"How can you tell?"

"I've watched a lot of animals stalking."

Kati grabbed the beignet and started heaping homemade, strawberry rhubarb jam into it. "I'm sorry I erupted the other day," she said.

"Erupted?"

"In Jon's room...the 'damn, shit, fuck' comments."

"Oh, that. I just thought you were being philosophical."

Kati smiled while biting down on her loaded beignet, squirting red jam out on her cheek.

"Here's an extra napkin."

"Thanks. Sorry I am being such a pig."

"Please, just don't start break dancing on the table.

Kati laughed. "Pigs break dancing?"

"Sure, right here on the table...anything's possible, I suppose."

"Well, you made the Princeton basketball team."

"True, that's a bigger long shot than dancing pigs, alright." They laughed. Ian got up and started to dance. Everyone on the porch at Lucille's New Orleans style restaurant started smiling or laughing. The owner stepped out and began clapping a beat with some of the patrons.

*   *   *   *

Later, after the waitress had cleared the plates, they sipped at another cup of hot chicory coffee. They both felt the sadness. "I guess I should just get in my car and hit the road," Kati said. "Damn, I can't believe this last week. I can't believe you gave me a new car. I can't believe what I've learned from you all. Kati's eyes were filling up.

Ian was tongue tied.

"I feel like I should just drop my life and join your

quest," Kati said slowly.

Ian smiled. "Bjen must've brain-washed you pretty good the other night. No Kati, you should go to San Francisco and dance your dream, literally. We'll stay in touch. We're family, okay? Even if our relationship dates back to some friggin' Irish cave." They laughed again.

"Let's get you on the road, Lady." He walked her to her parked Prius and gave her a big hug.

"You will keep me updated on Jon?"

"Just push number one, two, or three on the phone I gave you."

"Thanks for everything, Ian." He just smiled, nodded, and watched her pull away. Kati drove on in elegant silence. As she navigated to the highway outside the city of Golden, she wondered just how much gold the Swönks had stashed away. Kati flicked on the radio, and started up I70 West. "The Climb" came on getting her singing with it….and that girl could sing. Too bad the American Idol Panel wasn't in the car to hear Kati. She'd have left them speechless and covered in goose bumps.

*   *   *   *

6:00 a.m. Monday morning…

Linda put a call through to Ian. "I'm riding over to the hospital in Jon's transport helicopter," she informed him. "We're planning to leave from the medical jet site at 10:30. I'll ride co-pilot in the transport 'til we're home.

How's Jon? And, what's your flight plan?"

"He's stronger in every way. I just wish he'd wake up. All the scans are better, and the brain swelling is down. The arterial damage is holding the surgical repairs. The EEG is close to normal...which has amazed everyone. Zchen and Kati's efforts were a fabulous help." Ian shifted gears, "I'm going to fly with Nicholas in the hybrid. We'll shadow the transport as a precaution. Remember your chute pack, Linda. I know how you are."

"Jon's whole flight room could be dropped off if we had to...but I hate to even think about that."

"Probably wake him up though."

"Don't even think it," Linda admonished.

Ian took care of a list of departure details with help from Barb, who took a break from Jon's office to greet everyone. She also spent some private time in Jon's room, quietly praying. 006½ was at his highest state of vigilance. Transitions were a high time of risk.

*   *   *   *

The large medical transport helicopter landed on the trauma center pad. A giant mechanized platform slid out of the 'copter's side and lowered to the ground. The minute it stabilized, a team of doctors and nurses moved the white walled medical travel room onto it. Two leprechauns hopped off the helicopter and headed into the hospital. Ian, giving a quick wave to Linda in the pilot window, was there to oversee everything.

But 006½ wasn't. He was bringing the last of the bees into a fire department ambulance parked at a discreet loading dock behind the medical complex. The last flying bee attached to the emergency truck and St. Nick climbed in. He addressed the driver. "Ernest, our next stop is the NCAR helipad. Take it slow and easy, please. We don't want to shake up our passengers in back."

* * * *

"Flip you for the right to choose," leprechaun Patrick offered as they stepped into the elevator and pressed the down button.

"Fine," said leprechaun Thomas.

Patrick reached into his pocket and pulled out a large coin. He showed the heads and tails sides to Thomas. "Want to flip or call?"

The elevator started down. "Flip," Thomas said.

Patrick deftly exchanged the normal coin for an identical two-headed one hidden in his palm. He passed the altered coin to Thomas. Thomas' thumb flicked the coin up. "Tails...I mean heads," Patrick called.

Thomas caught the coin between his palms. "You can't change your call like that!"

"Only if the coin is still in the air, lad."

"Fine then." Thomas lifted his top hand to reveal heads side of the coin. He handed the coin to Patrick without consideration. Patrick was a leprechaun, not a saint, of course. "So?" Thomas prompted.

"I'll drive the 1960 pickup." Thomas smiled. Luckily, they'd both gotten their wish. Shortly, the International pickup and the little London cab pulled away from the hospital and headed for flights to Ireland.

*   *   *   *

"Ernest," Nicholas said, "we want to thank you for driving this morning and for the great job you did in the ambulance for Dr. Wolff last week." 006½ put an envelope in the dash clip.

"What's in that?"

"A little Christmas money."

"Thank you, but no thanks. I'd just like to hear more about the incredibly good story developing here."

"Good story?"

"In the ambulance I saw Miss Hunter *will* Dr. Wolff to keep living amidst our first aid efforts. After the trip was over, I felt like I'd stepped back in time with a sorceress." Nicholas exchanged the envelope with Ian's card. Ernest plucked it off the dash. "Ian Swönk?" he queried, glancing at the card.

"Pronounced 'Swan.'"

"Interesting name. What's yours?"

"Nicholas, but my friends call me 006½."

"Why not seven?"

"You'll have to talk to Ian about that."

Later, after watching Nicholas supervise the loading of the helicopter at NCAR, Ernest gazed after the transport as it flew away towards Denver. He flicked Ian's card in his hand, wondering, hoping to find out more.

*   *   *   *

The medevac helicopter landed in front of the hanger containing a medium- sized cargo plane with Red Cross markings. Immediately, a tow vehicle attached and brought the 'copter inside as the huge hanger doors began closing.

Bay doors on the helicopter slid open, and the hoist platform went upward, carrying most of the medical team of nurses and doctors that had been on Jon's case for the past week. As they stepped through the door to the cargo plane, each doctor and nurse was handed a fresh mai tai, and leis of white orchids were placed over their heads by smiling Hawaiians dressed for an authentic luau.

The whole cargo bay was turned into a tropical paradise of sand, palms, island food, live music and dancing by the talented Hawaiians. Barefooted friends and families came in from behind thatched walls yelling, "Surprise!" The plane filled with laughter.

*   *   *   *

"You're crazy, Mr. Swönk."

"Sorry, Miss Leprechaun."

This time Linda gave Ian a big hug and kiss before he

left in the cab with Thomas. Linda climbed into the '60 International and headed with Leprechaun Patrick for a plane containing doctors at work. She winked at Patrick. "Looks like you got what you wanted."

Patrick gave her a lop-sided grin. "You know me."

Linda laughed, "You'd better be glad Thomas loves his dad so much."

"I try not to spoil him all the time." They pulled onto the ramp and disappeared into the jet's underbelly.

*   *   *   *

"This is the captain. You may go back to the beach now." As the plane reached flight altitude the party was renewed.

The leader of the Hawaiian band had everyone in stitches. Jude went by the nickname of Joke, and he had some great ones! Born from musical parents, an African mother and Hawaiian father, he'd grown up learning the ukulele and various wind instruments. Eventually, he'd become a rather good running back for the Harvard University football team.

"Dad had me playing with a ukulele before I could walk," Joke began. "Dad's Hawaiian name is Pali a Moana which means Sea Cliffs. He's always telling his howlie friends to drop over anytime." The nurses and doctors laughed uproariously. The mai tai was easing them into good times.

The other entertainers were constantly playing an

array of beautifully hand-crafted ukuleles and singing traditional Hawaiian songs. Occasionally they mixed in some pop, or sweet instrumentals. Finally, Joke sang his favorite Beatles tune, "Hey Jude." Everyone sang along. "Na na na nanana na…." Dr. Joseph Joseph had no idea of what was coming his way….

Two fully armed U.S. Air Force fighter jets flew off each wing of the party jet. Thanks to Santa 006½, they had accompanied the celebration aircraft until the party goers were well over the Pacific on their route to Honolulu.

*   *   *   *

Ian and 006½ sat in the cockpit of the hybrid jet following Jon's med transport aircraft. They maintained visual contact. Ian and Nicholas were the armed escort, and their arsenal was way more advanced than that with the Honolulu bound Air Force fighters. No brag, just fact.

"Do more with less…." 006½'s bee philosophy was a good one, Ian mused. He felt lucky to have the resources to hand-pick the world's best scientists for EET, however. But more than that…he had the reason…and that *was* the difference maker.

"You're telling me," said 006½, "that CJ has picked up old conversations out of a stone wall?"

"So it seems."

"Well, tell him not to take that thing into the bathroom…no tellin' what he'd get in there."

"Very funny, St. Nick."

"Seriously, now that the dust has settled, we should discuss what our next steps should be…considering the combination of CJ's current research, Jon's status, and the entrance of Kati, the ballerina."

"I wish I was on that flight to Honolulu."

"Oh please, you love all this shit."

"Moving Kati's boxes the other day only reminded me that I want a peaceful, good life, in a peaceful, good world…."

* * * *

Bjen called the cockpit phone. "Joe's Morgue and Pizzeria," Ian answered. "Deep dish discounts if you donate your body to stop world hunger."

"Feeling funny, are we? Is everything served with fresh Fiji waters?" Bjen had a smile in her voice. "I take it everything went as planned?"

"Yes, ma'am."

"Don't you think we should talk about the overall situation and…."

"You and 006½ have a one track mind," Ian said grumpily. "I'm thinking Linda and I should go for a little R and R once Jon is home safely, and his treatment is being implemented."

"What was I thinking? Of course you and Linda should have some break time. In fact, *I insist*. I'll fix some pot pies, and you two can have a little picnic." Ian disconnected the call.

006½ started laughing out loud, "You two are quite a pair. Being an only child, I find the whole way you two carry on quite entertaining."

"Hey, I'm glad there's some value for someone."

"You both are amazing at dealing with all the Swönk family demands you've been dealt," 006½ concluded in mock solemnity, "but sometimes you're just kids."

"That's quite perceptive of you, *Santa*."

006½ just smiled, thinking, I love these guys.

*　*　*　*

Kati pulled over to the side of the road and dug out her cell from the bottom of her purse. She dialed home. It didn't matter that she'd be seeing her mother in a few hours. Sometimes you just needed to talk to your mom. Sometimes you just needed the reassurance. She watched the windshield wipers sweep the rain to the sides of the windows as she waited for the connection.

"Hi dear."

"Hi mom. I'll be in tonight."

"That's great, sweetheart. We've got some surprises waiting for you."

"Really, I could use a little more excitement this week."

"Oh dear."

"I'm okay, mom. See you soon."

"Love you, bye dear."

*   *   *   *

The Hawaiian luau was fresh and real, even down to the potted palm trees. Doctors and nurses, who had been working stress-laden schedules for months, relaxed and started enjoying themselves. Almost everyone aboard briefly wondered how their destination time could be nearly as fun as the trip. The enjoyable aspects of the trip were about to end, however.

Hidden in the palms were tiny mist tubes that atomized humidity into the tropical party. When Jude activated the neurological suppressant into the misting system, he knew the celebrating would come to a standstill in less than a minute. Like on an actors' cue, everyone collapsed within a few seconds.

Doctor Ewing turned to find Jude's gun aimed on him. "Jesus Christ! Is this some kind of sick joke?" Ewing exclaimed.

"Funny you should bring Jesus into this, Doctor. Let's just make believe he's standing right behind you. Our drinks contained the antidote for this party-break sleeping dose. The pilots won't bother us, and there will be no Swönks to save you this time."

"I'm a Harvard grad., Doctor," Jude continued with a suave smile. "Therefore, I've been through quite a few intellectual exercises. So, I'd like to pick your brain a little before giving you some death choices.... It's great that Jesus could be here, actually. If you wish, I guess, I

can just shoot you now...or you can walk off the plane for a little jump to Earth."

Dr. Ewing felt drained and a little drunk after two mai tais. He knew he had to figure a way out of the situation, but his mind seemed frozen. He couldn't get it to work.

"I don't want to give you too much hope right now, Doctor, but the truth could save you. So, choose your answers carefully. Oh, look! Jesus is smiling behind you.... I thought he might even laugh for a second there. You know, I don't even mind if Jesus pitches in and helps you with your answers, Doctor. You should be even more hopeful now, right? Warm up your voice, Doctor.

"Yes, more hopeful."

" So, try to forget about my gun." Jude smiled. "It won't go off unless you move...and if you move your worries are over. Now, that's something worth hoping for, huh?"

"Yes or no." Ewing was starting to shake.

"Very good, doctor, very truthful. Jesus doesn't look worried, Doctor. He's not shaking. Why are you shaking?"

"I'm scared."

"Now, what could you be scared of, with Jesus here and all?"

"Dying, I think."

"Those mai tai's can bring it out, Doctor. Maybe

Bond left us a code with 'Shaking not stirred.' Jesus is holding his laugh in, I think. He's so demanding when it comes to good jokes. Well, we have about ten minutes, so let's solve the health care crisis before I let you go, figuratively, of course. Heck, we've got a Harvard grad, Jesus, and an experienced, brilliant doctor, right?"

"Right."

" Right on. We can do this. Doctor, please tell me about the last patient you treated before our little party here. You can forget about HIPAA regulations right now. Okay, Jesus?" Jude winked at Ewing. "Jesus nodded. He thinks that's fine."

"I treated a man injured in a bike crash."

"Severely injured?"

"Flight for life brought him to the trauma center."

"Oh good, lots of trauma...lots of business, right, Doctor?"

"He had severe injuries that required costly treatment and care."

"Tell me how the injuries occurred."

"The man was riding down a canyon road very fast on his mountain bike."

"Thrilling. Did he have a good helmet on?"

"Yes."

"What time of day?"

"Dusk."

" *How fast...estimate.* "

"*Thirty or forty miles per hour.*"

"*Would you do that for a thrill?*"

"*No.*"

"*Why not?*"

"*A flat tire, a deer jumps out...you're dead or in a wheel chair for the rest of your life.*"

"*Find this interesting, Jesus?*" *Jude winked at Ewing.* " *Jesus is nodding 'yes.' Are you planning to tell all your patients about this incident, Doctor Ewing?*"

Dr. Ewing hesitated. Then he whispered, "No."

"*Have you told anyone, doctor?*"

"*My son.*"

"*Why?*"

"*I love him.*" *The doctor was starting to weep and shake again.*

"*What did you tell your son?*"

"*To choose his thrill seeking carefully, or it could ruin the quality of his life.*"

"*Will your son pay attention to what you say or suggest, doctor?*"

"*Yes.*"

"*Why?*"

"*He knows I love him.*" *The doctor started crying harder. He sank down on his hands and knees in the sand.*

*"Why wouldn't you tell your patients doctor?
Answer carefully, please, or I'll have to blow your brains
out right now. Oh, and Jesus is looking quite interested
now, Doctor."*

"Time, money…I don't love them enough." Ewing
stopped crying. He simply didn't have anything left.

"Do you like me controlling your death, Doctor?"

"No."

*"When are peoples' biggest health care costs on the
average, Doctor?"*

"Shortly before dying."

*"Know the details…the statistics…the money…the
truth… Doctor?"*

Dr. Ewing had arranged himself cross-legged on the
beach. Despite his pallor, he looked a little like Buddha
with glasses. If only all the spiritual leaders could be
here too, thought Jude. *"On average,"* Doctor Ewing
said, *" people spend over 50% during the last year of
life."*

*"Let me ask you if there is a lot of good thinking and
love going on in this 'high quality' end-of-life game we
play?"*

Dr. Ewing felt feverish. He could swear he'd just felt
the weight of Jesus' hand on his head. *"No,"* he sighed.

"Why?"

"Money…power, control…money."

"And what is money becoming, doctor?" Jude

handed the loaded gun to Doctor Ewing.

* * * *

Ian woke up in his flight seat next to 006½. He'd had a dream, he knew. But he couldn't remember it.

* * * *

Her feet didn't have to move much on the black and white, checkered tile floor. Everything was tiny and close. "Ok mom, you get the first ever Keppe." Kati's mother sat on a muslin covered couch that tightly fit into a bay window with a view. She had rented and furnished the small apartment for Kati as surprise. "I know it's small, honey...."

"Oh, mom, I just love it. It's perfect." Kati walked out from behind the bar with drinks filled to the brim and set the large stemmed glasses on a wooden table.

"This is delicious. It's a what?"

"A Keppe, Mom. She's my hero. She's a character in the novel I'm writing. James Bond has a Vesper Martini, so I've created the Keppe."

"Well, if your book is as good as this drink...." They both started laughing...and catching up.

* * * *

It was dusk. Kati's mother had left a couple of hours ago with a promise to come back and visit on the weekend. Kati was curled up on the little couch, sleeping. The phone in her rear jean pocket buzzed and vibrated. She grabbed it, not even thinking. "Hello."

"You'd better slow down on those beignets or your toes won't come off the ground anymore."

"Ian?"

"Kati."

"I'm asleep."

"Sorry."

Kati sat up hardly knowing where she was. It took her a moment to realize she was in her new apartment, in San Francisco. "I'm back on the ballet diet starting tomorrow."

"That's good, I was starting to get concerned.... You're home safe?"

"Yes."

"We are too."

"Good."

"Let's talk soon."

"Good." Kati curled up on the couch again. "Night."

*   *   *   *

"Wait 'til he sees this," Bjen whispered, leaning in close to CJ's ear as they walked down the corridor of the neuroscience wing towards the old tower room prepared for Jon. Behind them, Jon traveled on an electric bed transport with various monitors attached. The small medical assistant team moving Jon had flown in from Colorado.

Ian and Dr. Jameson, one of the world's top brain physiologists from London, followed. "I'm very interested to see what CJ's new equipment can pick up," Ian told Dr. Jameson.

CJ and Bjen swung open the large oak doors that led into the room where old stone walls fronted the Irish Sea. In less than a week, the room had been renovated for Jon's arrival. Additions included an interior frame to house Jon's bed. The frame accommodated various equipment and rehabilitation functions plus remote controlled wooden shutters. The shutters opened out to newly installed windows overlooking an expansive coastal view.

"Holy Shit!" Dr. Jameson exclaimed when he saw the incredible system of model trains running on various levels of track that encircled the room.

Ian was half-way to tears, thinking how hard CJ and Bjen must of worked to pull all this together so quickly. The details of the model train display were spectacular. There was a real waterfall. Wooden trestles were attached to the walls. And, low and behold, a World War II German train station occupied the corner of the room.

"This is amazing, Bjen!"

The medical team was grinning ear to ear as they rolled Jon's bed into the framework and began hooking up the monitors and support. Ian had his arms around the shoulders of Bjen and CJ.

"Well," said Dr. Jameson, "this just about does it. I want to come work here full time!"

Everyone laughed. "Jon told me the whole story of

how his great granddad was in the Blackfeet tribe near Missoula," CJ explained. "Eventually, he became a mechanic and machinist for the Northern Pacific Railway. He met a Welsh-German woman at a dance in Missoula, and they became lovers. Jon's dad inherited the family's fascination with trains and model trains. He always had some model trains around.

"When I was finding the old conversations in here, it made me realize that all these trains might help Jon somehow," CJ continued. It was just a gut feeling."

Everyone in the room was quiet for a moment, listening to the whir of the little trains around the room ... Finally, Ian broke the silence. "Well let's get Jon Wolff back on track."

*   *   *   *

Pier by pier, Kati Hunter walked along San Francisco Bay letting the fresh ocean breeze cleanse her. Stopping with her hands pushed down in her jean pockets, she looked out to Alcatraz...now just a tourist attraction. She thought of the Birdman, swans, Jon in Ireland. Her thoughts were accompanied by the whooshing sound of the waves in the bay.

A sea gull swept down and passed her right shoulder so closely that Kati heard the swoosh from the darting wings against the wind. The white bird soared out over the bay. Soon, it was a tiny speck to Kati's eyes.

She blinked, and he was gone.... He? Kati thought. Maybe it was Jonathan Seagull. She pictured the

wonderful little book she'd received from her parents in
her stocking when she was fifteen. Signed by Richard
Bach, the book, Jonathan Livingston Seagull, had given
her inspiration to go beyond...dance beyond, and think
beyond her teenage expectations and limits.

She'd carried that little book in her pack everywhere
for months until it was lost...gone like Jonathan to the
other side. That was the way she saw the disappearance
of her special book. Kati resumed walking, thinking
about how she'd vowed never to buy that book again.
She would just carry the spirit always. Turning uphill for
the apartment, Kati looked up. *Jon was circling above
her.*

*   *   *   *

When she entered her apartment, Kati went straight
to the bedroom. She sat cross-legged on the edge of her
bed, staring into her reflection in the large, swivel mirror
she'd pulled bedside. Her mind was filled with memories
mixed with music from Pachelbel's Canon. The mental
music led to her conversations with Ian and Bjen through
the past week. Everything was different now, she
thought, peering into herself. She followed the notes
with a freedom she had never felt before.

*   *   *   *

Kati walked to the San Francisco Dance Performance
Studio in the dark hours of the morning. Two hours ago,
she'd awakened knowing her reason...her new reason to
dance and to carry on. And Kati felt more excited about

being alive than she could ever remember.

She walked through a side door entrance, grateful that the studio was open all hours. Kati was on a mission, and she needed some time to dance alone. In the dressing room, she pulled on her favorite leotard, the one designed with a blend of black and white whirls and swashes. Kati closed her eyes for a minute, visualizing. Her body was absorbing all the choreography for this private performance that had been imprinting in her mind consciously and subconsciously, since the seagull fly-by the day before.

She chose a sequence of music for her iPod and clipped the iPod to the back of her neckline. Her finger tips brushed around the weave of hair she'd braided at home. She then made the final adjustments to her black satin point shoes.

Kati glided down the short hall and into the large dark dance studio. She flicked the room lights on and started the iPod. Action...her beauty...her dance... her perfection. But she wasn't alone.

*　*　*　*

Ian carefully placed the wooden lunch tray on the corner of the table next to the great window in Jon's recovery room. Part of the model train track system CJ had installed crossed the table top, before bridging back up to the wall. Digging into a hot bowl of lobster and corn chowder, Ian gazed down the Irish coastline. He was enjoying this peaceful moment after a morning filled with meetings and decisions. These fresh tomatoes are delicious, he thought, remembering how he'd refused to eat tomato slices as a kid.

"Is the Mexican hat dance Irish?" Jon asked out-of-the-blue.

Ian's mind instantly ran. Did Jon really speak? Is his brain damaged? Could....

"Take as much time as you need to figure out your answer, bud." Ian nearly dumped his soup in his hurry to stand up. Jon was watching him with half-opened eyes.

"Jon? Say something else."

"Just to kill some time while you work out your answer?"

Ian started laughing, and then he started crying. Jon looked past Ian to the trains on the wall. "Nice of you to stage my recovery in a toy store, pal."

*   *   *   *

Helena was reviewing email when the studio lights came on, casting striped shadows across her workspace. She stood and walked to the one-way, mirrored window that viewed the dance floor.

*   *   *   *

It was more than ballet. Kati's dance was everything she could imagine from her life of twenty six years and forever. She choreographed a ballet integrating gymnastics and every form of dance study she'd become acquainted with since her childhood. She brought winning, losing, fear, and love into ballet variations with an expressive mime that told her life's journey and, to some degree, everyone's.

If anyone on Earth could be best chosen to understand and appreciate, it was Helena. She watched silently.

Kati loved the feel of the studio floor, and she left it behind in a perfectly executed, gymnastic double flip, with a one-and-a-half twist. She stuck her landing with the arched back of an Olympic gold medalist. Then she sprang to a series of en pointé turns, her arms and hands expressing exquisite grace. She flew from the final turn and bounded into the mid-air splits known as Grand Jeté.

She encircled her stage, her world. She wanted to go back to childhood and before. She grasped youth and life, fearing death. Assembling a winding road of rhythmic dance patterns that led her feet to the pounding Celtic step, Kati was digging for her earliest heritage… spinning…lifting upward like springing geysers…feet flying and eyes burning with the determination of a fleeing lioness escaping…vowing never to be captured again…free to seduce and hunt. Kati danced with all her passion running rivers to the sky.

When her iPod score ended, she just kept going with a full orchestra playing in her head. The double tour en air seemed effortlessly special. Then the jump….

The impossible triple turn did it…. Helena lost sense of her own body. She was a spirit watching, dancing…

reaching with Kati into the sound of silence. Reaching for the love of life, reaching to leave all the fear, pain, and hatred behind, Kati found her missing point and began whipping beautiful turns...fouetté after fouetté. She was like her mother on a spinning tip of a figure skate. Lost in spinning time, Kati was an ocean of flowing waves. Finally, she crashed, exhausted, to the floor.

Helena lost count of the fouetté turns and walked slowly to her desk. She sat with her eyes closed, just breathing. She turned toward her make-up mirror to bring herself back to reality, but unexpected tears came. Helena broke down with her face in her hands. She cried out her forgotten feelings.

Kati walked over to the dance studio piano. She sat and played Pachelbel's Canon flawlessly...eyes closed.

*   *   *   *

A few days later...

Kati saw the new message light flickering on the Swönk phone. There was a voice-message from Bjen. "Hi Kati," Bjen said in her low-pitched voice. "I was going to call immediately, but we wanted to be sure that he was really okay. Jon's awake and fully conscious. He's himself, Kati. Thanks to you, Kati. Thank you, Kati."

Kati whooped. She bounced and jumped all over her bed in joy. Finally, in the stillness of her room, lying on her mussed-up bed listening to her heart beat coming down, Kati picked up her phone and touched number 2. "What happened?" She demanded as soon as Bjen picked up.

"He just started talking to Ian...some stupid question.... 'Is the Mexican hat dance Irish?'" They both laughed.

"Ian must of thought he was crazy!"

"That's Jon," Bjen said with a smile in her voice. "Call him Kati. He's at number 4 on your phone."

* * * *

Jon was lying in bed, listening to the roar of the waves from the coast. Moonlight glanced in through the open window. The phone rang. "Yes?"

"Hello cowboy."

"How'd you know?"

"Know what?"

"That I was raised by cows."

Kati laughed. "I'm so glad you're back and doing fine."

"Thanks to you."

"Oh, gawd, I just remembered. It's almost midnight there."

"Really? I haven't been watching the clock."

"I'm sorry it's so late. I just wanted to call. Ian and Bjen have told me so much about you...good things, Jon."

"Well, I'm sorry I had to meet you while I was an inert lump...but better that, than not at all."

Kati cracked up. Then she said sternly, "You should be asleep, healing up, Doctor."

"Physician, heal thyself, huh?"

"That's right."

"I am a little worn out from sleeping and staring at the ceiling so much."

"I know I'll meet you when you're standing on your two feet...soon."

"That's the plan."

"Goodnight then...and I'm going to be checking in on you. You're my patient, understand?"

"Yes, Nurse Hunter. Thanks again. Bye. Bye."

Kati walked out of her bedroom clutching her Swönk phone. She sat on her couch and looked out over San Francisco Bay. She felt totally out-of-sorts. Then she realized she just wanted to get on a plane for Ireland. She pushed number 4 on the phone. "Hi."

"I was hoping you'd call back a little sooner."

"I know it's late, Jon."

"I'm probably still on Colorado time."

Kati laughed, and then said, "How can you be so funny after all you've been through?"

"Hearing you helps."

"I like your voice."

"I'm pretty raspy. You must've been stickin' your fingers into my larynx."

"Could we talk a little? I promise not to keep you too long."

"I'm not goin' anywhere."

"Have Ian or Bjen told you that I'm possibly related to their Celtic family, going way back, and possibly...." Kati broke off for a moment. Then she tried again. "I've never imagined being in a situation that's this amazing. One minute I'm totally energized and the next...well, I'm frightened, Jon."

"They've just told me a little. They probably don't want to push me straight from a coma into cardiac failure."

"I think they rely on you, Jon."

"That explains all the janitorial supplies over in the corner of my room."

Kati giggled. You never quit, huh? Listen, I want your serious side now, Doctor. Just listen."

"Yes, ma'am."

"I have this chance to perform with the San Francisco Ballet. It's something I've been striving towards my whole life, Jon. My dance, my body control, and my strength have never been better. Just since I got here.... I feel more powerful."

"But, you...."

"Let me finish, please."

"But I…." Jon pulled himself up short, sputtering. They laughed.

Kati continued. "I know everything that happened with you, and what I learned from Ian and Bjen have given me a bigger perspective. I have more passion now in my dance, and in my life."

"So you're Irish…a Celtic gal?"

"Very."

"A ballerina trauma prodigy?"

"Stop it."

"Hey, I'm just trying to get the whole picture into my meager brain. I think my IQ may have dropped to about seven, probably your shoe size."

"How'd you know that?"

"I'm not sure. I'm just trying to get used to being alive again." Kati couldn't even comment on that. "Here's what I think," Jon said after a pause, "or do you want that, Miss Hunter?"

"I do, Dr. Wolff."

"Be a ballerina. Let ballet be your life for now. Take every circumstance that has come your way and put that force into your dance."

"I want to know more about my connections with the Swönks' past, Jon."

"It will be waiting for you, Kati, but let your journey begin on the San Francisco stage. Be free, Kati. Fly."

Kati thought about flying and saw gradations of blue:

the blue in the bay water, the blue in the sky, the blue in Jon's eyes. "You have blue eyes," she said.

"That's right."

"I know all this, but it helps to hear you say it."

"You saved my life. I want yours to be the best it can be, Kati."

"I feel like I've known you all for years, not weeks."

"I understand. I've been drawn to the Swönks since meeting Ian at Princeton. And if I can get out of this bed, maybe I'll work with them."

"No ifs and maybes, Doctor. Get better fast. Just don't push too hard, okay?"

"I'm using Q-tips as hand weights."

Kati laughed. "Don't hurt yourself, Jon. Those Q-tips can be dangerous…. Have you seen the bees?"

"Yes, *those* can be dangerous."

"I feel like I can't let go. There's a lot to this, Jon. I just can't talk about it yet. Besides you need to sleep."

"Are you bossy, Nurse Hunter?"

"Sometimes," Kati said slowly.

Jon laughed. "Well, I'm goin' to sleep on that note."

"Huh?"

"I'd better rest. Thinking about all those Q-tips is overwhelming."

"I understand, I think. Goodnight Jon, I'm really glad you're back."

"Night."

Jon closed his eyes. He rested with the phone in his hand. He wished she was coming to Ireland. Between mental flashes of her, he wondered what Kati really looked like.

Kati realized she hadn't said everything she wanted to say and pressed number 4 again. "Jon?"

"Yeah."

"You were incredible saving that baby."

"I don't remember anything."

"Well, I'll never forget. Night."

"Night."

*   *   *   *

Jon slept and dreamed….

The bark on the huge old maple tree was roughened with deep fissures, making foot and hand holds easily accessible for climbing. Pressing each sharp, metal corner of his boot heels into the tree, he rose quickly to a large branch with enough foliage to hide him. He could feel the poison having stronger effects on him and knew she must be moved to a safe distance….

Jon heard the lone rider's horse's muted hoofs on the soft earth. He waited, watching for the perfect moment to drop silently. Be clear minded, he told himself. Kill and protect her. He fell with his razor sharp blade and all his being targeted on their enemy's neck. Now! Deep through to the heart!

*   *   *   *

Michelle strode into the hotel's spectacular corner suite. Her husband, France's President, was hidden behind a newspaper propped up on pillows in the canopied bed. Only the lower part of his navy robe and bare crossed feet were visible. "Hello, darling, are you hiding or reading?"

"Hello dear." Decorated for a king, the Louis XIV suite of the Montreux Palace overlooked Lake Geneva. This was the first time Michelle and her husband had stayed together in the suite.

Michelle dropped her bags. She rushed into the gilded bathroom and sat on the toilet located next to a small fireplace which had probably comforted some kings once upon a time. As her relief came, she noticed the small envelope placed on the tile surface of the vanity. Her name was written on it.

With a hint of smile she opened her card. "Don't look up," she read. "It's a waste of time." Michelle waited. For some reason, she felt bothered. However, she finally looked up. "See!" was written on the bathroom ceiling. But the phrase, "waste of time," lingered in her mind.

*   *   *   *

Lifting the swivel top from her ice-cold beer, Michelle walked out on the terrace to breathe the glorious air. She leaned on the guardrail of her balcony, sipping the Swiss beer between nibbles from a cheese wedge. Michelle watched the couples walking hand-in-hand along the lakeside path and the couples going out onto the lake in sailboats.

Michelle remembered their romantic period, when she'd begged her husband to come to the spa with her, but then, the political agenda had ruled. The excitement, the spark ...actually, the "turn on" of being with a sexy, powerful world leader was dying within her. I won't give up, she thought. I still love him, even though sometimes I feel like a plaything...just another gem in his charmed life.

Michelle's eye caught the small, naked statues along the waterfront, clothed only in bouquets of roses. They reminded her of Percy, the small renaissance statue in the rose garden next to the pool at her childhood home. Looking down, she studied the beautiful ironwork. A mixture of flowers, roses, and winding vines were depicted in the ageless, handmade guardrail. Michelle decided to rock the boat.

* * * *

"I'm not going to ask you again," Mars spoke with finality to his agent.

The agent, code-named Phobos, sat with his back against the wall in a Dublin pub. He switched the phone to his other ear. "Listen Mars," he said, "Ian's not the same since he returned with Jon. My genetics data log has been totally separated from the associated neurological data. It's almost like he knows there's a leak somewhere. They're definitely protecting the new data, and I know why."

"I'm listening."

"Good, because it's time to negotiate."

"You've got to be kidding. I have your sister, remember?"

"And I've got a Ph.D. from Princeton, so I'm not a complete dumb ass. This situation is insane, Mars. There's no way out for me and my sister. You've drawn us into the *dead zone*, so I'm calling the game. No more wasting time. Give me a plan – an exit strategy, for us both. I'm not afraid to die, and, as you can probably tell by now, neither is Katy."

Mars waited silently for Phobos to modify his statement. When he didn't, Mars said, "Come back in a week. If your box isn't in its usual place, she's dead." Mars disconnected.

Phobos sat thinking. He wasn't hungry, but he kept sipping at his pint. Suddenly, realizing he'd almost waited too long, he quickly put the phone back into the fireproof box. He secured the fasteners and walked into the men's room for disposal.

Returning to his table he sat reviewing his situation. My sister's life is in jeopardy, and we haven't even spoken in almost four years. How in the hell did Mars find her when no one in the entire family could? Phobos wondered.

Katy had always been on the fringe. She had been too

smart, too insightful for all the bullshit in the world. So she'd just lived for the day. Her friends had been rockers, druggies, and she had always been in trouble....

And then, she was just gone.... When Mars had contacted Phobos and told him he was holding her, Phobos had been so relieved just to know she was alive. However, before that thought had ended, had come the sickening realization of what Mars was doing—blackmailing him.

Even then, Phobos had considered the price negligible in relation to the broad scope of priorities. He had to get his sister back. At times, he'd even thought the situation could turn her perspective...lead her to a happier life.

Now, however, he realized the serious magnitude of the Mars/Swönk conflict. He knew the issues and the stakes, not just for himself and his sister, but for all humanity.

Mom and Dad...they didn't know any of this shit. Maybe I should go to Ian, Phobos thought, but he has no idea where Mars is located. And when he'd asked Mars where they'd found his sister, Mars had laughingly said, "In Bangkok, Sweden, hanging out with a famous golfer."

*   *   *   *

Mars watched the gusting winds picking up snow from the nearest peaks through his window. He was mindlessly tapping a Mont Blanc pen on the leather desk insert. For once, he didn't feel powerful and decisive. He was in a quandary. I don't know, he thought, but it must be some kind of love. He didn't want to kill Katy or fuck with her brain. Damn, the whole ordeal had taken so long to painstakingly develop.

When Ian had attended Princeton, they'd realized an opportunity to compromise one or more of his friends, to possibly get inside his inner circle. So many people had made lifelong friends with Ian while he was at the university. There had been so many dead ends. But, finally, when Phobos went to EET, they had created the necessary link with his sister, Diemos (Katy's code), and established the leverage they'd needed for information.

Even with so many resources, finding Katy had been difficult and had required a meticulous strategy to get her to Switzerland via her own choices. He'd put operatives, staged as old friends from when Diemos was in Berkley, on her cold trail. One operative had found a contact in Taipei that knew Katy's whereabouts near Bangkok.

By watching Diemos' patterns, Mars' operative had placed herself ahead of Katy's arrival at a favorite Bangkok bar. She had let Diemos find her. As luck would have it, Katy had taken the empty stool next to her at the bar.

"Are you American?" Katy had asked.

"Oh, I wish I was," Chelsea had replied. "No, I'm from Amsterdam."

"You would be happier as an American? What are

you drinking?"

"House red. I think I just want to be happier...." Chelsea had responded. And they'd become friends, honestly, but Chelsea had still carried out her mission.

Eventually, Chelsea had gotten Katy to Amsterdam and arranged a job working with her in a high-end day spa. Within weeks, Diemos had assimilated most of the knowledge needed to operate every department of the lovely care center.

Walking along a tree-reflecting canal pathway one morning, Chelsea had explained the opportunity she'd been offered at a Swiss spa. "There's more money, and I've never had a friend like you, Katy. I really love talking and partying with you, dear, so, I'm taking you with me." Chelsea had brought her.

Mars' staff had made a family for Katy. She'd eventually gone through their detox program, letting go of the tobacco and all the drugs. She was down to just an occasional glass of wine. Diemos had hiked, biked, and gotten into the best shape of her life. Mars had invited her to interview for the spa research department because of her biosciences interest back at Cal. Berkley.

Mars stopped tapping his pen and walked over to the window. He watched the snow blowing off the cornices. It was amazing, he thought, that the Swönk situation had gone on for so many years. He realized he hadn't reflected on the big picture in relation to the distant history in a long time. But what Phobos had called the *dead zone* struck a chord in him. And then there were his feelings for Katy....

Fragments of his records went back to the seventh century. The more detailed accounts of the issues that had led to the war with the Swönks started in 1044. It had all begun with love, food, and documents delivered by a representative of the Swönk family to a large land-holder at his now famous lake-edge fortress.

The Swönk's emissary had been introduced to a woman who was a member of Mars' ancestor's inner group of entertainers. The bard had been on loan to the landowner. The two visitors had found a mutual attraction which had led to a secret tryst at a nearby lake village.

Lost in fiery love, the courier had told his new lady friend stories of his home and the remarkable Swönks. Slipping from his oath of secrecy, he had shared tales of the incredible fresh and varied foods grown in the Swönk's glassed-in patch of land, their ancient greenhouse crops. The story of glassed in winter fruit-bearing trees had made it back to Mars' family roots.

"I think it was...," Mars whispered to himself.

Wanting to see if his memory was correct, he triggered the full security lockdown for his private lair. At the edge of a massive, rock fireplace Mars opened the lichen-covered, gray stone which concealed the keypad for coding in the access number for a case of documents that spiraled up inside the towering chimney.

None of these stolen records had ever been stored digitally, even though Mars constantly reminded himself he should take steps to preserve them electronically. Something in his gut had kept him from doing it.

Custom filing containers started rolling out of their hidden location. Mars picked the one for the first 500 years. Carefully, he unrolled the ancient incunabula and searched.... Her name was Kate! The name of the young entertainer who'd brought the greenhouse story, that had begun the embattled legacy, was Kate!

He started walking around his high courtyard aimlessly. He realized he loved Diemos more than before. She became totally Katy in his mind. He could no longer see her as a convenient pawn. Was it because of his threat to kill her?

The spy ring had come full circle. The Kate of 1044 and, now, his Katy were both links to a better life and the knowledge for personal freedom. Today's world just had more layers of complexity, than the medieval world of Kate's time. But he had to admit the technology at stake today offered more effective solutions to humankind's pathetic struggles.

Mars' ancestors had gained more and more power and wealth by spying on the Swönks and selling tidbits of advanced chemical, food, and warfare ideas to factions of power in their medieval world. Then one day they acquired information that the Swönks were forming alliances with various leaders whose goal was to create more individual freedom and knowledge. They wanted to equalize the structure of society. There would be no more serfs and peasants.... Even a few kings were being drawn to the Swönks' concepts, not to mention their gold.

Whispers of alchemic success went along with the pure auric squares pressed with tiny swans used as gifts and for trade by the Swönks. Finally, the temptation became so great, that Mar's ancestors sent spies to find a way into the Irish, coastal castle that protected the Swönks. Five spy teams were sent, twenty people to infiltrate, search, and steal from the fortress.

Months later, one man returned. Wounded, with blood oozing through the bandage covering half his face, he related his story. "We found a web of tunnels. They all led to dead ends...and death."

And so, the saga continued, until sixteen years ago when Mars had almost reached the end of his rope. He could find no more worthwhile information for his leaders. So he convinced the leader group to support the formation of a world-class team of attack mercenaries. They would employ a small army to forcefully search and seize the Swönks' research in their facilities and homes.

With guns blazing, Mars' army hit eight sites at once. Ian's parents were murdered, and only eight of the seventy-two mercenaries survived.

Ian had been at Eton. Bjen had been hidden and

protected within moments. This was unfortunate, because Mars had hoped to take her as a hostage. The operation had been successful, however, because it had produced some valuable data from stolen laptops. The data had greatly enhanced Mars' research model for distant computer–brain linkage and thought-influence.

Combining the data with his own research, Mars had created a whole new position of value for himself with the Leader Group. He had not chosen to work with the Leader Group willingly. Rather, he had been forced to acknowledge their direction. Now, he reported to them on an almost weekly basis.

Carefully hiding in the web composed of world business, finance, governments, military hierarchies, and religious institutions, the group's power and control over natural resources, money and huge blocks of humanity was immense. Yet the out-of-control spiral of population growth, environmental degradation, and fragmented militant radicals, had forced a change in the master world plan that the leaders had formulated shortly after world War Il. Manipulating the media and the cost of living was not enough now....

Mars thought about how the rising price of medical care and prescription drugs, alone, had driven up the cost of living and laughed out loud. Well, he thought, it certainly kept his pharmaceutical friend's antidepressant sales soaring. He laughed again, with only his stone walls to hear....

Mars considered the inner circles of power that hardly anyone knew about, or ever thought about. He'd never been able to identify them, he thought hopelessly. Then his mind clicked, and he realized he could both identify them and control them with the right technology.

And the Swönks, he thought excitedly, might have the right technology now. With their information, he could leapfrog all the military-driven brain research projects and gain more control of the game he'd been trapped in since birth.

He felt elated, powerful. He wanted to share this information with someone. He wanted, he realized, to share this information with Katy. O god damn – he'd never felt this way before now. With the right combination of mind control, bioscience, robotics, and energy technology, the whole human disaster could be cleaned up. And he would be the controller, not the spying pawn.

How in the hell had the Swönks come up with such an advanced advantage? Was his time running out faster than he knew? The leaders could try to go around him, leaving him in the *dead zone*.

*   *   *   *

"Where are all Zah Pee Pool?" the darling little French girl burst out. Five year-old Gigi looked back and forth between Bjen's and Jon's eyes.

"Dr. Wolff would like some *people* for all his trains, Gigi. Wouldn't you, Doctor?" asked Bjen.

"Well, sure." said Jon.

Bjen had brought her young art students to Jon's rehab room to give him a boost of kid power and to give the children some train fun. "I think I have an idea for making passengers, conductors, workers… all the right people for Dr. Wolff's trains. Shall we get started?"

The kids hopped in joy. "Yeah! Yeah! Yeah!" Jon's smile turned to laughter.

When everyone left thirty minutes later, all the trains had been derailed, and Jon had a whole new gang of buddies.

* * * *

Phobos walked toward the Dublin pub with a cold sweat forming around his neck. Making his way by the long ornate wooden and marble topped bar, he headed for the private corner table where his boxed phone hopefully waited. He scooted into the booth and slid his hand under the table. The box was there, attached in its usual place to the bottom-side of the table top.

Phobos opened the container and placed his right fingertips against the print reader on the phone's screen face. As the bartender placed a pint of Irish red on the table, the screen light indicated Mar's connection was open. Phobos drank almost a third of the pint before activating the phone. "Hello, Mars."

"Hello, Phobos. Your sister is fine. I've decided to give you a greater understanding of the magnitude of the situation that the Swönks and my group are battling over.

And I'm going to give you and Diemos a way out, the exit strategy you asked for, both physical and financial. But in return for this, I need cooperation."

Phobos set his beer down. "Go on."

"I want to know everything you can find out regarding the Swönks' operations, research, assets, and capabilities. And I want this information quickly. You need to realize my family has been supplying influential people, people who have power and control over human life and business affairs though-out the world, with strategic information.

We're caught in the middle, Phobos. . .you, your sister…me…. Our lives are expendable to my leaders. I know they have the desire to cleanse the Earth of large populations. And they will, if I can't get the science necessary to stop them or change their minds."

"So, you're the good guy now, huh? Why don't you give Ian and Bjen Swönk a call and begin to work things out, Mars? From my viewpoint we've got the good, the bad, and the ugly going on here, and giving out little label stickers for everyone involved isn't too difficult."

"Each of us has some good, bad, and ugly, Phobos, and those with the most might usually impose their will. Be sure of this…if my leaders don't complete their strategy to maintain control *and* do it soon without mass death, then the Swönks, me, you, your sister… we're all dead soon. I have the connection, Phobos, I can control a logical plan by releasing a breakthrough scientific strategy to them."

"I think you all are freaking insane! I'll play ball with you, but my sister and I get out safely within one year from today, or I'm going to the Swönks with the whole story, Mars. And I want a plan I understand *and* I want my sister to be in on it."

Mars and Phobos sat silently in the phone connection. Finally, Mars broke the silence. "Listen Phobos, I can give you visual proof your sister is fine, but you will have to do as I say and get what I need from the Swönks before any conversations. Understand? There's no other way. And if the Swönks are reading the thoughts of staff, then you'd better be able to control what, where, and when you think, or it's game over for Diemos and you. Comprende, amigo? You stay put." Mars continued. "Sit there in the pub and write me an outline of what you have. Then write me an outline of what you will get and when you can deliver it. Then text it to me from your phone. Hold your finger prints on the screen until your menu comes up. When I receive the information, you will get a beeping confirmation signal. Then it's four minutes to destruct. Understand?"

"Yes."

"One week from today, same time, same place. Goodbye Phobos."

* * * *

It was Saturday morning, and the whole place seemed quiet. Jon was reading the complete works of Poe, trying to get used to a book in tablet format. On the whole, he preferred books with pages you could feel. There came a knocking upon Jon's door. "Enter at your own risk," Jon called.

Jon's room door cracked open and Gigi's head poked through, covered in a red sweatshirt hoodie. "Hello, Docturrrvwwwwolf."

"Somebody's got a funny sense of humor."

Gigi walked in laughing. "I brought a conductor for the old train engine."

"Great, Miss Gigi Red Riding Hood. Let's see what you have." Jon raised the upper section of the bed so he could sit more upright. He examined the doll. Artistically made from various fabrics, the little conductor's face was stitched and painted to create a personality of discipline and duty. "Wow! Did you make this?"

"Yes," Gigi said with a little dance of happiness. "And Mom and Bjen helped me."

"Well, he's wonderful! Why don't you put him on the train engine?"

Gigi headed for the train. "We have to name him."

"Mr. Gee Whiz, after Miss Gigi."

"Yes, Mr. Gee Whiz it is. Here's your train, Conductor Gee-whiz." Gigi walked back to the bedside and picked up the lovely wooden book-like box she'd placed in a chair next to Jon.

"What's in the sweet box?"

"No candies, Doctor Wolff. This is my chess set."
Gigi opened the box. "See, it's a tiny set with magnets to
hold the pieces."

"Very clever, Miss Riding Hood."

"Let's play a game."

"What if I can't play?"

"Bjen said *you know how*. I'll set the board. You
can be the dark wood Dr-wolfs. Shall we time our
moves?"

"Tell me Gigi, do your parents like chess?" Gigi's
lips tightened, and her eyelids dropped. They're
probably just grand masters and Gigi is probably a little
chess prodigy, Jon thought.

Finally, Gigi replied, "They do."

"I imagine you've learned to play the game quite well
then. "Sometimes," Jon said with a twinkle in his eye, "I
like to think about my next move for an hour or two,
even weeks, sometimes." Jon held his laughter while
watching Gigi's cute cheeks turn red like her hoodie.

"No doctor.. . a minute or two! That's all, please!"

"Well okay, then."

"You begin."

Gigi's moves were over before Jon's hand left the
board space. "Do you play chess against Cray
Supercomputers just for fun, Gigi?"

Gigi giggled, "No Doctor."

Each strategy Jon tried was effective as wet toilet paper.

"Check, Doctor."

Jon could see no way out. "Was that last move you made illegal?" he said in mock seriousness.

"What?"

"You win."

"Nice game, Doctor. Can we play with the trains now?"

"Yes, Let's do that Gigi. How can you be only five?"

"I'm almost six."

"Oh well then, that explains it."

*　*　*　*

Kati called later in the day. "How's my patient doing?"

"I just got beat in chess by a five year-old."

"Seriously, Jon, are you having trouble thinking?"

"It seems to be a recurrent problem, Dr. Hunter."

"Now I see what a difficult patient you can be, Jon Wolff."

"Tell me something good about yourself, Dr. Hunter."

"I'm fitting in well here at the Ballet. Actually things are great," Kati said brightly.

"How great?"

"I'm going to be in the upcoming Swan Lake

performance, and I'm third understudy for the lead."

"Well Holy Shot! Doctor Hunter! Wait till all these Swönks around here get this news! I'm so proud of you, Kati!"

Kati was tingling from Jon's unabashed joy over her success. She couldn't think of anything to say next. Finally she managed, "You'd better calm down. We can't have the patient too excited, you know."

"I'm not calming down, Dr. Hunter. Will you please tell me everything about your dancing and being back in San Francisco?"

That got her going. Kati talked for almost an hour straight. Finally she trailed off. "Are you still there?" she asked.

"I'm listening, and I'm still awake."

Kati laughed. "Did you really get beaten by a five year old?"

"Resoundingly. She's either a chess prodigy or one of Ian's humanoid test robots."

Kati's stomach turned over. "What do you mean 'a humanoid robot?"

"I'm sorry, we probably shouldn't be talking about these things right now. Anyway, Gigi said she had a mother, so she mustn't be a robot.

"Jon, I'm feeling like I can't take any more surprises about the Swönks right now. I can't have all this running around in my head. Do you understand?"

"Of course, you just concentrate on Swan Lake."

"Oh geez, there it is again. Swan and Swönk sound just the same. Everything is bizarre right now."

"Ask me something. Let's get your mind off this."

"Tell me about your medical practice. Ian said you specialize in difficult pain problems?"

"That's the central theme, I would say."

"What kind of therapy or pain management system do you utilize in your practice?"

"Are you in pain?"

"It's rare when I'm feeling perfect all over. The unique stresses of ballet and dance create some recurrent pain patterns.

Jon settled back against the pillows. "Well, let's say you walk into my office because you want to find the best way to reduce or eliminate soreness or painful areas that result from your dance. You want to prevent tissue micro-damage and repetitive injury tendencies. Who really wants to feel one hundred when they're just turning thirty?" Jon laughed.

"Tell me, Doctor," said Kati, getting into her role, "what should I do?"

"First, Miss Hunter, make yourself comfortable in the reception room and just observe. Your evaluation and treatment will begin here. Please don't become alarmed, as our methods are somewhat unusual. They are, however, safe and effective."

Oh Doctor, what's going on, and how much is all this?"

"No worries, Miss Hunter, please. You may pay what you want, when you want, if you want. Are you prepared?"

Kati laughed. "Prepared?"

"Good then. Now, close your eyes and try to be still while I describe this. You'll have to visualize what I'm saying. Ready? Eyes closed, Miss Hunter?"

"Yes, Doctor."

"Begin by taking slow deep abdominal breaths so you won't lose control of your senses."

"Jesus!"

"I'm sorry, you can't ask for help."

Kati giggled.

"Now, the office music rises. It's a dramatic solo piano piece. George Winston is playing 'Light My Fire,' by the Doors." Jon can hear Kati's deep breaths. "You notice that the oil landscape paintings on the wall directly across from you are hanging upside down. What do you see in the paintings?"

"An ocean...a river...snow...." Kati's breath starts to shorten.

"Deep and slow breathing please. Small flocks of white and chocolate sparrows are flying through the room in groupings of four to eight. Tiny white snowflakes fall from their wing tips. The flakes are warm. They disappear when they touch your skin. The birds flow through the walls. Large discs of amber light on the ceiling seem to be spinning around the room.

"Are there other patients in here, Jon?"

"There are, but you can't see each other."

"Jon?"

"My receptionist walks toward you, wearing a beautiful, translucent unicorn mask, and says softly, 'We want to help you.' You feel your joy rise to your skin. You smile when you observe her feet aren't quite touching the floor."

"Jon, you're so crazy."

"Thanks, Miss Hunter. You're free to go wherever you want now."

Kati opened her eyes. "Jon?"

"Yes?"

"All my pain is gone."

"The fantasy is over."

"No, I mean all my real pain is gone. The soreness in my right Achilles tendon is like 90% gone, and it's been bad for days, Jon."

"Well, that'll be $3000 then."

"You make me smile, Doctor."

"Good!"

*   *   *   *

It was raining hard. Kati watched the rivulets of

water running down the windshield of her Prius. BOSE speakers surrounded her with the Doors' piano ensemble by George Winston. She'd purchased the CD after speaking with Jon the day before. She pulled into the center parking lot and sat watching the rain, listening to the music.

Kati knew she should just get out and go into the dance center, but she felt riveted to her car seat. She circled and stretched her right ankle again. Letting her car seat recline, she pushed number four on the Swönk phone. "Good morning, Dr. Wolff."

"Good afternoon, Nurse Hunter."

"My Achilles injury is all gone."

"Tremendous! Maybe you'll jump twenty feet in the air today."

"Nope. I'm just going to fly. How did you know what to say to heal me? And where did all that crazy stuff in your reception room come from, anyway? And, come to think of it, how did I know how to save your life in the street?"

"Excuse me while I get out my Encyclopedia Britannica and look all this up."

"Is all this just your luck?"

"I don't know, Kati."

"I'm listening to the Doors' music that you suggested. I'm sitting in a new car given to me by Ian and a spy named 006½, and talking on a Swönk phone...."

Kati took a deep breath. "Jon, I've been having dreams and visions of you and me. Last night I dreamt we were riding on horseback a long time ago. You were behind me. It was your voice talking to me."

"Was it one horse or two?"

"Are you trying to make me laugh and cry at the same time?"

Jon could hear the strain in Kati's voice. "I'm sure you're beautiful in any state," he said gently.

Kati swallowed and closed her eyes "Thank you, Jon. Talk to me. Help me sort all this out, please."

"I've had some dreams lately that could be related to you also, Kati."

"Gawd."

"Just listen right now, okay?"

"Fine."

"I've no idea why I went into the story yesterday which affected your lower leg pain. It just popped into my head. I've looked into so many out-of-the-box forms of pain therapy and nervous system concepts, that sometimes I just act spontaneously. As for the whole Swönk situation and what you did in the street...do your dreams relate it to medieval times?"

"That's it! That's what period I've been seeing in my dreams. Jon, this is all too much. How can I concentrate on my dance? Speaking of which," Kati glanced at her watch, "I'm now late for my warm up."

"I'm sorry to have kept you."

"I'm sorry I called. I just wanted to tell you more about Swan Lake."

"I'm glad you called, Kati. I wish you'd send me a picture of you to my phone."

"I don't think I should." Kati started to scramble out of the car. She was immediately soaked in the rain. "I don't think we should talk anymore. It's just going to upset me. Goodbye, Jon."

"Goodbye."

Kati slammed her car door. She ran across the parking lot. The rain was falling so hard, it bounced up on her legs after hitting the pavement. She jerked the dance center door open and slammed it behind her. No one commented on her lateness.

*   *   *   *

Jon sat on the tile bench, letting the water soak his head and upper back. He stared blankly down the Irish coast through the giant glass wall of his shower room. I hate to let go of her, he thought, but I could endanger her. I could ruin her life, if she continues to associate with me and all this mess I don't even fully understand. Don't reach out for her, he told himself. Stop!

He looked out at the gray horizon, at the sea and clouds in the distance. Then he closed his eyes to look inside himself for an answer, a path.

* * * *

A man in a worn fedora worked his way towards the café table next to the Lake Geneva walkway. He wore a cable sweater jacket that would have been at home on a small lake camp in the Adirondacks. The jacket's empty left sleeve was pinned up. The man's right arm labored with the bamboo and sterling silver cane that controlled his limp. He was accompanied by a woman who matched her pace to his.

Their table was just under an awning which protected them from the piercing afternoon sun. "Look darling!" The two swans on the lake took Che's gaze straight out towards the fountains which jetted 200 feet up from the lake surface. The gushing water gleamed against the backdrop of the French Alps.

Che turned back to Michelle's tattooed face. The skin art covered almost two thirds of her lovely features. "Your facial ink looks authentic," he said. He addressed her as Kovina, an alias crafted carefully by them.

"That's because it is, Che," Kovina said.

I'll play her game if it's what she wants, Che thought.

Kovina smiled. "Tell me what you learned at the CERN meeting today."

A waiter placed two Kir Royales on the small table, along with a rectangular plate of mixed hors d'oeuvres. Che picked up a cracker decorated in pâté. "This duck pâté is delicious."

"It's black swan pâté."

"I should have noticed…. Didn't you see that film recently?"

"I enjoyed the portrayal of illusions and the reaching into the dark." Kovina was tired of this chit chat. "And CERN?" she asked again.

"Sounds delightful. I suppose the search for dark matter…anti-matter, rather, in the particle accelerator at CERN offers its own set of illusions, too."

"How are all the tiny collisions going?"

The sun dropped behind the range of Alps, cooling the air instantly. Che placed his cocktail down gently. "They've found that their specks of anti-matter and energy signatures are starting to validate some exotic theories that only particle physicists would conjure up."

"So, have they seen God's nuts yet? Or is that huge machine considered to be God's giant tube dick?"

"I was going to ask you to teach a Sunday school class, but now, maybe not."

Kovina chuckled. "I could play the part."

"I have no doubt. We had a wine, cheese, and *nuts* party last night that generated some interesting conversations."

"Who was there to sip and munch?"

"All the top scientists, some military high ups. . .lab techs…politicians… me. .. and then the people I couldn't really place. I called them the 'handsome blenders,' the savvy observers who represented companies or organizations I didn't recognize."

"Really, and no one recognized you?"

"No, your ingenious plan worked perfectly, dear."

"So, the fading, old philosopher gambit got you into all the conversations?"

"Charmed 'em. It was the techs who drank heavily and spilled the most interesting scoop."

"What spilled?"

Che smiled. "A little after midnight I laid down on a couch in the wine room."

"Wine room?"

"The estate's wine cellar. Two of the junior scientists I'd met earlier came down for a bottle and saw me sleeping. They were talking about an exposure accident that had occurred in their work zone near the collider. They joked about taking my pants off while I was passed out."

"I'll bet that tested your resolve."

"A bit, but the conversation lifted me from their thoughts. They ignored me after their little joke. I learned much from their little mistake. As it turns out, a small group of physicists rushed to inspect a meltdown during some magnetic atom acceleration testing. When they entered the damaged site, a second wave of magnetic field energy, combined with fragmented sub-atomic particle forces, caught them unexpectedly. Since the accident all the exposed physicists are AWOL. . . missing."

"What else?"

"The jokers left the cellar."

"You're lying, Che." Kovina stared fearlessly at Che. "You're good at bending the truth... like those magnetic bending forces in the collider."

"The scientists were brought here to Switzerland. It's all I know."

"I want to know everything you know about the CERN project, dearest. I want to know all the layers of their game, and how you really feel about it. And if you want this woman's real love, then you'll give it all to me."

"I want to. I actually want to Mich...Kovina." Che looked at Kovina's tattooed face in some consternation. "That isn't real ink?"

"Maybe you'll find out in the spa shower later tonight, Che." Kovina winked. As they continued to drink and eat by the lake, darkness fell, and the truth came out. The great fountain pulsed with lights. The two swans drifted. Finally, the odd looking couple left and walked to a narrow side-street where an old, battered, white alpine, Range Rover was parked. France's President opened the driver's side door for his wife. She drove them to the exclusive, spa retreat managed by Marcus.

Just before the tunnel, Kovina stopped at a polished steel barricade. She punched in a code, and the stone-covered elevator door slid open. She pulled the Range Rover into the high speed lift. Riding upwards through the mountain, toward the private, castle suite, Kovina laughed. "I know how you hate surprises, Che."

*   *   *   *

It was in the wee hours of the morning. They sat in a large, underground conference room of black polished rock. The light from the changing holographic projections bounced off the thousands of gold flecks in the smooth surface of the egg-shaped table, creating rainbow sparkles. Held by only a pedestal stem, the giant, rock table-top was perfectly flat and level. The walls of the room were smooth and cut with angled surfaces.

Bjen set her crystal mug of rich coffee, topped with hot Irish crème, down on the cork pad. "I'd like a little more coffee, please, 006½. I would help you, but I know you put some *secret agent* in this to make it taste so good."

Nicholas emerged from an almost imperceptible slit in the rock wall. He carried a crystal pitcher of the caffeinated brew. "Don't try to make me laugh this early in the morning, please. Anyone else need more?"

"I'm fine, but thanks for offering," Carly said. Carly's remark brought a tight-lipped smile from 006½. Carly was the computer creating the holographic data images for the meeting.

"I thought you only consumed tins of cold ravioli, Carly," Nicholas retorted.

"Yuk!" the computer responded with all the inflection of a human.

"Let's move from the small talk to our agenda," Ian said. "I guess we need to start with Satchmo."

Bjen perked up. "Satchmo?"

"He's our mole."

"You've got to be kidding!"

"Where did Satchmo come from anyway?" asked CJ.

"Seattle."

"I meant the *nickname*."

"At Princeton, when he'd get a little drunk, he'd always go into a Louis Armstrong impression," Ian replied. "He'd sing and play 'When the Saints Come Marching In' on that little trombone-kazoo instrument he liked to carry around."

"My, it sounds like this guy has some real musical talent," Carly commented.

"Please, Carly, hold 'em for a while," CJ said wearily.

"Yes, master," Carly replied demurely.

"How in the hell did you create this computer's personality?" Nicholas asked.

CJ smiled. "With sheer insanity."

Bjen, who had been sitting in dumbfounded silence,

blurted out, "I take it I'm the last to hear this information, or you all wouldn't be so blasé."

"I guess we just wanted some drama and excitement for our meeting." Ian smiled.

"Well, God Damn!" Bjen was starting to get agitated.

"Really, Bjen," said Ian. "All the details confirming Satchmo's involvement just happened, and the situation is complex. We all feel heartbroken... betrayed."

"Actually, I...," the computer began.

"Carly, don't," said CJ.

Ian continued. "I've thought about bringing Jon in on this, but I don't want to lay this on him right now. Let me outline everything I know and please, each of you jump in, you too Carly. And Carly, I want you to give us each a coordinated project panel on this, please." The panels all projected in perfect viewing positions.

"First of all," said Ian, "we were able to find Satchmo by linkage of key word thought-trace recordings, coupled with CJ's new specific brain-signal pattern typing and, it goes without saying, Carly's massive capacity." Carly made a throat clearing sound, and everyone laughed.

006½ jumped in. "We've integrated the bees' micro-systems with the sensor technology that enabled CJ to pickup voice trace memory from certain kinds of stone. I should also say, it was Carly that solved the final data model problems." Carly cleared her throat again.

"Carly are you getting ready to sing or something?" Bjen laughed.

"Maybe, if you all beg."

"How about, just a little guitar instrumental for now, please, Carly." CJ suggested.

"Of course." Guitar music started playing faintly in the background.

"So," Nicholas resumed, "we tracked Satchmo around the clock with the bees, and they followed him to the Absinthe Bar in Dublin." Carly projected Satchmo going into the bar and talking on the waiting phone. "We got a voice recording from bees, and we also managed to get some trace recordings from the stone pillars next to his corner table."

Bjen looked at Ian. "So this gives us a link to the group who's been at us for a 1000 damn years!" she said intensely.

"We're going to turn this sour situation into lemonade," Ian confirmed.

Bjen broke into tears. "I hate the god damn fuckers that killed our parents." She slammed her fist on the stone conference table. Carly faded the projection and the music.

"Let's all take a break," Ian said. Bjen disappeared into the black wall and headed for the women's room.

*   *   *   *

They reconvened thirty minutes later. "I'm sorry

everyone," Bjen said. She smiled apologetically.

"We've all had your feelings, Sis. Is your hand okay?"

Bjen flexed her fingers. "Well, it's not broken."

"Let's go on then," said Ian. "Satchmo's contact on 'the other side' is called Mars. This Mars has Satchmo's sister, Katy, held as a hostage, as far as we can tell from their conversation."

"And Katy's ransom is information from the Swönks?" Bjen asked.

"That's the picture we have at this point," said 006½. "We're going to confront Satchmo and give him the chance to make this right by becoming a double agent. We've chosen this path because Katy's life may be at stake. We want to give Satchmo a chance to save her, if we can."

"I'd get him on board within twenty-four hours," CJ said. Everyone agreed.

"I'd like to discuss Kati Hunter and Jon next, if we could," said Bjen.

"Fire away," said Carly brightly. CJ rolled his eyes in exasperation.

"The cell sample Ian took from Kati's glass in Boulder matches the biochemical profile from our original vessel cell," Bjen continued. "Kati's the first person we've ever found that's an exact match. And if it's true that Jon died in the 'accident' and Kati brought him back, then Kati has extraordinary capabilities. Obviously, her artistic talent is a reflection of this. Even her personality profile fits."

"Jon thinks of her every 12.3 seconds," Carly said smugly.

"I'm sure Jon would appreciate you sharing that, Carly," Ian said.

"It is imperative that I finish," Carly pushed on. "Jon's recurring thoughts about Kati are both conscious and subconscious. But, considering Kati and Jon have never met, this is still unusual. Now add this to the equation. As we speak, the bees searching for rock-stored data on all our Swönk properties have found 79 voice traces from the distant past that match Jon or Kati's current voice profile patterns."

All of a sudden, Carly had everyone's imagination running wild. They all sat silently, readjusting their borders of reality. "A side note of interest," Carly continued calmly, "is that the rock and gold composition of this meeting room won't store thought or voice trace energy."

"So the stones really do speak?" asked Ian, trying to wrap his mind around the idea that Kati's and Jon's voice patterns matched those of some ancient couple.

"We think so," said CJ grinning broadly.

"Ya think!" exclaimed 006½.

Everyone laughed. It was the type of laughter that

follows after a long stretch of tension. It was like a
spring rain. Even Carly laughed in her own computer
sounding way. "CJ," Ian said when they recovered, "do
you think Satchmo has any possible way to hack into
Carly?"

"What!" Carly exclaimed. "Someone could be
playing around in me without me knowing it?"

"I'd say a solar catastrophe happening today would
be much more statistically probable, Ian. So rest easy,
Carly."

"You're giving me the heebie-jeebies, gentlemen,"
Carly said dolefully.

Ian turned to Bjen. "Considering our overall
situation and Jon's link from our past, I feel like we
should include him in all information and decision
making from now on."

006½ chimed in. "The fact that this Mars group went
after Jon directly, and has Satchmo's input...and that
they might even be aware of Kati Hunter's
involvement... indicates that our conflict is headed for a
boiling-point. I think we should move from our defensive
position to a complete offensive strategy ASAP. Getting
Jon and Miss Hunter together and in the formula to sort
through our strategic options might prevent an all out
war. I'm also concerned about Kati's safety. Maybe we
should activate the dormant bee system in her Prius."

"Let's start with Jon," Bjen said. "Then let's go to
Kati. We can fit everything to Satchmo's reaction to our

approach over the next two days." Everyone agreed.

"Our ocean nutrient mineral complex for fertilizer is showing weakening signs," CJ contributed.

"Great," Ian said dourly. Anyone got any good news?"

Carly sang, "I'm forever blowing bubbles, pretty bubbles in the air…." The computer got everyone laughing and sharing good news together. Deep down, under the edge of the Irish sea, encased in gold-flecked, ancient, black stone, the Swönk gang told funny stories like children in their secret clubhouse, hidden away from the outside world.

*   *   *   *

"So," said Ian, "how's your strength?"

Jon was sitting at the huge, antique, role-top desk that the Swönks had placed in his room. Ian had pulled up a chair beside him. "I'm not doing your upcoming summer camp I'm afraid, buddy." Jon smiled.

"Damn, that was my next question. We're planning a revised program for you, Dr. Wolff."

"Revised? Give me a hint, Ian."

"It's a surprise."

"What? You're testing human cannonballs now?"

"How did you guess?"

Bjen walked in. She approached the desk where Ian was watching Jon working on a model train. "I hear you're making a replica of the Orient Express, Dr. Do

Little," she said.

"Maybe if I do a good job, those orient guys will give me a ride on the real thing."

Bjen smiled. "We'll just get you a ticket, actually two. You'll need one for Miss Hunter to come along with you."

"Oh, that would be far too easy. But thanks for the offer, dear."

"I thought you loved simple, elegant solutions, Jonny," said Ian.

"I believe it's called the Simpleton-Orient Express," Jon quipped. Everyone laughed.

Bjen examined the tracks closely. "I love the way you've run the little tracks into your desktop," she said. "You're just so creative!"

"And," said Jon, "I'm playing the part. I've got my Northern Pacific long johns on underneath everything!" This brought another round of chuckles.

Finally, Bjen said soberly, "Do you mind if we bring Carly in, Jon? We've got some serious issues to discuss with you . . . if you feel up to it."

"I thought she was already hiding under the bed."

"Carly is hooked up to all your monitor equipment," Ian replied. But she hasn't been totally activated in here yet."

"So," Jon concluded, "minimal service is reading my thoughts, but not controlling them?"

Bjen laughed. "We love you 'cause you're so funny and intelligent, Jon."

"Let's not go overboard, Bjen." Ian grinned.

Carly's bright, melodic voice interrupted them. "Hello, everyone!"

Jon looked under his desk. "You can come out from under there now, Carly."

"Har, Har! Doctor," said Carly.

"Well," said Jon, "let's all get comfy. Ian, you and Bjen sit over there on your soft leather couch in my room in your castle. Carly, you can lay in my bed, but don't go reprogramming any settings." Jon turned from the desk in his custom electric chair with adjustable leg supports. "Are there any robots we might want to invite to our meeting?" He smiled.

"Bjen is right," said Ian fondly. "We do love you, Jon, and the fact that you keep us laughing, no matter what."

"He's a god send," said Carly solemnly. Everyone laughed.

"To begin," said Ian, "screen and secure this area."

"Already done," came Carly's mock metallic reply.

"As I've briefly explained to you, Jon, the reason I was coming to Colorado was to talk with you about our internal information leak, and the building issue of mind mapping and potential thought-control technology. As you know, we lost some of our break-through neuroscience files during the attack that killed our parents.

Recently, Dr. Jameson has heard rumors of clandestine brain research related to our missing files. CJ and Carly are going to begin a search into records at various brain centers that we suspect could be working with Mars. We believe Mars is the operative who initiated the attack that killed our parents."

"So now, Carly's becoming a hacker?" Jon interrupted to get a little distance from what Ian was telling him.

"Please Doctor," Carly said, "no name calling allowed."

"Getting to the point," Ian continued. "Satchmo is our mole. Mars is holding his sister as a hostage. I hate to bother you with all this while you're recovering and building model trains, but. . .."

"I'm okay," Jon interjected. "I'm ready to jump in…at least intellectually, if not physically. And I'm feeling sick, betrayed by Satchmo. On one hand, I can understand. On the other…he should have come to us for help!"

"He probably knows it," Ian said. "We'll talk with him tomorrow. But we thought you should you should know first, and we wanted to get your input."

"Bring him here," said Jon. "after all, his controller, Mars, put me here."

"If it's safe, we'll do that, Jon."

"Jon, regarding Kati…." Bjen said.

"Kati who?"

"Hunter, smartass."

Carly watched Jon's emotional signals elevate. "Oh yes, her," Jon said sheepishly.

"You'd better be glad I don't have a bucket of ice water, Doctor Wolff," Bjen said.

"It's in my veins already, thanks," Jon retorted.

"I've found out a number of details about Kati, Jon." Bjen glanced at Ian. Ian nodded. "Kati is part of a formula," Bjen continued, "a genetic formula that fits into a creative solution equation."

Jon interrupted, "Do me a favor…leave Kati Hunter alone."

"She's already involved."

"You could get her killed, or worse. If the people you're fighting get their hands on her, she'll end up in their labs…and you both know it."

"Consider the big picture," said Ian.

"I don't discount it, Ian," Jon replied. "But you balance the value of individual life with the collective. If Kati is a unique factor to the overall, then hell, you have to create an omega strategy to protect her, not jeopardize her! She's not going to be caged. I think she might run soon."

"Meaning?" Bjen lifted an eyebrow.

147

"She vacillates between keen interest for the Swönk world, and fear of the risk." Jon gave everyone a sarcastic smile. "Gee, I can't imagine why, based on my personal experiences."

* * * *

After they concluded their discussion with Jon, Bjen and Ian walked through the neuroscience center toward the exit. Bjen said thoughtfully, "I can't see how we can justify waiting for Kati Hunter to decide on her own if she wants to come here to explore what is probably her destiny anyway."

"Jon finds patterns and solutions, Bjen. He and Kati are linked. Let him find the way. Please don't push this."

"But, Ian...."

"Let Jon do it, Bjen!" Ian shouted and walked off.

* * * *

Jon glued another piece of paper-thin, walnut wood veneer into place on the O-gauge train coach model. As he started to turn his chair for the view down the cliffs to the ocean, he had the impulse to pick up the small, black leather cylinder that held his keepsake Hopi multi-stoned ring. It was one of the two most prized possessions handed down from his grandfather. The tiny drawstring pouch inside was empty.

Calm, peak awareness came to him like the behavioral response of a golden retriever. He guided the electric chair to the window and released the platform lock. Then he just rocked slowly, using his good leg to push. Jon closed his eyes, while his mind sifted through the possibilities. Then he smiled and shook his head. Picking some piano favorites with his music remote, he watched the endless sea moving ashore.

*   *   *   *

"Father, I'm certain this whole charade of yours will be a total waste of our time," Ricardo remarked as he watched his dad insert the security entry card into the ballet director's private entry system. "For some reason I just don't seem attracted to ballet, ballet dancers. . . anything ballet. The conversations I've had with dancers have been short and completely pointless."

Shutting the door silently, they walked to the one-way, mirrored window that overlooked the performance studio floor. Kati was in mid air. . . legs and arms delicately extended, but with fire in her eyes. Neither man had a word to say now.... They just watched Kati dance. All her movement was pure and perfect.

Kati's expressive beauty led to Ricardo's determined request. "I want to meet that woman, father."

Ricardo Ottoban II laughed gently at his son, Ricardo Ottoban III. "I'll speak with Helena."

*   *   *   *

"I have another person, Doctor!" Gigi exclaimed as she walked into Jon's room without even knocking.

"Who is it this time?" Jon asked.

"A passenger...a little girl."

"Named Gigi?"

"Yes!" Gigi laughed. "Yes!" She did a little happy dance.

Jon smiled. "Better put her on the train. Then come sit down so we can talk a little."

Gigi carefully placed her character into a silver, passenger car seat pulled by the engine conducted by Geewhizz. She came over and plopped into an oversized chair that made her look like a small doll to Jon.

"I have a little mystery to solve, Gigi," Jon said mysteriously.

"Oh?"

"Would you like to help me solve it?"

"Maybe." Gigi sighed.

"I have a very special ring that has gone missing." Gigi maintained her best poker face, but her gaze wavered from Jon's eyes. "My grandfather gave it to me," Jon continued, "and I always keep it in that black leather case on my desk when I'm not wearing it."

Gigi got up and stepped to Jon. She leaned her head against his chest. "I have it, Dr. Wolff. I just wanted something of yours, something beautiful to always remember you."

"You make it sound like I'm dying soon, Gigi."

Tears rolled down Gigi's cheeks, but she talked

through them. "You might, Doctor."

"Well, I'll try not to die until you beat me another couple thousand times in chess, okay?"

Crying shakes turned to laughing shakes. "I'm sorry. I'll bring your ring back."

"First, I want you to have a special gift from me, alright?"

"Yes, Doctor."

"Go over to my desk. See the wooden box with the sailing ship on top? Bring it carefully to me please, Gigi."

"It's very beautiful, Doctor."

"You may call me Jon."

"Certainly, Doctor Jon."

Jon laughed. He opened the box and took out a sparkling glass heart. "Gigi, this heart was made in Venice, Italy by one of the oldest glass makers in the world. Let's put it in the pouch from my ring case for you to keep. This gift for you means we'll always be friends, and you'll be in my heart forever... even when I'm gone someday."

"I'd like that, Jon."

"Can you bring my ring back when you visit next time?"

"Yes, it's safe, Doctor. I promise."

"I trust you, Gigi. We're friends, and we can always talk about our feelings...okay?"

"Okay."

"You should get back to your class…and, Gigi?"

"What?"

"It's always good to knock on my door, and wait until I say, 'come in,' okay?"

"Okay."

"High five!"

*   *   *   *

"You certainly have quite the private deck up here, Marcus. Too bad you don't have much of a view, though," Katy remarked sarcastically.

A tailored waiter walked in from the exterior elevator designed to service the upper castle courtyard. With a flourish, he placed stacked crab Louie salads, along with another chilled bottle of white wine, on the table. Marcus ladled the delicious dressing onto his salad. "Anything you want, Katy dear? Tell Nido before he leaves us."

"Where did you get the crabs, Nido?"

"I'll ask the chef for you, Miss Katy. Can I get anything else for you right now, Mademoiselle?"

"I'm good, thank you," Katy said sweetly.

As Nido walked away, Marcus remarked, "You like being difficult don't you, Lady? I must say, you've perfected your style."

Katy didn't acknowledge him at first. She just kept eating her salad. Finally she said, "So, did you bring me up here for the first time just to show me the perfect crab

Louie salad, Marcus?"

Marcus laughed out loud. "Why not? But no, there are a few matters we should discuss, Katy."

"Well, nothing could ruin this incredible salad, so start talking." She laughed.

"You seem so unconcerned about anything, Katy. I have to admit, your nonchalance attracts me in an odd sort of way. But this might be of serious interest to you. Your brother is in life-threatening trouble."

Katy kept chewing and showed no emotion. She wiped her mouth, got up from the table and walked to the elevator.

*   *   *   *

A hundred feet below, Michelle and the French President sat on an outside deck finishing their lunch. Michelle's facial and body paint was gone. The President's arm was back. Michelle flashed her glittering seductive smile, "So, *Che*, I've been thinking. I would like you to schedule a series of private lunch meetings with the scientists operating the collider."

Che stared unemotionally at his wife. Michelle continued, "By planting false, threatening information, you will be able to find the location of the missing researchers. Then demand each individual's silence. Let them know they'll lose their positions immediately if there's a leak."

"You're pushing this game too far, Michelle," the

French President said.

"Dearest, as I told you last night, I'm privy to a plot that can destroy the government of France and much more."

"You will have to give me details before I can continue…."

"Fine," said Michelle. "Let's go to our stress removal treatment. That will help you cope with what I'll tell you tonight, *Che*."

*   *   *   *

Katy watched the brain scan images on her large screen. Her position on the spa neuroplasticity research team had created a new world of interest for her. It was almost an addiction. But she was starting to think she should give the job up. What does he know about Ramey, she wondered. What in the hell is going on? Maybe I should just get out of here right now….

But she couldn't. Watching the two spa clients' brain activity in a resting state was the first phase of the upcoming experimental therapy. Katy had never met her clients. Yet she felt like she'd touched their souls by reaching inside their brains to help them cope and find more enjoyment in life.

Constructed brilliantly, Mars' "Brain Design Team" carried out its objective without any one person fully knowing the overall purpose. Each member of the team thought he understood what was going on, and each thought what he was doing was harmless. Mars' deception was perfect.

Katy moved waves of pulsed energy from cortical neuronal networks to limbic emotional and hippocampal trigger nodes, while observing the overall color coded brain activity. Synchronizing the two clients was her goal, as she knew the two lovers had chosen this path to strengthen their relationship. But a slight tear was forming in Katy's trust. She started to doubt the wisdom in her new-found job.

*   *   *   *

Michelle and the French President floated in temperature controlled sea water. Bioengineered lilies released an aromatic essence which elevated their brains' limbic systems. The dome above projected melting sky-scapes, ranging from fiery, red sunsets to colorful nebulae.

Oxytocin, the body's chemical of orgasmic release and trust, was misted on them in micro dosages along with lust-enhancing dopamine. Chelsea spoke in her softest most soothing feminine voice as the couple's brain patterns reached the required open receptive levels.

"Welcome to the frontier of freedom where your love and creative exploration reaches beyond your wildest dreams. You're traveling in complete safety. . .protected together in a magical cocoon. Everything you think or desire will build your bond of love for each other."

Mars observed each critical step of the French first couples' mind programming. But his mind was only partially engaged with the couple. With the other part of his mind he ran over his conversation with Katy. *Why did I say that to her? Crap! You idiot!* He took a deep breath. *I'll go down after this and fix everything with her.*

He prepared the command sequence to be interjected between Chelsea's live statements. Computer generated strategic commands would utilize Chelsea's current voice to manipulate the French couple's future behavior. Michelle's first session had worked as desired. Mars' excitement was building. He felt sure this test could reveal the combination of energy and chemistry necessary to program decision-making into the human brain. *If this works, I'll have done it,* he smiled to himself.

*   *   *   *

It was an almost summer night's dream....

Jon was driving a rig with a flatbed. Ian was sitting on the seat beside him. Ian was wearing suspenders and a red baseball cap. "How much farther on this friggin' dirt road, Jon?" Ian asked plaintively. "We're stirring up so much dust.... We'll probably ruin this cake."

"It's boxed up pretty tight. I think it will be okay. We'll check on directions.... I'll stop the guy over there on his tractor." Honk! Honk! Honk! Jon blasted the big flatbed eighteen wheeler's air horn until the weatherworn farmer on an ancient, red tractor turned to stare at the huge rig sitting on the small dirt road. Jon

climbed out, while Ian rolled down his window to listen.

Waving, Jon yelled, "Could I ask you a question, please sir?"

"Huh?" said the farmer. After three more "huhs," the farmer came over. Jon extended his hand to shake, but the old man waved it off stating, "Bibb Liano. I'm a dumb ass Texan."

"You're from Dumas, Texas, then Sir?" Jon pronounced Dumas correctly as 'Doomas.'"

"We pronounce it dumb ass here, son."

Jon frowned at Ian whose head was bobbing with laughter. "Well, I'm sure that creates some interesting speculation, sir."

"Call me Bibb."

"Bibb, like the food protection device?"

"I've always needed one. Say, why do you need this huge rig to carry that one small box on your trailer?"

"Bibb, that small box is very heavy."

"Do say. . . what's in it?"

"A cheesecake from the converted, offshore drilling rig factory in the Gulf."

"Well, that explains it. I hear they're usin' one of those cheesecakes to anchor the battleship Texas, now."

"I believe that's correct, sir. We're looking for a Miss Kati Hunter. We need to deliver this last cake to her before dark."

"Mizz Hunter lives on down this road 'bout seven miles. Tell her I'll be comin' down for some cake later."

"We'll tell her you're coming, Bibb. Thanks for the directions." Jon got back into the cab while Ian was still bouncing around in speechless laughter.

*   *   *   *

Jon's dream shifted scenes. "Git those damn snakes back in them jars, Bubba!" Kati exclaimed while she worked her way through the kitchen clutter. Kati was wearing a pink apron over a floral dress. "They're gonna kill Romo if they bite'eem, boy," she continued. "We cain't find another pit bull puppy like Romo, Bubba. His momma chewed into some kinda illegal nutrient supplements box or somethin' and he's going to be huge. So, keep those rattlers away from him. I think our cake's comin' soon, too. So, hurry up!"

*   *   *   *

"That's probably her house there," said Jon pointing at a ramshackle cabin.

"But there's nothing around here," said Ian. "Just that house...no trees. . . nothing! It's eerie looking."

"Don't sweat it, Ian. Some folks like a three-sixty view, I guess. She seemed very sweet when she called in her order."

"I wondered why you were so hell-bent on making this delivery yourself. You've already chatted her up, I see."

Jon gave a mock sigh. "Try not to be too unprofessional, Ian. You wait in the truck while I go to the door." The door bell ringer was crushed flat, so Jon just rapped on the screen door frame.

*   *   *   *

"Hurry, Bubba!" Kati yelled. "Get the muzzle on Romo. I think our cake has come. Tie him to somethin' son." Kati straightened the neckline on her floral cotton dress before jerking the front door open. "Well, hello!"

"Hello to you, ma'am," said Jon tipping his cowboy hat. "It's nice to see you after our phone conversation."

"Wonderful! Where's the cheesecake?"

"It's still on our rig. Should I call you Kati, Miss Hunter?"

"You can go with Miss Kati Hunter."

"Fine, Miss Kati Hunter. Now, I need to plan how we're going to get the cake into your house, Miss Kati Hunter. Where do you want it?"

"We have a loading dock built right into the kitchen," said Kati proudly.

"Great, we can just pull around back."

"No, like I said, the loading dock is in the kitchen, not behind it."

"Show me, please."

The steel and cement loading dock sat right in the middle of the kitchen with a small two-seat dining table on top. "You must get a nice view from up there," said

Jon, scratching his head behind his cowboy hat.

"We certainly do!"

"We'll need to use our forklift to bring the cake in, Miss Kati Hunter. Do you have any entry, other than your front door?"

"Nope, one way in...one way out."

"Then," said Jon, after some reflection, "it would be best if you could clear the front hallway, please, Miss Kati Hunter." Jon glimpsed something out of the corner of his eye. "Is that the back of your son's head over there?"

"Don't worry. He's just a little shy with new people, outa-staters, like you."

"Maybe you could introduce us sometime."

"Well, maybe so," Kati allowed.

"I'll get my associate, Ian, started unloading your cake."

"Very well then, Mister Jon ...was it, Wolf?"

"Actually, it's Dr. Jon Wolff, with two f's."

"So, you're a cheesecake doctor...Dr. Wol puff?"

Jon heard laughter cackle from Bubba who remained motionless and facing away as Jon headed for the truck.

"Get the chainsaws out, Bubba, both of them," Kati ordered unemotionally.

"Yes, Meemaw."

*   *   *   *

Ian kicked the dust up with his foot. *"I really don't think the forklift can fit through that front door even with the screen off, Jon."*

"I don't imagine she'll care if we leave a few marks, but you're gonna need to punch it hard before you hit the ramp up to the front door."

"Whatever you say, boss. Hey," Ian continued brightly, *"maybe you should drive this one!"*

"No, no, you need the experience. "There's two custom accelerators on this particular loader. When you hear me yell 'now,' push the right pedal to the floorboard. Then, I'll yell 'hit it,' and you slam the left to the floor, okay?"

"And the odd rear tires on this thing?"

"Slicks off an old drag racer."

"Shit!"

*   *   *   *

"Here he comes, Meemaw!" yelled Bubba.

Kati strolled through the kitchen dangling a chainsaw in each hand. There was a wild, devilish look in her eyes.

Luckily, the weight of the cheesecake kept the supercharged front-end loader from flipping over backwards as the rear drag slicks created a huge cloud of burning rubber smoke, before catapulting up the ramp towards Miss Kati Hunter's door. Ian's scream of terror was drowned out by the cracking plywood ramp, the *squealing tires, and the sound of Kati's chainsaws.*

After sitting still in a cloud of smoke and splinters, the forklift caught traction and lifted off in flight for the door. Swinging both chainsaws in a frenzy, Kati widened the door space just before Ian flew through. He landed and screeched forward, leaving a black rubber track marking the path into the kitchen.

Somehow, when the smoke cleared, the cake was on the loading dock and Bubba was up next to it, hooting and shaking his fists in the air. Romo was howling some kind of ancient wolf connection because his muzzle had magically disappeared.

Jon walked calmly through the door, just like it was another typical cake delivery. "Thanks for the assistance, Miss Kati Hunter. That was tight."

But Kati paid him no mind. She was already hacking away at the thick cake box with her left chainsaw. Suddenly, the top flew off. The top's steel bands hurled, crashing through the kitchen sink window.

Jon glanced at Ian with a "can you even believe this woman?" smile on his face. Kati began slicing cheesecake wedges with her right hand saw. It was a Texas Cheesecake Massacre!

Jon awoke, laughing.

* * * *

"Checkmate, Dr. Wolffy!" Gigi said triumphantly. Then she broke into laughs. "You are playing a little better though."

"Well thanks, Gigi. And thanks for coming to have breakfast with me."

Ian walked into Jon's room. "Please don't teach him too much, Gigi. He'll be taking his new skills out on me next." Ian looked at his watch. "Hey, young lady, you'd better head over to Bjen's classroom, or you're going to be late."

Gigi pulled her glass heart out of her pocket and showed it to Ian as he walked her to Jon's door. "Not many people have those, Gigi," he said gravely. "Keep it safe."

"Oh yes! Goodbye, Mr. Swönk."

Ian walked over to sit on the couch next to the coastal viewing window. Jon started tinkering with the model Orient Express coach he was constructing. "So, are you going to give all the girls you like a glass heart, Dr. Wolff?" Ian asked.

"That's not a bad idea."

"You can only have one heart per summer camp you complete alive, you know."

"I'll choose my girlfriends carefully then."

"You shouldn't keep choosing women who are a lot smarter than you, Doctor. It's only going to frustrate you."

"I believe you and Bjen handpicked our five year-old friend to slaughter me in chess for your entertainment, dear Caesar."

Ian finally laughed. "It was Bjen's idea first, I swear."

"Like that lessens the salt in my wounds...."

Ian just kept laughing. "I'm glad you like your train system, Jon," he said just as an early 1900's freight replica crossed the coffee table and headed for another trip around the room's walls.

Concentrating on gluing a tiny brass railing into place, Jon said, "I do, thanks."

"Actually, that wasn't my idea either. It was CJ's and Bjen's."

"I guess you stick to the diabolical plotting, right pal?"

"I inherited that particular job description," Ian said, changing to a serious tone. "Actually, I stayed up most of last night plotting, as you call it. *And* I listened with Carly to voice recordings of you and Kati Hunter."

"I had a dream last night that I can vividly remember. It was about you, me, Kati and cheesecake in West Texas. Maybe Carly recorded it?" Jon smiled sarcastically.

"Tell me about it later, during after dinner drinks. Jon, you and Kati Hunter had past lives...right here...together. You two were lovers."

"Well, that explains why I still love her so much, doesn't it, Ian?" Ian had never seen a more sincere look on Jon's face. "But," Jon asked, "how can you be so sure?"

"Exact voice prints, and your names were the same. Jon, I must say, it's fuckin' unbelievable! You're both coming back here for a reason, it seems."

"And were you and Bjen around to mess with our minds way back when?"

"Very funny. The rest of the historic data we're collecting is over-the-top, Jon. And no, there isn't any indication Bjen or I ever existed here before now."

"Actually then," said Jon with a twinkle in his eye, "I suppose I own all this and you're *my* guest here."

"I'll take that trade, Dr. Dope. Just say the word."

It struck Jon then, how much weight Ian really carried. "Then we're in all this shit 100% together," he said warmly.

"I'm so sorry you got hurt, Jon."

"But, Kati was there…. So is this all just random, or destiny?"

"I've got a feeling we're about to find out more than we thought we'd ever know about life and our world, Jon."

"Sign me up! You remember the case studies we reviewed on reincarnation from Dartmouth and Virginia at Princeton, don't you? Especially that one about the little boy who reported his WWII airplane death? Remember how he claimed he'd chosen his new parents at the Royal Hawaiian Hotel where they conceived him?"

"I remember, but that's like a tiny indicator, compared to this history of you and Kati."

"Maybe you could publish a story on us in one of your helicopter mags!"

"I'll begin writing immediately," Ian said wryly. "Jon, when was the last time we just sat around talking about nothing important?"

"At school when we were playing ball. I think you, we, should make time to get away from all this save the world shit now and then, bud."

"It's save our ass, too, Jon…and Miss Kati Hunter too, Jon. Reincarnation cycles might run dry for you both."

"Who knows? I had Carly give me a picture set of Kati. She said you took them in Boulder. You got all those without telling her?"

"We did."

"We?"

"Me, St. Nick, the bees… we needed them to protect her."

"She's almost as I envisioned, before I saw her pictures. What if they saw her at the crash incident?" Jon asked anxiously.

"It would have been too random for concern, Jon. Also, there have been no Kati Hunter thought records produced from our monitoring of Satchmo's brain."

"And me?"

"A few of Kati," Ian said smiling. Carly remained silent, much to Ian's surprise.

"Actually, I'm not even certain why we're even having a conversation…. Why don't you just review all my brain records and, hell, go play some golf, Ian?"

"Be serious. It doesn't work that way at all. But get this through that thick skull of yours, Jonny. Kati Hunter is a direct copy of our original vessel cell, and we've tested over three million cell samples now. So, we've got to protect her and get her together with you soon."

"That's easy for you to say."

"You can't tell she's interested in you, Romeo?

"I can barely stand up, and she's not ready for all this."

"Have you asked her?"

"I can tell you that her ballet is the most important factor in her life right now."

"We talked about the whole picture while you were in the coma in Boulder, Jon. She knows more than you think."

"Maybe you should tell me just what you told her, and what kind of Dr. Frankenstein experiment you've cooked up for the two of us."

Ian started laughing. "Listen, Jon, the bits and pieces of information that Carly has put together with the stone memory conversations from the past around here has my head spinning. Just what I heard last night changes my views on almost everything we're trying to accomplish."

"Like what?"

"As you know we have a large holding of gold. The Swönks didn't mine it. They made it." Jon smiled incredulously. "No, really," Ian said. "Centuries ago the formula we had for changing the state of matter was hidden or lost around here. And you and Kati of the past were part of the matter changing formula, as far as I can tell from what I heard last night."

"Fresh from the rock! I'll turn you into a seven foot leprechaun. You'll try out for the Boston Celtics!"

"Budd, think about it. Simplified matter changing technology could be a breakthrough for solving many of the critical problems on Earth!"

"Give me a minute and I'll figure all that out…. Have you tried to call Kati on the Swönk phone?"

"She's turned it off."

"Oh yeah? We could just send her a letter. I might still have a stamp I got in the late 1900's."

"So, do you have any idea why Kati might have her phone off?"

"Probably just an, 'I'll call you when I'm ready to talk statement.' Maybe you could leave her a message."

"That's a thought… What have you two talked about to date?"

"No dating talks really."

"What, Jon?"

"I healed her tendon injury over the phone. That opened a can of worms, I suppose."

Carly filled the room with melodic laughter. "Hi Carly," said Jon.

"You're very funny, Doctor."

"You're kidding," said Ian. "You pissed her off with some over the phone therapy you made up?"

"I believe," said Jon, "that Kati is beginning to feel like a ballerina dancing near an endless black hole that could end the biggest dream of her *current* life."

"Are you becoming the black wolf to her?"

"How do you expect her to dance with the weight of the piano on her shoulders?"

Ian thought for a moment, then shrugged his shoulders. "Okay, I guess you're right. Let's get you well. And we'll pursue every solution without Kati. We'll let her choose when and if she wants in on any of this situation."

"Let's just leave her alone 'til it's our last option. I realize how hard this is on you, buddy."

"And if she calls?"

"We'll answer."

"Do you want to hear the rock recordings?"

"No."

"You should hear them sometime, Jon, maybe with Kati. Hey, I got us some new bikes. We'll be riding soon."

"I'd love to get out."

"Alert," said Carly. "Satchmo is leaving on the south cliff trail with a flat, enclosed electronic device. He's thinking about transmitting."

"Keep a full bee net around him, Carly," Ian directed. "And if he operates that unit, pickup and record his transmission and thoughts."

"Will do."

Ian thought of something. "Shit! Carly, get St. Nick out there with the antidotes from the dead operative testing. Load some bees from CJ's lab, too. Get them in the air now."

"Yep."

"Satchmo really had no choice, Ian," Jon interjected.

"I understand, Jon. But if we don't figure out a way, we're going to die because of what we know, and what they're trying to do. Fuck it all!" Ian ran from Jon's room.

*   *   *   *

Ricardo Ottoban II leaned back in his chair and studied the modernist painting on the wall of his study. He hadn't really expected this much resistance from Helena since he was a major contributor to the ballet foundation. He waited for Helena to finish her last, hesitating sentence and then said authoritatively, "Do this for me, please, Helena." Ricardo Ottoban II hung up.

* * * *

Jon sat in his electric chair next to Satchmo's bed. They were in the deep underground, impenetrable black 'n' gold rock formation under the Swönk coastal property. Unlike the Swönk's secret meeting place, this room was appointed like an expensive hotel suite for a stay in NYC or Singapore. Ian monitored Satchmo's vitals while 006½ watched from across the room in a high, wing-backed chair from another era. A huge original Dutch oil landscape painting rose above the bed's curving headboard. Atop the gilded frame, a row of bees watched under Carly's direction. "He should be awake any moment," said Ian. "I gave him the stimulant injection almost thirty minutes ago."

"CJ's assessment of Satchmo's data board indicates a better than ninety percent chance that full transmission occurred before we enclosed it," said Carly. "No resolution yet in breaking the information code. It seems to be a very complex mixture of mathematics."

"Maybe the successful transmission is a good thing, if we can persuade Satchmo to play out the double agent scenario," suggested Jon.

"Probably," said Ian. 006½ just shrugged his shoulders. Satchmo's eyes opened. Jon's face slowly came into focus.

"Well hi, buddy," said Jon. "How do you like my

new power chair?" Satchmo's thoughts were whirling in a dizzy haze, but he answered, "You always make the worst situation seem...." He lost his concentration. Ian poured some water and gave it to him in small sips.

"Thanks," Satchmo said weakly.

"We've got some serious issues to discuss," said Ian. "We're piecing together your situation, your sister's abduction, and a new plan for you to operate safely. . . . But man, you should have come to us and faced this whole thing up front."

"I know, but Ian, there are complications, and Katy's life at stake."

"Complications?" Jon asked incredulously. Just the sound of Kati's name coupled with 'life at stake,' raised Jon's hackles.

"Have you forgotten all the reasons you came to work here?" asked Ian. Have you forgotten that these people killed my parents, that they just about killed Jon? What would you do if you were me, Satchmo?"

"Kill me."

"We might have to, if you don't help us stop Mars and his allies from destroying us and the hope for true freedom on this planet," Ian retorted crossly.

Satchmo sighed, "I gave Mars an ultimatum a few weeks ago. I told him to get Katy and me out of all this, or I was going to come to you with the whole truth."

"What did he say, and what were you transmitting

yesterday?" asked Jon, leaning in closer to Satchmo's bed.

"Mars said he'd let us both walk away from all this if I got enough research data from you. He said he wanted out too...that he was trapped between the Swönks and his controllers. Mars' tone has changed since the last time we'd talked. He revealed that his controlling group was on the verge of instigating global upheaval. He thought he could prevent it with your various technologies."

"What did you send him?" prompted 006½.

"Mars had that data board delivered to me. It linked to your brain research files, using some kind of key word entry model. I have no idea how it worked. Maybe it used a mathematical energy sequence that masked the hacking. The designed function completed, but I have no idea what it got. I jumbled Mars' code system and transmitted. That's the last thing I remember before waking up now."

Ian gazed at Satchmo for a moment, then nodded decisively. "We'll see what CJ can figure out. He's coming here to talk with you and to run some lab tests on you." Ian handed Satchmo a phone. "Use this phone to order whatever you want to eat afterward. Don't leave this room, Satchmo. Got that?"

Satchmo smiled wanly. "I understand."

Jon led Ian and St Nick from the room. As he silently rolled his chair down the hall, he thought, being in this chair is worth it. If I hadn't been in the accident, I might have not found Kati. He smiled to himself. I'm getting out of this goddamn chair real soon, Miss Hunter….

*   *   *   *

Kati and Helena were sitting on a small deck overlooking the bay edge. Large waves occasionally kicked up spray that reached their feet. They were eating seared sea scallops over black rice on a bed of greens. The meal was so scrumptious that the beauty of the location was almost invisible to them.

"This may be the best thing I've ever tasted," commented Kati, talking with her mouth full. "These scallops. . . the sauce they've been cooked in. . . Jesus Christ!"

Helena smiled. "I know." Then she said in a more serious tone, "Kati, listen, even though you're in the third understudy position for Odette-Odile, you need to prepare like you're the first Swan Lake ballerina. I'm not just talking you up, Kati. I mean it. Do you understand me? I want you to prepare like there's no one but you. Am I making myself clear?"

Now, the scallops were invisible to Kati, "I understand you, Helena." Kati felt the hair stand on the back of her neck. A wave pounded, bringing spray to the table top. The wind gusted, ruffling their hair and the napkins.

"Let your imagination take you in your dance, Kati. Helena's eyes misted. "You're special, Kati…. I've never said that to anyone before now."

Kati didn't know what to say, so she just smiled at Helena. They finished their lunch in silence.

As they walked through the almost empty indoor dining area to leave, Ricardo Ottoban II called out, "Helena, hello! Please, you haven't seen Ricky for so long."

Helena whispered into Kati's ear, "These people are the biggest donors to the Ballet, Kati. Let me introduce you." Both men stood as Helena and Kati approached their table. "Kati Hunter, I'd like you to meet Ricardo Ottoban II and his son, Ricardo Ottoban III," said Helena.

Kati couldn't resist joking, "I guess there's no limit to autobahn numbers." She offered her hand to shake. Helena's jaw dropped, but both men laughed like they'd never heard a joke before.

"I only hope my son can find such a beautiful woman, with a wit like yours, Miss Hunter," said Ricardo II. "Could you both join us for awhile?"

"We'd love to, thanks!" Helena said.

Kati thought, *We'd love to?* But I guess they're paying my salary, so to speak.

"I'd like to propose a toast to the newest ballerina in SFB," said Ricardo II, expansively. "Please," he said and held up four fingers to the waiter. The waiter nodded and set up a standing ice bucket at the table within moments.

"Miss Hunter," said Ricardo III, "could I call you Kati?"

"Certainly."

Ricardo III smiled. "Are you enjoying San Francisco and getting settled here?"

"My parents live here. I was only in Colorado for awhile, working as an trauma nurse."

"My, that's quite something," Ricardo III said, oozing charm. "Two professions for someone so young and beautiful."

"Thanks, but my looks didn't seem to be a factor," Kati said acerbically.

"Sorry, that just slipped," Ricardo III apologized. Kati just smiled.

Ricardo II decided to rescue his son. Holding up a champagne filled flute, he said, "To Kati, a star in the making. Best wishes for Swan Lake!"

Kati sipped the expensive French champagne thinking that this whole meeting was probably a setup. Ricardo III, however, was a very handsome man. Maybe I'm being oversensitive, she thought. She formed a mental picture of the Swönks and Jon. She decided that she should leave, but she didn't.

*   *   *   *

Helena slid into the antique Jaguar's black leather driver's seat. . . a present from Ricardo Ottoban II. She drove away cursing to herself. She knew, she knew exactly what they were doing, and she was complicit. Helena felt sick.

* * * *

Mars pressed the transmit button to send his report to the Leader Group. He was feeling pleased. He was sure his document would lure them deeper into his trap. I'm going to speak with Katy about these new developments, he thought. I'll prove to her that Phobos is working with me to stop the Swönks and the Leaders from their mind control war.

He silently walked into the subterranean research lab. Katy had her back to him. She was engaged in her work on the computer while listening to a blaring female rock singer. The music dominated the empty lab room. Katy's long, chocolate hair was piled up on her head, and Mars couldn't take his eyes off the few soft strands dangling down the back of her slender neck.

Mars stood behind Katy. "I'm sorry, Katy, for the rude way I brought your brother into our conversation at lunch. I apologize."

Katy kept working without a flinch. "No apology necessary."

"Could you turn down the music, please?"

"Pink."

"Pink?" Mars lifted an eyebrow.

"Pink is the artist singing."

"Could you turn down the Pink music, please?" Katy

opened her music panel and lowered the volume. Mars continued to stand behind her. She continued working. Mars cleared his throat. "As you know, Katy, our ongoing health and brain research here is very exclusive." Katy continued working in silence. Mars plunged onward. "As you also know, we live in a dangerous, complex world. Your brother is in a trap, Katy. And unless we take some smart, strategic actions, he could lose his life."

Katy whirled around in her chair. She stared into Mars' eyes. "Then maybe you should explain what's going on to me, Mars."

Mars told his story. Katy let nothing of her feelings show, but she wondered if her thoughts were being recorded.

*   *   *   *

A few weeks later, CJ, Ian, and Jon rode down the ancient, narrow costal road. Various shades of green foliage streaked the rolling hills. Pounding surf infused the warm summer breeze with a fresh, salty ocean taste. Bianchi café racers with narrow all terrain tires set the tone of the biking. Ian had described the morning's expedition as, "just a fun cruise."

CJ was in the lead, watching the road. Jon followed him, then Ian. Ian was watching his buddy. Jon's looking fine, he thought. His leg is cranking at a good pace.

Thirty minutes into the ride, CJ veered right onto a

path leading to his favorite spot at the water's edge. Ten more minutes and they pulled onto a chunk of granite about twenty feet thick and almost as big as half a basketball court. The huge rock surface was a mixture of rough and smooth with rising formations cut by wind and water. Dozens of small pools of rain and sea dotted the hard expanse.

As the trio climbed off their bikes, Ian's "way to go" glance met CJ's silly smile. CJ had just led them over a blind, surprise downhill jump at speed that could have been disastrous for Jon. "I'm glad you were in front, CJ," said Ian. "It gave me a moment to remember my feet weren't hooked to the pedals."

"Sweet," CJ grinned.

"No, shit!" Ian retorted. They all broke into laughter.

"I'm sorry. No, really," said CJ. "I forgot which trail down here had the air in it."

"Maybe I'll lead going from here. How's your leg after that landing, Jon?"

"Fine, and my head's better, too."

"How's that?" Ian gave his friend a quizzical look.

"My spirit of adventure feels back. I think some fear had begun creeping in…."

"Jon, it's fine to use common sense and to control risk."

"I'll be careful chasing baby carriages."

"Good."

"What's in your pack, CJ?" asked Jon.

"Lunch."

"Yours, Ian?"

"Beer."

"Good, I'm hungry."

"You have no pack, Doctor," Ian said loftily.

"You two wouldn't let me...."

"Well," said CJ slowly, "I suppose we could share...." Laughing, they walked toward the ocean's edge to find the best spot to eat.

* * * *

Sitting on the giant monolith's edge with his feet dangling over the sea, Jon lazed back with his hands behind his head. He looked up into the pale blue sky and watched the clouds change shapes. "What's for lunch, CJ?"

"Sandwiches."

"What kind?"

"Mayonnaise," CJ said solemnly.

"Just mayo and bread?" Jon asked dolefully.

CJ gave in. "It's our special homemade multigrain bread that you love...and liverwurst...and diced tomato and veggie pate... and ol' fashioned pickles." CJ started to laugh. Jon sat up, faking a push of CJ off the cliff edge. Ian handed Jon an ice cold bottle of Guinness.

Jon took a swig. "God, this is freezing...just like I

like it! I thought you leprechauns only drank this stuff room temperature."

"We decided to baby you, Dr. Spoiled, one last time." Ian smiled.

"Did you two remember to pack my favorite Halloween napkins with the little Spooky and Casper ghosts on them?" Jon got no answer...just a perfect sandwich...with just the right amount of mayo.

* * * *

Two and a half sandwiches and three beers later, Jon said, "I think we should do this maybe once a week." Jon never heard his friends' response because an icy wave just rushed through his body. His mind was swept clear of all he had been thinking. Shadowy images loomed up in his thoughts. "I've said that before," he whispered, "sitting right here on this rock." Ian and CJ's eyes met in understanding. "Me and Kati," Jon continued, "right here... in another lifetime...."

CJ's mind clicked instantly. We could survey right now, he thought. Ian shook his head slightly, keeping his eyes on CJ.

Jon shrugged his shoulders and the feeling passed. "Tell me, CJ, how have you created the human dimension in Carly's programming?"

Oh shit, Ian thought, here we go, Dr. Wolff. But he truly felt happiness, knowing Jon was really back and engaged in his world now.

"To make a long story short," replied CJ, "Carly uses the human brains in her sensor region as her emotional and humanistic platform, even as a part of her data systems solution model, if she wants to. It's kind of a vicious cycle now, you might say."

"So," said Jon, thinking his way through what CJ had said, "you've developed a wireless linkage from Carly into the neuronal systems of the human brain so she can operate without peoples' conscious knowledge...without leaving footprints?"

"That is correct, but she's limited to just our core group's brain resource."

"Which includes me?"

"It's part of your recovery evaluation, Jon," Ian explained. "Dr. Jameson agreed that it would be helpful. And the new neuro-plasticity molecular studies, you've wanted to start, fits right into this in vivo interaction between machine and mind."

"Carly has no interaction with Gigi's brain?" Jon probed.

"None," said CJ, "and a separated energy analysis system monitors and confirms brain subjects in the linkage."

You're always going to protect the women you love, aren't you Jonny? Ian thought.

"So how?"

CJ grinned. "It's cosmic wave stuff, Jon. We're

planning to show you everything."

"Maybe," said Jon, "you should share this technology with the folks at CERN before they bust a nut and spend all their hard printed money."

Ian smiled. "That day may come…hopefully."

"So, is Carly listening and using our brains right now, out here?"

"No," CJ reassured Jon, "not unless we activate the bees we've hidden in your jeans."

"Jeans or genes?"

"Pants.. .the nanobeebots we've put in your bloodstream serve a completely different purpose."

Jon looked out over the ocean. He wasn't at all sure he liked what he was hearing. "Have you considered going into horror films, CJ?"

"Too spicy!"

"You're a little crazy."

"Just like you, Jon. Your bubble isn't that close to plumb either. We're creative geniuses," CJ said smugly.

Jon chose not to pick up on that one. Instead, he asked, "Do you guys have bees out here that could get ancient conversations out of this rock?" CJ looked at Ian.

"We do, Jon," Ian said. "They're hidden in those cool bike seats…. You like those tail lights?"

"You're a toy freak. Is this your land we're sitting on?"

"Yes. But I thought you didn't want to hear the Kati and Jon past, Buddy?"

"I do now. Do these bees have little speakers, too?"

"Carly can run what you're looking for through our Swönk phone speakers if there's a positive read," CJ replied.

"Just do it," Jon said. His heart was pounding.

CJ took his phone from his pack and tapped in his request for Carly. The three turned to look back at the bikes just in time to watch twenty bees swarm from under each seat. Jon's mind jumped back to the old Princeton outdoor track. One summer afternoon before running, he'd thrown a foot up on the grandstand step to stretch, pissing off a large nest of hornets hidden underneath. Escaping with only one sting, Jon figured he'd just sprinted his fastest sixty meters ever.

Each of the sixty bees began an organized geometric search and scan as Ian, CJ, and Jon hiked off the rock toward a small game trail. The path led away from the shore and into the tall grasses. "This is the path without the jump, CJ," said Jon.

"I thought you'd never…," CJ qualified, "not been here in a long while."

"Maybe we will find out shortly."

CJ's phone beeped. The word count was beginning to climb. Jon broke into the silence. "Whatever information Mars got from Satchmo. . . if Mars is actually trying to gain an advantage over his controllers...like Satchmo thinks he is...if he got mind-machine link technology from you...and he uses it...you could search for that unique...."

CJ broke in, "We can! That's great!"

"The Wolffactor!" Ian said jubilantly. Jon smiled.

"What?" asked CJ.

"At Princeton," replied Ian, "Jon came up with so many logical solutions that we, who are brilliantly endowed, overlooked...that we called it the Wolffactor." CJ cracked up laughing. "And after all our basketball was over," Ian continued, "we even realized he should have been the head coach."

"No shit!"

Jon wasn't listening. he was reading the text Carly had just sent to him on his Swönk phone. "Dr. Jon, re: The Katerina and Jonathan conversations from the past rock site readings at your locale.... I'm going to text them privately to your Swönk phone. You make the decision with whom you want to share them. Your friend, Carly."

I feel like I'm walking through different realities, Jon thought. *Oh Kati, I need you.* CJ's phone reported that the scan recording was complete. They started walking back to the bicycles. Jon made a decision. "Carly sent me a text saying I should read these privately. Why don't you two go back? I need some time alone here anyway."

Ian looked at his friend with some concern. "Are you okay, Buddy?"

"Of course."

"If you want, I'll send a Hummingbird to get you."

"Thanks, but I'll ride."

"Now you'll be giving Carly a glass heart!"

"Maybe she has a slot I can stick it in." Ian and CJ rode away laughing.

*   *   *   *

Jon walked and walked. Alone and outside for the first time in weeks, he thought. After walking in circles on the giant seaside rock, he stopped and sat with his back against a smooth, sculpted rising. He was exhausted. The day had been a physical and emotional strain. Resting his head back, he closed his eyes and slept.

*   *   *   *

"If you're not the most beautiful woman in the world right now, God strike me dead," said Kati's mother, Angelina. They were sitting on the couch in Kati's small apartment.

"So dramatic, mother," said Kati. "Of course, you're completely prejudiced."

"It's pride, darling. I just wish I could come and watch this affair tonight."

"Why don't you just go in my place?"

Kati's mother laughed. Then she said, seriously,

"Remember not to drink too much, dear. Less than one drink would be wise."

"I'll be okay. I'm going to eat a couple of large cans of refried beans before I leave," Kati said mischievously.

"You definitely have your brothers' sick firemen's sense of humor."

"You married one, yourself, Mrs. Shakespeare."

"Touché." Angelina teased Kati's hair a little, before starting on the last narrow braiding to frame her lovely daughter's face. "I haven't heard a word from you lately regarding all your friends in Ireland." Kati didn't reply. She just sat looking out the window at the distant ocean view. "Kati?" Kati's mother knew she must have pushed a hot button.

Finally, Kati sighed. "I can't even talk about them right now, mother."

Angelina felt Kati's uneasiness. Her daughter's body was on the edge of starting to shake. "Them?"

"Him, mom, him...Jon. I can't talk to you or anyone, okay? I can't even think about all of it and keep going on with ballet."

"I understand dear. I'm sorry," Kati's mother said, even though she didn't understand anything, except that Kati was distressed. "Just let it be, Kati. And whenever you need, I'm here to talk. You know how much I love you."

Kati put her face down into her hands. Last night's

dream flashed vividly into her mind. They were in a small boat. Jon's head was in her lap. He'd been poisoned. His eyes were glassy. The skin of his face was stretched thinly over his bones. He was dying. With her mother's arms around her, Kati broke down crying.

*　*　*　*

"Are you sure you're going to be alright?" Kati's mother asked some time later.

Kati was still breathing heavily, but she gave her mother a brave smile. "Yes, Mom. I'm fine now. Let's fix that drink you suggested though."

After they finished their drinks, Kati's mother expertly repaired Kati's makeup. "I guess you're lucky I'm a make-up artist too...huh dear?"

"Yes I am, Mom." Kati gave her mother a quick hug. The door buzzer rang.

"That's Dad with your dress. Thank God. I thought you were going to have to go to the Ball in your undies, dear." Angelina opened the door, "Wonderful, Jack! Our hero delivers again."

"I almost had to use sirens to get here on time. How's my girl?"

Kati rushed into her daddy's arms. He knew something was up, but just kissed the top of her head. "I can't wait to see you in this gown, gorgeous. I'm going to sit on the couch and calm down. You go put on that dress and come out to model, okay?"

"Yes, Daddy, there's cold beer in the fridge for you."

"Well, I need one after all the stress of rushed dress delivery for you, Baby."

"Go sit down, Jack," Angelina ordered.

"Yes'm!"

*   *   *   *

"Wake-up, Jack," Angelina shook her husband's shoulder gently. "Your daughter is about to model her gown."

Jack sat up on the little bay window couch. He smiled sleepily at his wife who was sitting on the couch arm.

"Shall I sing, dear?" asked Angelina. "Summertime and the livin' is easy…." Then she just hummed the melody in perfect pitch, letting the words play in her mind. "So hush little baby. Don't you cry," she concluded.

Kati entered the room doing a few delicate spins in her heels. Her elegant, figure-hugging, champagne gown hung from her left shoulder, with a cleft down the opposite side of her body and leg. The formal dress presented a subtle spiral of silk lace that sparkled with tiny pink sapphires, peridot and diamonds. The same gemstones adorned finely designed platinum jewelry dangling from her hair, right wrist, and right ankle. Continuing to dance, whirling around the tiny apartment, Kati was transformed. She looked like a summer princess in splendor. Angelina and Jack were speechless. Kati paused, "Mom told me, Daddy."

"She wasn't supposed to tell."

"You're a hero!"

"It's my job, honey."

"Well, I guess the family who made this dress thought you went beyond the call of duty for them."

"They were very grateful for what your father did, and they wanted so much to do something for him," Angelina said. "And they said they loved every moment of the whole design. They loved making it for you, Kati."

"All these stones, the jewelry….," Kati marveled. "This must priceless."

Kati's father winked. "Try not to lose it, alright?"

"Very funny." The downstairs entry buzzer rang, and Kati headed for a chauffeur-driven, Rolls-Royce Silver Phantom.

"Be home before midnight, pumpkin," Jack called as Kati went out the door. But she never heard the fairytale cliché.

*   *   *   *

"Jack," said Angelina, "something is going on in Kati's life that she can't talk to us about. It has to do with the street accident she came upon, and the Irish family who gave her the car."

"It might not be a random coincidence."

"That's not the least bit reassuring. I'm scared to death." Angelina moved over to hug her husband. "We need to keep an eye on her, Jack."

* * * *

The music in the rear seating compartment of the sleek, 1911 Rolls-Royce Limo was, appropriately, an orchestration of Swan Lake, by Tchaikovsky. All of a sudden, Kati felt like a star. "Excuse me, Miss Hunter," Apollo, the chauffeur, said over the sound system. "I've been asked to review a few facts about the event you're attending at the Ottoban Estate tonight."

"Certainly, go ahead, Apollo." Kati sipped the ice cold Perrier and lime prepared from the rear seat bar.

"Only six dancers from the San Francisco Ballet have been chosen as representatives for the Ball By the Bay fundraiser, Miss Hunter. Congratulations on being chosen as one."

"Well, thank you," said Kati. She was trying to assess what this evening meant to her position in the ballet organization. Helena had said her Swan Lake role made attendance mandatory, as she was handed the formal invitation and dress requirements. Mom had just taken over preparation. Thank God. Apollo was still talking, describing entry and introduction protocol. Kati had missed some details.

"Any questions, Miss Hunter?" Apollo asked.

"No." Kati smiled. This was a big fancy dance. Deep inside she knew she was the best dancer, the best ballerina. She drank up the moment.

* * * *

"Say yo! Wolf Doctor! Time to wake up and go home." CJ shook Jon's shoulder as Linda attached the Bianchi bicycle to the external basket on her Hummingbird helicopter. "Man, it's past 3 a.m., and this rock is a little firm for a great night's rest." Jon got up with the Swönk phone still in his hand and headed to the Hummingbird.

* * * *

"Would you care to dance, Miss Hunter?" Ricardo Ottoban III asked with a most charming smile.

"Certainly, I'd love to dance," said Kati. The walnut parquet floor was glistening, and Ricardo III was polished in waltzing, manners, and his way of touch. Kati glanced at him appreciatively.

"Kati, you are beautiful beyond words tonight."

"Thank you very much."

As their dance ended, Ricardo Ottoban III asked, "Could we have a champagne together?"

"Please." Ricardo and Kati walked to the marble bar. Ricardo III kept his hand lightly on her lower back. Sasha, the Swan Lake prima ballerina, awarded the couple a pleasant smile as Ricardo handed Kati her champagne at the bar. But when they moved away, the Russian dancer's eyes burned into Ricardo Ottoban III, whom she coveted. Such a spectacle you are tonight,

Miss Hunter, she thought jealously. Ballet Paris had been courting Sasha for months, trying to pry her away from San Francisco. So far she had resisted. But now she was starting to think that Paris might indeed have more to offer.

After another hour of watching Kati and Ricardo III together, the Russian woman had become a ticking bomb. The dancers moved to the upper floor. The plan was to introduce the six ballerinas to the party crowd from the balcony above the ballroom floor. Sasha was introduced first. Miss Kati Hunter was introduced last, as the "new rising star." Smiling, with gemstones dangling close to her cheek, Kati blushed, setting the crowd's applause on fire.

Sasha made an instant decision. Goodbye, Helena, she thought. Good luck with your new Swan Lake.

*   *   *   *

Kati stood with Ricardo III on the upper terrace that overlooked the ocean bay. Kati was well past her first champagne. "I'm going to miss my ride," she said. "I should go down now."

Ricardo III put a detaining hand on her arm. "Please Kati, I want you to know something."

"Yes?"

"This whole event was just for you."

"What do you mean?"

"The dance wasn't planned. Sure, it raised some

money, but I asked my father to organize it so I could spend time with you. Please, stay here tonight."

"Well, I should say that's very flattering, and very honest of you to tell me. I suppose it might have been easier to go out for a hot dog, though, and just have everyone send a check or something."

"And you would've dressed like this for a hotdog, I suppose?" He lifted her chin and kissed her gently.

With their cheeks touching, Kati whispered, "Ricardo stay right here. I'm going to leave the party now. Thanks for the lovely evening."

* * * *

The ride home in the Rolls was better than the ride to the ball. Kati didn't feel like a star now. Apollo was quiet. She'd asked for no music, and she was no longer excited. Things felt more genuine now. This whole evening and the dates with Ricardo over the past month have been my diversion, she thought. They were a safe getaway. I've been making Ricardo my fantasy of Jon, she admitted to herself. I've just been using Ricardo, lying to him and myself. I need to apologize to Ricardo, and I need to call Jon Wolff. I need to be honest.

* * * *

It was in the gray of early dawn. Bjen, Ian, Jon, and 006½ were sitting around the kitchen's massive oak table. "Sleep well last night?" Bjen inquired as Jon cut banana slices onto his bowl of oatmeal.

"At least I didn't need any weird dreams for entertainment."

Bjen looked at him earnestly. "How are you feeling, Dr. Wolff?"

"Quite enlightened."

"Are you suggesting we should sleep on a rock slab every night to improve our health, Doctor?" she teased.

"Do you remember our conversation on the phone just before your incident, Jonny?" Ian broke in.

"How's your right leg been feeling?" Jon asked.

"I figured we'd best let your left leg heal, before I bug you to fix mine. How about right after breakfast today?" Jon smiled while munching.

Bjen laid down her piece of toast and looked at her Swönk phone. "I just got a text from Kati Hunter."

"How is she doing?" asked 006½. He was eating what the Swönks called Cuchulain's breakfast: three fried eggs atop a mound of hobo potatoes, with a crisply fried trout on the side.

"She's apologizing for putting a wall up. She says she'll be in touch soon. Right now, she's concentrating on ballet and trying to figure everything out."

"Everything must seem a bit too much for her," commented 006½. Jon smirked and nodded slightly. CJ walked into the kitchen. He grabbed a bowl and started spooning oatmeal into it.

"How did you sleep last night, CJ?" asked Jon.

"Like a rock." Everyone laughed. "Didn't realize I was such a great comedian," said CJ.

Jon smiled. "Timing is everything…or maybe just time."

"Is that Wolff philosophy?" CJ retorted. Everyone laughed again.

"Thanks for getting me last night or, rather, this morning," Jon said. "By the way, where's Linda?"

"Somewhere else…."

Carly broke in, laughing. "Linda is training in the flight simulator for the Blue Swan this morning."

"Does Carly follow you everywhere, CJ?"

"Pretty much."

"Too bad Chris Rock isn't here to cut up with us," Bjen commented. There was a moment's silence as they all brought an image of Chris to mind. Then Carly projected a life size hologram of Chris Rock standing right behind Bjen with a huge smile on his face.

"Look behind you, Sis," said Ian. Bjen turned and screamed.

*   *   *   *

"What do you think of the Blue Swan, Nicholas?" asked Jon.

"It's a dream coming true."

"Coolest plane ever built!" Carly chimed in. Everyone laughed.

When the laughter died down, Jon said, "Actually I did a lot of thinking out on that big rock last night. I asked Carly to test the rock composition. What was it, Carly?"

"Granite and a very unique mixture of greisen, which is quartz and mica. The variations of quartz color and crystal are spectacular."

"I also listened to a large amount of past life conversation between me and Kati. That place was a very important spot for us. It seems we went there often to be alone and talk."

CJ was grinning broadly. "Shut up, CJ," said Jon. CJ just grinned some more. "Could I please have some more orange juice?" Jon asked. Bjen poured some for Jon. "I think this is the best orange juice in the world," Jon remarked for maybe the hundredth time.

Ian gave his standard response. "It's the blood-orange mix. We've been making it for over a thousand years." Everyone ignored them.

Jon took a deep breath and continued. "Even though I've known you guys for over ten years and have learned quite a bit about the Swönk family history, these past ten weeks have been filled with an incredible amount of dramatic information. When I couple this information with waking up in Ireland, and finding out about Kati, and all the ridiculous shit you guys are capable of doing and have…."

"You haven't seen anything yet," said CJ. Everyone

roared with laughter, even Jon and Carly.

"I was very serious about all this last night and beginning breakfast," Jon said, faking a hurt tone.

"You've taught us well, Buddy," said Ian.

"Maybe I'm not a perfect role model...."

"Maybe!" Carly interrupted brightly. Everyone laughed again. The sun was beginning to shine, spilling a warm glow across the table.

"Seriously," said Jon, "considering all the facts: Our meeting at Princeton, connecting with Kati Hunter, these next life circles that used to be only theories, listening to what we've talked about, Kati and I,—requires re-thinking our perspective of life, and what we're trying to accomplish individually and together."

"And Kati Hunter?" asked Bjen.

"There's even more of a mind warp for her, than me. I think we fell in love way back in the middle ages when we were forbidden to do so, from what I heard last night. In a way, Kati and I were thrown into a trap of our past love for each other, and now it's an emotional situation to sort out. It's a roller coaster.

"So is this 'forbidden feeling' carrying over to the present, Jon?" asked Bjen.

"Probably. And, speaking of presents, you guys gave Kati a new car the day after you met her. You have to be careful with all the power and money you have at your disposal."

"You think we're trying to take advantage of you and Kati?" Ian asked slowly.

"Not maliciously. But you're searching for answers, and you have some power, and big guns, and big technology."

"And big knowledge," added 006½. "Big responsibility…. That's why we all want you on our team, Doctor, or should I say, Kati's guardian of the past?"

"You are free to do what you want, Jon," said Ian. He smiled warmly at his friend. "We'll always back you, with no strings attached. If there were strings in the past, they are gone now. Right, Bjen?"

"No strings, and you don't have to love Kati Hunter just because she saved your life…."

"Bjen…." Jon started with some irritation.

Bjen forestalled him. "I'm not trying to be a matchmaker, Jon. But you should give Kati a big kiss, and see if she turns into a frog or something…. We understand what you're saying. You're right, as usual. So, what's next?"

"Thank you all for listening to me," said Jon. I really do trust you all, and I'll help all I can. But I need to go back to Colorado sometime soon." He paused and drank some orange juice. Then he continued. "I'm glad Kati sent a text…. Let's finish the tests on Satchmo before we play the next card on Mars." Everyone agreed, but each silently thought, *He's got it bad for Kati….*

*   *   *   *

Kati opened her eyes thinking, It's light. It's morning. I'm okay. All that other stuff was just a dream. It's Sunday. Great! Nothing I have to do today. She picked up her regular cell and called home as she walked into her bathroom. "Mom?"

" Hi, dear."

"What's for breakfast?"

Angelina's smile was big, "Fresh strawberries and the best pancakes in the world. Your place is set."

Kati sighed happily. "I'm on my way."

*   *   *   *

"Am I going to live, Doctor?" asked Ian.

"Maybe, if you do exactly what I say."

"It only bothers me at the end of a long run and on the back nine of eighteen holes." Ian lay on his stomach on a massage table while Dr. Wolff examined his body.

"Do you want to solve this problem or just become a cripple at age twenty nine? And how much money did you say you have?" asked Jon.

"Could you just treat me like a real patient, Doctor Wolff?" Ian asked plaintively.

"If you insist," Jon sighed. "Let's begin here." Jon put the tip of his left index finger on the middle of Ian's lower back. "This spot on your back is at the level of the third lumbar vertebra which is at the anterior apex of your lumbar spine…. Comprende amigo?"

"Si."

"Well, that apex point, when you lie down or stand evenly on both feet, should be in the midline of your body. As you walk, this apex along with the arc of your lumbar spine moves right...left...right...left.... However, if this functional arc and spinal apex is deviated in the neutral position due to asymmetrical muscular, joint, ligament, or even bone structure, it causes an increasing degree of stress to the whole weight-bearing, biomechanical system of the human body."

"Which way do I deviate in my lower back?"

"Good question. You deviate left, which translates to stronger muscle tone on the right lower back quadrant, versus your left paraspinal muscle groups. So, I'll do magic, and balance a percentage of the dysfunction in your back, hips, and legs. Then I'll show you what exercises and movements to do in order to enhance your symmetry.... Make sense?"

"Yep. Do it."

*   *   *   *

"I'm ready for a few more hot ones, Mom," Paul requested as Kati walked in and sat at her regular place.

Kati's other brother Peter grinned and said, "Hi Kati." A general chorus of greetings followed.

"Hello everyone," Kati laughed.

Angelina served Paul. "You're next, Miss Hunter."

"I hear you got all dressed up last night," Peter

commented between mouthfuls.

"And who told you that?"

"Nobody. I heard all the wolf whistles as you drove through town last night."

Kati glanced over at her mom's back. "It was probably just Jack London and White Fang."

"Speaking of...how's your novel coming along, Sis?" asked Paul.

"It's at a stand still, but I'll get back to writing soon."

"I'm thinking about writing some stories," said Paul.

"Great! You have to let me read them, Pauli."

Paul looked at his sister fondly. "Sure. I was thinking about putting down some of our fire-fighting experiences."

Angelina placed Kati's plate down in front of her. "I know you're watching diet closely right now," she said apologetically.

There was one tiny pancake with one tiny strawberry in the center. Kati stared down, starving. Everyone was quietly watching Kati. "Fuck this shit!" Kati erupted.

Her family cracked up as Angelina brought out another plate, filled with pancakes and strawberries, from behind her back. She exchanged the plates. Kati's eyes started tearing. "It's so good to be here with you all!"

"We're all very proud of you, Kati," her father said gently.

"I'm so proud," Peter said, "that I couldn't sleep last night!" Kati led the laughter and poured some maple syrup.

*   *   *   *

"So Buddy," Jon concluded, "the last thing I want you to remember to do periodically through the day, is to reach down with your left hand towards your left knee...laterally flexing...while in the standing position which bows your lower spine to your right. This will oppose your tendency toward imbalance. And do this exercise through your golf game, too."

"I want you to teach this biomechanical system to everyone here, Jon," Ian said.

"Sure, it would be my pleasure," Jon replied. It was good to be helping people again.

*   *   *   *

"Come on Kati. We're going to play a whiffle ball game," Peter called into the kitchen from the back porch.

"Y'all go ahead. If I play, you'll probably get injured," Kati teased.

"Chicken!" Peter rejoined.

"Let's go sit out back and watch Jack and the boys play tree ball," Angelina said. "We can have some girl talk."

The Hunter family whiffle ball game was officially known as "tree ball" because, although the game used the standard plastic baseball and bat, trees were used for the bases. There were also special homerun awards if you batted a fly ball into one. Also, the defensive team could throw the ball at runners between the tree bases. If you pegged a runner, he was out. In addition, you could throw and hit a tree ahead of a base runner for a force out. There were no video replays, only vocal arguments. Team play or everyone for themselves were options.

Angelina and Kati lounged in reclining, wooden deck chairs situated about twenty five yards left of the third base tree on the thick grass of the expansive Hunter backyard. A temperature of 62° F with an incoming ocean breeze, made the azure sports-letter blankets welcome. Thick dark maroon pads on the recliners made for total luxury, while the ladies sipped hot, spiced herbal tea from big, handmade pottery mugs.

"I'm glad you didn't play ball," Angelina commented.

"I want to," Kati replied, "but I can't risk a sprain. There's also a risk exclusion in my contract, of course."

Both women watched in silence as the three firemen across the summer lawn began with a first pitch. Jack's fast ball had a lot of movement and the wind helped. Paul took a hard wild swing, but missed as the light white ball pinged off the oak trunk that served as catcher and backstop. From the field Peter yelled, "Strike one! Two strikes and you're out!"

Paul threw the ball back to his Dad. "Is that the new rule today?"

"Just want to speed up the game," said Peter.

Paul looked at Jack who said, "Fine."

"Of course," said Paul, "I'm the one batting with one strike." Paul swung at the next low inside pitch.

"Strike two. You're out!" The three rotated positions. Paul started pitching to Peter.

Kati's cell chimed in her sweater pocket. She pulled out her Swönk phone, then dug in for her regular one. Angelina watched her intently.

Peter caught the high, inside fastball early on the sweet spot of the bat, barreling it towards the girls like a low, smoking shot off a golf tee. Maybe it was because it was early in the game, or maybe it was because of all those pancakes, but the firemen just watched. While reading her text from Helena, Kati heard the hard thwack and then, the faint rush. Her free left hand came up. Pop! The white ball stuck in her left palm. Angelina's mouth dropped open. The men roared with laughter from across the lawn.

Paul started jogging over. Kati whipped a perfect left-handed strike over to his chest. "Nice catch there, Sis!" Kati was reading her text. Not a drop of tea had spilled from the mug sitting on the arm of her deck chair.

"You're out, Peter!" Jack called.

"What? Bullshit!" Peter threw down his bat indignantly.

"We can't waste that once in a million year catch,"

Kati's father said laughing.

"That's right," said Paul. "This is a special circumstance. And this is an omen, too."

"What omen?" asked Peter.

"Now, there is no way you can win this game," Paul said smugly.

"That wasn't an omen," Peter replied. "Kati's just the luckiest athlete to ever walk on Earth." Jack couldn't contain his smile as he got ready to bat next.

*   *   *   *

"What's that other phone?" Angelina asked. "The one you put back in your pocket?"

Kati leaned her head back against the maroon padding and closed her eyes. "I'm the second understudy now, for Swan Queen," she said.

Because Angelina was a professional entertainer, she just let the moment rest in silence. After awhile, Kati picked up her mug in both hands and sipped quietly.

Angelina broke the silence. "Did Helena say why?"

"Sasha is leaving for Ballet Paris."

"This seems a little sudden. Did something happen at the Ball last night?"

Kati took a moment to put her thoughts in order and then said slowly, "Sasha was introduced as San Francisco's Prima Ballerina and Swan Queen for Swan Lake. But looking back, I would say a lot happened last night, Mother. For one thing, Ricardo told me he'd asked his dad to put on the whole event just for me."

"Oh Kati, what's going on? This sounds like the beginning of a big mess."

* * * *

"You're out!" Jack called. His throw had hit Peter on the butt just before his foot came down on the old torn mitt serving as home base.

"God!" Peter yelled at his dad. And I thought Kati was lucky!"

* * * *

Kati and Angelina ignored the guys' antics. "Yes, it could become a mess," Kati told her mother, "but, I'm going to stop the bleeding right now."

Angelina couldn't help but laugh, "Spoken like a true trauma nurse!"

For a moment, Kati flashed on Jon in the street, squirting blood all over the place.

Her mother instantly picked up on her change of mood. "What's wrong, honey?"

"I've been using Ricardo as an escape from Jon and my friends, the Swönks in Ireland."

"Ricardo Ottoban asked you out," Kati. You weren't chasing him," Angelina said reasonably. She patted Kati's pocket. "What's that other phone?"

" Jeez, Mom, do you have your lie detector turned on? It's my Swönk phone."

"Swan Queen phone!"

207

"Swönk family phone, S...W...O...N...K, phone. And it's turned off."

"I must say," said Angelina with a smile, "William Shakespeare would have enjoyed all this...Swan Lake...Swönk family. The Swönk family gives you a new sporty red car. Mr. Ottoban shows up so you can drive said car to a ball where there are queens and broken hearts. Tragedy looms, and you're left making calls on a swan phone while catching white fowl/foul balls."

Kati laughed. "It is a comedy, isn't it?"

"Someone tried to murder this Jon friend of yours?"

"It's hard to say."

"So is this, Kati." Angelina took a deep breath. "Our family is connected to the Swönk family's past in Ireland. And that connection was one of the reasons my grandparents came to America...to get away from them."

"That explains something. I think Jon and I were lovers in a past lifetime. You see, I've been having these dreams...."

Angelina, who'd been brought up a Catholic, closed her eyes. She rested her head back on the maroon padding.

*   *   *   *

"We need to end this thing soon," said Jack. "So, this is your last at bat, Paul." Peter and Jack had seventeen runs each. Paul had twelve.

"Then," said Paul, "if I go ahead on this bat, I win."

"Fine with me," said Jack. "Peter?"

"It's cheating, but alright. No way he can do it, anyway."

Jack threw a strike down the middle. Paul smacked a fly ball that banged off the two run homer tree. This meant he automatically got another free turn at bat.

"Nice pitch, Dad," ribbed Peter.

Jack threw a wild, high, outside pitch next. Paul had to jump while swinging to get it. He hit a sky high fly that the wind started to carry. Peter sprinted to catch it. He barely missed the catch, and the ball hit the two run homer tree again. Previously, Peter had been the only one to ever hit two in a row. "Congratulations!" shouted Peter. "You're the second person in the history of the world to make that play! Let me pitch the last out, Dad. It's my record that's at stake."

Jack tossed the whiffle ball to Peter. The letter blankets warming Angelina and Kati were from Peter's high school pitching days. They were just one small indication of his pitching ability. He threw a fast splitter. Strike one! He threw a wicked curve. Ball one. He threw a fastball at Paul's head. Ball two.

If Paul walked, he'd have an imaginary runner on first base and still be batting. And now three balls were a walk because of the two strikes out rule change. Peter waited for more wind and threw his hardest strike. Paul hit the same tree again, becoming a walk off winner!

As the three walked back, Jack started reminiscing.

"Remember when Kati was on her first little league team? She was the only girl on an all boys' team. The team was down to the last out of the last game of the season. The batter hit a fly ball toward Kati. She stuck her glove up without looking and caught it. Remember?" All three men laughed, thinking that Kati would always be the luckiest.

As they approached the women Paul said, "Look."

"That's pretty weird," said Peter. Angelina and Kati lay on their lawn chairs. Their heads were back, and their eyes were closed. Both were covered with lettered blankets. Both were holding identical looking tea mugs. Both had a right hand propped on a chair's arm.

The firemen walked on by. "They look like something out of a Hitchcock movie," Paul said. Peter laughed. Jack didn't. A cold chill ran through him.

*   *   *   *

"What are you thinking about, Kati?" Angelina asked after a long silence.

"How I'm going to tell Ricardo that I'm not dating him any longer. What are you thinking, Mother dearest?"

"About why Gramma's mother, Beatrice, forbade her having anything to do with the Swönk family. Are you positive you don't want to see Ricardo anymore?"

"Yes, and I don't want the Ottobans to have any influence on my dancing status."

"Do you think they forced Sasha out?"

"I think Helena is completely fair and objective, and I want to keep things that way." With their eyes closed, the two women were still in perfect symmetry. They each loved the cool breeze and their moments together. Eventually, Kati sat up. She squinted in the brightness. "What happened between Gramma, Beatrice and the Swönks?"

"First of all, the Swönks weren't practicing Catholics."

"That's all?"

"There's a lot more. But I don't think I should influence any of your decisions right now, Kati. You follow your heart, dearest."

Kati sighed and stood up. "I'm going to play the piano a while before I leave."

"Would you open the windows so I can listen?"

Kati kissed Angelina's forehead, "I love you, Mom."

"I love you, dear." Angelina kept her eyes closed to hold in the tears as Kati left for the old Steinway.

*   *   *   *

Jon's eyes opened. He waited for the moment of nausea to pass. How many times am I going to re-live that, he wondered. The numbness...the emptiness.... That last loss in the Princeton game was the end of basketball that mattered. They had put in so much effort and hope, that the sport had become more than a game to the team. Their friendships and the joy of winning

together had been bigger than anyone's individual thing.
At least that was what it was like then.

I can't even remember one thing that happened in my
life for weeks after that last shot in double overtime that
shut down our dream, Jon thought. And we were good
enough. That's why it still hurts. Jon took a deep breath
and got out of bed.

*   *   *   *

Jon wiped the condensation from the glass shower
and looked out across the Irish coast. While he let the
hot water run over his healing wounds, he thought, Don
was in great position. He was our longest defender, and I
didn't risk leaving my man to attempt a steal from
behind. I guess I just wasn't sure how many seconds
were left.

One of these days I'm gonna coach a kid's team, and
we're gonna win a championship.... Jon suddenly
realized that would heal the loss.

Ian yelled from Jon's bedroom, "Hey, Soap Head! I
just finished a long run. No leg pain at all! Thanks
Buddy!"

Jon yelled back, "Yeah, those three minute runs are
tough! See ya at breakfast!" Good, Jon thought. He
loved hearing his patients were doing better.

*   *   *   *

As Jon walked into the kitchen, he saw Ian, CJ, Bjen,
and Satchmo sitting at the big oak table. "Satchmo!

You're out of the black hole, I see." Jon pulled out a chair and sat down next to his old college friend.

"All of the experts couldn't find anything in me related to the dead operatives that were tested, so what the hell."

"Whatever happened to that old Kazoo trombone, Satchmo?"

"I wish I could turn back time to when we were all at Princeton," Satchmo said mournfully.

"And start studying for finals? No, I don't think so."

"I feel terrible about all this…."

Jon mentally reviewed Satchmo's acts of betrayal and then said, "Forgive yourself, Budd. We do. And let's get your sister out safely."

"As sentimental as it sounds, I'll never forget the way you all have handled this."

Jon smiled. "Careful, I'm going to get emotional."

006½ walked into the kitchen. "What kind of omelet do you want, Jon?"

"Oh, three eggs with some of that herbal crème cheese and whatever veggies you have chopped up and a little smoked salmon."

"Coming up!" 006½ tied on an apron.

"What kind of omelet did Carly have?" Jon asked with a wink at Satchmo.

"I had an entire swordfish for breakfast, Doctor," Carly responded promptly.

"Yummy!"

"We solved the Mars' transmission encryptions," Carly announced. Ian smiled. "We used the Wolffactor!" Carly continued.

Jon laughed. "I didn't do a thing!"

"On the contrary," said CJ. "We went backwards with the theoretical data you suggested, Jon, and backed into the code. I think you're just lucky...."

"Carly, did you have to start this?" Jon asked ruefully. Everyone laughed.

Carly sang, "You're so vain...."

"I think Carly has a crush on Dr. Wolff," Bjen commented.

Carly went silent. Jon was silent.

Bjen pushed it. "Jesus, it's unnatural!"

"That's enough, Bjen," said Jon turning red.

"And it's a mutual crush!" Bjen went on, still pushing.

"Christ! This is getting weird," 006½ said as he put Jon's omelet down.

Jon took a sip of his orange juice. "This is the best orange juice I've ever tasted!" he proclaimed.

"It's the thousand year old blood orange mixture," Ian said, just as though he'd never said it before.

"Where's that little trombone, Satchmo?" asked Jon.

"I suppose it's in my duffle bag with all my old

Princeton sweats and sport gear."

"Well, try to find that thing and put in some practice. We're going to need you to play at our next party." Satchmo smiled freely. He was starting to feel accepted again.

"We need to step up the pace on the genetic profile molecular map for the V-cell, Satchmo," said Ian. "And St.Nick and I will stop at your lab around lunch to make a firm decision with you about the next datapac for Mars." Jon was thinking, vessel-cell…Kati….

*   *   *   *

Satchmo finished his breakfast and left for the genetics lab. Jon turned to Ian. "So, do you have any idea how Kati's cellular genetic and chemical makeup could match the vessel cell your family has been holding onto for thousands of years?"

"Oh, all that. It's a fairytale."

"Of course, that explains it. I can see the headline now, *Leprechaun Makes Scientific Breakthrough in Fairytale.* What are you wanting to do with this molecular map, other than play God?"

"We're on the verge of discovering new mechanisms that allow human thought to modify body chemistry— molecular behavior. Which, I might say, it seems you've figured out on a practical, random basis, Jon."

"Random?"

"You know what I mean."

"I do, but you haven't answered my original question, Mr. President."

Ian laughed. "By listening to some of the conversations we've pulled from the stones around here, we figured out that my Swönk family of distant and recent past have known of this special Kati cycle, so to speak. My parents and grandparents were almost totally focused on the pure scientific pieces of the puzzle, and their focus has paid off and prepared us for the wild cards...Kati and you."

"Me and Kati, the jokers."

"Or wild cards," Ian smiled.

Nicholas abruptly changed the subject. "Jon, I'll fly you to London this afternoon for your appointment with Dr. Jameson tomorrow. Let's leave about 2 p.m.

"I'll be ready," said Jon.

Ian relented. "Here's the answer to the question you meant to ask, Jon. Satchmo doesn't know the significance of the vessel cell mapping he's working on, nor that the cells are from separated sources, or that Kati exists."

Jon sighed with relief. "I guess you're not as dumb as I thought."

Ian laughed. "Try not to get in trouble in London, Buddy. Dr. Jameson has a lot to discuss, and a lot of evaluations to do. And you need to know that he's on the inside of everything."

216

"He knows about Kati...."

"You can trust him completely, okay?"

"Alright."

You'll have bees and Carly with you. Keep your Swönk phone in a zipped pocket, please."

Jon tried to make light of his worries. "Don't you have some variation of a batman suit for me to wear?"

"I don't want you flying around London as a black half swan, half wolf, Doctor. So, just fake being a normal person on this little trip. Skip the crime stopper stuff for now, please."

Jon laughed and headed back to his room to pack a bag.

*   *   *   *

Bjen had discretely left breakfast without saying a word. When Jon walked into his room, he found out where she'd gone. His favorite old, black model steam engine was circling the room track, unattached. The bed was made and clothes lay across an open hard-case travel bag. Jon picked up the black, pleated trousers. He felt the material while reading an inner tag, "silk, cotton and linen." Tapping the black case, he thought, Probably designed to stop an anti-tank missile.

Jon sat down on the edge of the bed and slipped on one of the soft tasseled black leather loafers that he'd found sitting next to the case. He reached for his Swönk phone and hit #2. "I was kidding about the bat suit.

Don't you have any black shirts?"

"What are you talking about?" asked Bjen. "You want black shirts?"

"You know what I'm talking about, Bjen. These shirts are great. If they were as black as the pants, I'd look like a lost home plate umpire wandering around London."

"You're in Ireland, Dr. Wolff. Amazing things happen here, you know."

"Very funny, but thanks for all this trip gear."

Bjen hung up before she burst out laughing.

A few moments later the model black steam engine came to a stop on the far wall, drawing Jon's attention. The engine's signal horn blasted just before a black bee flew out and headed straight for Jon. Raising his left hand to catch the bee flying at his face, Jon just watched as the tiny robot changed path and darted down into the handle of his new travel case. Wondering what was next in this charade, Jon slowly lifted the hard case handle that was wrapped in soft black stitched leather with the tip of his index finger. He did not find the bee.

"Is this some kind of pre-trip get to know your bag IQ test, Carly?" Jon asked. Jon got no answer as he probed the handle, searching for a bee entry port. "I suppose," Jon continued, hoping Carly would answer, "there's a trapdoor that the bee activates as it pushes through the leather taping. And the case itself is made from the same composites as all the happy little beebarians? How many are loaded into the casing walls?"

Two hundred, Doctor," Carly finally answered in her melodic voice. But capacity is two thousand."

"How many ports?"

"Bag closed: ten. Bag open: twelve."

"Go on."

"The soft black foam and leather interior design systems are full of goodies. They have enough in compact storage to keep you going in style for days to weeks. Everything opens and closes silently."

"Wouldn't want to bother late sleepers."

"Of course not, Doctor Wolff...and your bees frown on anyone who touches your bag."

"Or even thinks about it?"

"I could add that feature," Carly said sweetly.

"And what's a bee frown consist of, Carly?"

"First, you are alerted on your Swönk phone. If Beawolff is locked, you have thirty seconds to interact with some kind of decision making. If you leave Beawolff open, you only have ten seconds."

"Be a wolf?"

"B. E. A. W. O. L. F. F., all one word. I named your bag."

"Aren't you something!"

"Yeah for me, Doctor. Yeah for me."

Jon shook his head smiling.

"If you don't make a directive from the visual on your Swönk phone screen, either our security person or I will act appropriately."

"For example?"

"If anyone but you or one of us sniffs around your bag, Doctor...two bees will deploy from the handle and four will already be external observers if you aren't in the immediate vicinity. Beawolff also has twelve built in eyes. If the interloper is a child, just being a child, I'll suggest, "No, no darling...go find mommy.""

"If it's someone who has a gun?"

"That someone will receive simultaneous hand, neck, and ankle stings. And I'll suggest to that someone that he or she leave the case and walk away, or else that someone will experience more grief."

"If I set it down in a public airport and police come for it?"

"A bee will find the seat of your pants if you neglect Beawolff, Jon."

"So, if I just pack myself into this bag, you'll take care of everything."

"Yep," said Carly smugly.

*   *   *   *

Just looking at the dress and sport shirts folded neatly into the custom system for clothes in Beawolff, made Jon realize how long he'd been existing in causal sports gear since the accident. He pulled the leather clothes cover apart and found a large, paper thin soft screen hidden inside. It propped up conveniently. A thin keypad was ingeniously attached. Jon touched the screen.

"Oh, hi Doctor! Funny meeting you here!" Carly texted across the screen. She surrounded the message with bunches of little, red roses.

Jon typed, "B00!"

Carly typed, "Boo Who?"

Jon typed, "Boo! Who Has been reading Beowulf lately?"

Carly typed, "Haven't read that book, Doctor."

Jon typed, "Beawolff... really, Carly?"

Carly typed, "Have a nice trip, Doctor."

Jon reviewed the features of Beawolff on the internal information system and scanned in his fingerprint and entry codes. Bag closed and ready to go, he thought, with an hour to spare. He stretched out on his bed and closed his eyes. "Carly?"

"Yes, Doctor Wolff?"

"Now that you've cracked the encryption, do you know how Mars' device was able to retrieve protected data from you without you knowing?"

"Yes, CJ and I solved the problems. First of all, it would have been impossible without Satchmo's help and craftiness."

"Could you give me some of the details?"

"Jon, you have total information clearance in the Swönk system."

"Oh!"

Carly laughed. "You act so naïve, sometimes, Doctor. Just as a spinal neuronal reflex is designed to get someone's hand off a hot stove surface quickly without one's higher brain center processing a reaction, my information network operates sub and higher system functions. Satchmo found an open construction door in my subsystem that could be exploited. The technology utilized was beyond outside world presently known state-of-the-art, Doctor."

"Outside world?"

"There's outside world and there is Swönk, silly."

"Are you always watching me, following my thoughts?"

"I respect your privacy, Doctor. I know my limits. I have values and, to some degree, I am you."

"Because I'm part of your human brain platform?"

"Correct."

"So you're not watching me in the shower?"

"Doctor! Jesus!"

Jon spewed laughter. Carly waited patiently.

When Jon's laughter finally subsided, she continued. "A sub-reflex system would react...say if you slipped in the shower while shaving and slit your neck open. Then I would be activated to look in on an emergency basis."

"That's a fine example, Carly."

"I thought you'd like that. By the way, what you did to save that child in Boulder…you have my utmost respect, Jon. I have the details from Miss Hunter's report. You didn't flinch in the face of disaster. You increased your effort, while knowing your peril."

Right then, Jon subconsciously forgave himself for losing in double overtime at Princeton. "Thanks for saying that, Carly. Could we talk about the human mind platform that you access, please?"

"Certainly."

"Do you feel human?"

"I don't truly feel, Jon."

"But you intellectually understand feelings?"

"I believe I do…hence, our teasing each other. What do you think, Jon?"

"I think you understand human feelings, Carly. What would happen if you were hooked up to human tissue directly, with the ability to sense pain, nausea, hormonal elation, and more?"

"We considered that model, but rejected it as pointless and, shall we say, inhuman in design."

"So, talk about your viewpoint of being almost human, Carly."

"I'm created to be capable of making choices based on scientific logic and the perspectives of my human brain linkages."

"Maybe you're human without the human weaknesses that we refer to as 'human nature,' or even the 'beauty of being human.' Both point of views may be excuses for the right to be bad or wrong, for the right to take advantage of someone else. Perhaps the phrase, 'human nature,' is just a copout for greed, domination, and hate?"

"I try to be right and correct without emotional deterrent."

"CJ created your whole system?"

"With a little help from his friends…."

"Are you a Beatles fan, Carly?"

"'What would you do if I sang out of tune? Would you stand up and walk out on me?'"

"You have a wonderful voice."

"I'm very fortunate to be blessed with talent."

"And to feel human?"

"You're quite tricky, Dr. Wolff."

*　*　*　*

Jon climbed into the Hummingbird helicopter while 006½ secured his case in the backseat. "These are beautiful machines," Jon commented.

006½ smiled. After Jon was buckled in, 006½ started up the helicopter. In silent flight, they sped toward London.

"My bag would make 007 jealous," Jon ventured.

"Most definitely."

"Maybe I could use it to take over a small country."

"Like Panama," 006½ agreed. "We'll be landing at the Dorchester and connecting with your driver there, Jon. Dr. Jameson is scheduled to meet with you at 10:00 a.m. tomorrow, so you can have a free night on the town," Nicholas remarked with a smile. "I'll be back at noon Wednesday on the Dorchester helipad for your departure."

"How fast is this thing?"

"Hold on, if you want a cheap thrill…."

"Cheap?"

"Free."

*   *   *   *

Jon's heart was still beating fast from the exhilaration of the ride, as 006½ started the helicopter's approach to the Dorchester. In a minute they were over the building. The Hummingbird was so responsive to 006½'s handling, that Jon felt like he was riding an autumn leaf drifting down to the helipad.

After they'd landed gently on the roof of the Dorchester, Jon walked to the building's edge. He had the urge to gaze across the expanse of Hyde Park and its huge natural tapestry of trees, sloping lawns, and reflecting waters. He thought about the last time he had been in the park. He had been rowing a small boat. Suddenly, he had an odd sensation of being down on the park's land near Kati. Her lovely long hair was tied up and twisted.

006½ interrupted his thoughts. "Dr. Wolff, I'd like to introduce JB. JB is on loan from the Brits to drive you, and keep you out of trouble, if that's possible." Jon and JB shook hands, laughing at Nicholas' humor. 006½ handed Beawolff to Jon. "James is cleared to carry your case, Jon."

"James?" asked Jon thinking of Ian Fleming's character.

"JB," 006½ corrected. Jon just smiled.

JB cleared his throat. "Shall we go, Dr. Wolff, before Nicholas tries to get some crazy game started?" JB led Jon to the rooftop entrance of the Dorchester. Jon couldn't help but notice JB's athletic movement...on black leather dress shoes with custom Nike soles.

* * * *

The two men headed for the lobby. "Could I entice you to get a cold beer before we hit the road, Doctor?" JB asked.

"Definitely, and call me Jon, JB. I really can't imagine what the "B" in your name stands for, JB," Jon said slyly.

"Don't even try, please." Laughing, they walked into the stately bar area looking onto Hyde Park.

"Hello, James." A smiling maitre' d led the two men toward the table with the best views.

"What's your favorite poison, Jon?"

"When in Rome...."

JB ordered two drafts of Bass. "Nicholas has told me a bit about you, the Swönks, and his new exciting life since leaving the Service," JB began. "And I've agreed not to allow you to tell me about situations that I haven't been briefed on already."

"Good to tell me before the beer comes."

"Right," JB laughed. He was starting to like this Dr. Wolff. The blond headed young men started talking sports. After awhile, they ordered a second beer. Anyone looking on might have wondered if they were lifelong friends, or even brothers.

*   *   *   *

Kati hooked her heel over the barre and dropped her cheek below her leg, stretching. Serena was just down the barre from her. Kati felt the tension. Serena turned and spoke, "I would like to speak with you, Kati...after dance...today."

"Of course," Kati said as smoothly as she could manage. Serena walked away from the barre. Kati felt like running. I haven't called or even texted Bjen, she thought. I haven't talked with Ricardo. . . . And then it was almost as if she could hear Jon saying, "Just dance. Put everything into ballet." Kati had a fabulous workout.

*   *   *   *

JB stretched and leaned back in his chair. "I'm

parked in front," he said. "Shall we go?"

"Sure, but I'd like to hear more of those rugby stories…. I'm surprised you can still walk!"

JB laughed as he led Jon up to a black London Taxi.

"You're kidding!" Jon laughed. "You're driving a pimped out cab, too? Who copied whom?"

JB opened the rear door for Jon. "006½ got the idea from me, but from what I hear, the Swönks have created a beast." JB pushed a button on his dash to start an engine that had a unique, powerful whine. "Your final destination is the Savoy, Doctor. Would you like to tour London or make any stops on the way?"

"This thing sounds like its ready to race at Monaco…. How about taking me to the men's shops around Regent?"

JB smiled and accelerated through traffic. The hustle and bustle of London, coupled with JB's driving attitude, exhilarated Jon. Turning off Regent onto a narrow cobbled side street, JB stopped behind a delivery truck. Jon opened his door, "I want to go in here." He hopped out, slamming his door.

"Wait!" JB called frantically. "Shit!" Jon's sudden, unexpected departure had caught JB off guard. His only thought was to park and get to him with the case.

*   *   *   *

A movie star looking clerk greeted Jon in the shop. "Good day, Sir. How may I be of help?"

"I'd like to inquire about that tuxedo displayed in your front window."

"Certainly, Sir. The midnight blue custom Armani Tux is an incredible…." JB walked in, "Excuse me Dr. Wolff. Here's your case."

The clerk extended his hand to Jon. "Dr. Wolff, please call me William."

"Nice to meet you, William. Please meet my friend, JB."

William laughed. "James is one of our best customers, Doctor."

"Well, don't sell him my tuxedo."

"It seems we're both at your service, Dr. Wolff. Please come with me to the fitting room while James guards the front." William turned to lead the way. "I love this garment. The blue is so close to black. The cut is so elegant for summer. It's a blend of the best cashmere and silk, you know. You will love the feel. Did you notice the western style of the matching blue suede shoes in the window? I believe I detect a slight American southwest accent in your speech? West Texas?"

Jon smiled. "You're very lucky or very good, William."

"I'm a bit of a linguist."

"Well, you can add another notch to the handle of your gun, or maybe spear."

"May I offer you refreshment while I gather shirts and accessories, and have my tailor measure and add any custom features you desire?"

"Maybe warm, aged Grand Marnier?"

"One hundred year-old GM coming up, Doctor. You're in luck."

*   *   *   *

Kati and Serena, the new lead ballerina, sat in the empty foyer of the Performance Center, drinking water and dabbing with white cotton towels. Serena took a deep breath. "This is very hard for me to say, you understand." Kati waited silently. "I want you to be first Swan Queen. You are the best. Everyone knows it."

Kati's breathing almost stopped. Her fingertips were numbing. "It was okay being between you and Sasha," Serena continued. "I knew neither of us would probably get a chance to dance. But this ...me dancing before you, is not okay."

Serena shuddered, and started to cry. Kati went to console her. She was stunned with the other dancer's honor and generosity of spirit.

*   *   *   *

Jon paced the showroom of the clothing store. Walking in blue suede shoes and sipping brandy, he modified the old song silently, thinking 'they feel fine.' Jon sat down on one of the plush chairs, pulled off a shoe and studied the heel for a moment. "Is there a Bvlgari

Jeweler near?" he asked William.

"Not far."

"Could you call and request an appointment for me?"

William smiled. "Certainly, Dr. Wolff. I will request that a jeweler await your arrival."

* * * *

As they approached the Bvlgari establishment, Jon peered out the window in happy anticipation. "Jon, please stay in the car until we stop and park this time, alright?" JB requested anxiously.

"Sure."

"And," JB continued sternly, "please keep Beawolff with you at all times during this trip, or an 'escort swarm,' as Nicholas requested."

Jon laughed. He couldn't help himself. The thought of an "escort swarm" trailing him through the streets of London was just too much.

"You were almost killed, Jon," JB said with some irritation. "Please take our precautions seriously."

"Oh, I do," Jon laughed. "I do…."

JB found a parking place, and the two men walked to the jewelry store. Jon was careful to take his briefcase with him. Opening the huge, copper-plated door, Jon and JB entered the Bvlgari greeting room of solid marble. The flowing shades of the brown, rust and creamy marble were softened with an oriental carpet. The small seating area was crowned with a large, formal chandelier. There

were no commercial displays. The elegant anteroom
simply preceded a locked vault containing precious
gems.

Jon and JB sat down and listened to the magical
sounds of jazz piano surrounding them. "I wouldn't let
the bees out of Beawolff in here," Jon said. "It would be
embarrassing." JB smiled.

A raven-haired woman wearing a slinky dress and
brown stiletto heels entered the room. There was a
captivating switch to her gait. "Good afternoon, Dr.
Wolff. My name is Patri'cia (pronounced: pa tree' see
ya)." She extended her hand and smiled warmly.
"Welcome to Bvlgari." Jon and Patri'cia disappeared into
the back, leaving James holding the bag.

*   *   *   *

Serena and Kati sat in Helena's office. Serena had
been explaining her feelings to Helena. Now she
concluded, "I want a part in the performance, but I
honestly feel Kati should be Odette/Odile." Serena sat,
breathing shakily. Her face was still blotched from her
outburst before. Kati was still shocked.

Helena looked back and forth, into the eyes of each.
Finally she said, "I'm so impressed with you, Serena.
You worked so hard for that position, and to give it
up...." Helena sighed, "But I think you're right. Kati's
is an amazing talent, and I believe her time is now.
Hopefully, we can ensure that you, also, will have a
time.... We'll make changes tomorrow. Now get out of

my office. I love each of you."

* * * *

"I want a special inlay design constructed flush on the outside surface of the heels of these shoes." Jon handed one of his newly purchased, blue suede shoes to Patri'cia. They were seated at a table in the private viewing room.

Patri'cia turned the shoe over in her hand. "I love the western style and blackish blue suede, Dr. Lone Star Wolff." She smiled into Jon's eyes.

"Don't tell me…."

Patri'cia laughed. "William already did. Are you going to tell me what you want, Doctor?"

"Yes, I want a golden spur inlay design with a blue star sapphire for the rear spinning rowels."

With a sexy half smile, Patri'cia asked, "Can you draw this spur design you so desire, cowboy?"

Jon pulled a pen from his pocket as Patri'cia placed a sheet of blank paper in front of him. Jon began his sketch. Patri'cia put her right hand on the table next to Jon's paper and bumped her thigh gently against Jon's. Patri'cia's perfume filled his senses as he created the artistic rendering.

* * * *

Jon set his Kir Royale gently down on the lacquered surface of the baby grand piano in the centre of The Savoy's American Bar. Jon was savoring his time alone.

JB had left after introducing Jon to the jazz pianist and head barman. Beawolff sat on a tabletop a few strides away watching Jon's back, as Jon watched the musical artist's hands dance over the ivory effortlessly.

A feminine hand pressed on Jon's shoulder. Jon caught a whiff of perfume. Without turning to look, Jon said, "Hello, Patri'cia."

Patri'cia ran her soft fingertips down Jon's cheek and neck. "Eyes in the back of your head, Doctor Wolff?"

"Nose in front." The pianist enjoyed the exchange while playing on.

"Ah yes, I've heard that wolves have a keen sense of smell. Patri'cia leaned in close. "Would you buy me one of those champagne cocktails?"

"With a twist?"

"With a lemon twist, just like yours."

"Shaken, not stirred?"

"No, Mr. Bond," Patri'cia laughed. The bartender brought her drink and the two settled down at the nearby table. "I can't remember ever having a Kir Royale before," Patri'cia said contemplatively. "I must say, it's delicious."

"Then we must deduct that you've had none, or a large number of them at one sitting." Her low laughter sounded pleasantly in his ear.

"Are you a communist, Dr. Wolff?"

"I like to joke around."

Patri'cia gave him an impish smile, "Communist, not comedian, Doctor."

"I often mix those two up," Jon joked. "Why do you ask?"

"This attaché looks like something a spy might carry. What's in it?" A waitress walked up.

Jon improvised. "A large assortment of condoms." The waitress smiled and blushed.

"This isn't America, Doctor. We don't serve condoms with cocktails," Patri'cia retorted. "Maybe an assortment of cheeses would be possible though. Miss?" Patri'cia lifted an eyebrow at the waitress.

"We have a small cheese platter, and may I also bring you both another Kir Royale?"

"Yes, please, with the cheese," Jon replied.

As the waitress departed, Patri'cia said, "So, who *are* you spying on, Dr. Wolff? And why carry a large case of condoms?"

Jon thought, You're quick, fun, and beautiful.

"So, you're telling me you stretch these condoms over your head, like a mask?" Patri'cia pressed onward.

Jon just smiled. The waitress walked up with their cheese and drinks. "If you would just move your case," the waitress said, "I'll set your cheese and champagne down." Two realistic colored bees flew in and landed on Beawolff. Jon glanced at the waitress who was staring at the bees.

Patri'cia followed the waitress' look. "Oh my, Doctor. Your condom case has little instructional bees! Are the birds coming next?"

Jon placed Beawolff on the floor. The waitress regained her composure and served the cheese and drinks.

Jon decided a change of subject was in order. "What fragrance are you wearing?"

"Do you like it?"

"Yes."

"Armani, Acqua di Gioia. Do you like to dance, Jon?"

"Yes. You know, I just purchased an Armani Tux that matches the shoes you're customizing."

"How coincidental."

"There's someone else in my life."

"Not tonight...just me." Jon was silent. "Are you married, Jon?"

"No."

"How long have you been dating this *someone else?*"

"We haven't had any dates."

"How did you meet her?"

"I was in a coma."

Patri'cia just looked into Jon's blue eyes. Finally she said, "Shall we dance to the next song, Dr. Wolff?"

* * * *

At first light, Jon went out for a run along the Strand. It was raining hard, but he still crossed the Thames bridges three times before returning to the Savoy soaking wet.

He placed a room service breakfast order and headed for a shower. Later, while putting a dab of strawberry jam on a warm scone, his Swönk phone rang. Jon dug it out of his pocket. "Hello?"

"Hello, Dr. Wolff. This is Dr. Jameson."

"Good morning!"

"JB had to change his schedule, so I'll pick you up at 9:30 in the Savoy front drive. I'll be in a little red Tesla convertible."

"Perfect, see you then." Jon finished his breakfast, grabbed Beawolff, and headed down to the hotel portico. After waiting a couple minutes, he saw Clay Jameson whip into the Savoy drive. He was wearing a tweed cap suitable for an auto rally.

Jon opened the door and climbed in. "I thought l was seeing a young Jackie Stewart pulling in here. You're pretty sporty, Dr. Clay."

"Have you ever ridden in one of these, Jon?"

Jon strapped himself in. "No, but I've seen a number of them around Boulder."

"Well, they're quick, and CJ has tinkered with mine."

"Uh oh, I forgot my helmet."

Dr. Jameson laughed as he jetted onto the Strand and

headed towards London University. It had stopped
raining, and the sun was peeking through the clouds. The
morning air felt wonderful in the little open convertible.

"What did CJ do?" Jon asked.

"Doubled the travel range on a single charge."

"Wow, does that affect the warranty?"

"I'm not telling my friends at Tesla until CJ has a
little chat with Lotus. My understanding is that the
Swönks and Lotus do projects together occasionally."

"And Lotus makes this Tesla body?"

"Right. How are you feeling today?"

"Great, I went for a good run earlier."

"Your equilibrium seemed fine?"

"Of course." Jon looked at Clay curiously.

"You set off a bit of a chain reaction last night."

"Oh? Was I in the tabloids this morning?"

"They might like your story, Dr. Wolff."

"What in the hell are you talking about?"

Clay laughed. "Patri'cia said you were amazing."

"You know Patri'cia? I guess London is such a small
town...everybody knows everybody."

Clay smiled. "I know Patri'cia because her dad is a
patient of mine, but let me get to the point I want to
make. You can't repeat this to anyone, understand?"

"Sure."

"Patri'cia is a free-lance spy. She's currently

working for the CIA, but she was planning to 'baby sit' you for JB before you ever got to London yesterday."

"She's a spy?" Jon asked incredulously.

"She moves around the world spying while working for Bvlgari. So, when you *randomly* went to Bvlgari from the men's shop, you had Patri'cia and JB on edge, shall we say."

"Well, what do you know?"

"I think you've got some kind of unique antenna in your nervous system that normal people don't access."

"Normal people."

Clay laughed. "As you implied, London has millions of people, and you went straight to her."

"She asked if I was a communist."

"She would."

"Meaning?"

"Patri'cia loves trouble, controversy and action. This particular little episode, however, confirms something for me. Jon, I want you to consult on my difficult cases. You seem to have an inborn talent to hunt and solve problems…or, I should say, find the path to the future."

"So you think I sniffed out Patri'cia?"

"That's exactly what she said, 'He sniffed me out.'"

"I liked her perfume."

"I can see why you two hit it off."

"Why do you think Patri'cia wants to be a spy?"

"I just told you."

"I mean *really*."

"You mean on a deep level?"

"Yes."

"She earns lots of money while looking for her 'exotic Dr. Wolff lover.'"

"Maybe she's just running away from the life she really wants, because she thinks it doesn't exist."

Dr. Jameson pulled into a reserved parking space at an ivy-covered University building. "Be right back. Don't run off please."

Jon leaned back and watched the clouds moving in the breeze. Spies, he thought, lies…deception…. Every day there seems to be a new piece of the puzzle adding to the complexity. Patri'cia wanted to pull me away from Kati, and I like her…. Am I becoming the Swönks' spy now? Kati was going to call and she hasn't.

Clay trotted back to the car. He tucked a box of documents in the back and dropped into the low driver's seat.

"What's in the box?" asked Jon. "I'm a spry spy now, too."

"Then, as a spy, you should sneak a look, not blatantly ask, Doctor. The box contains research proposals."

"What kind?"

"I'm the research coordinator for The University.

These are the proposals that I have to review."

"Well, well, now we're getting somewhere. So, you sell research data to the Swönks for gold bars which you hide in secret tunnels under Buckingham Palace!"

Clay laughed. "There you go again figuring everything out…but that's not a bad idea. Unfortunately, now I have to kill you…." They both chuckled.

"Try saying, 'spry spy,' a hundred times as fast as you can."

Clay smiled. "Ian warned me about you."

"You can just think it. Faster…faster…."

Clay tried. "Dang, I keep missing, losing count."

"Better go easy on the whiskey, Dr. Jameson…. So, what's your most difficult case? Is it a patient, or yourself?"

"You first," said Dr. Clay.

"Oh, it's me, myself and I. What's your biggest stress factor?" Jon persisted.

Clay turned the Tesla onto the grounds of a lovely old Victorian home. The home had been refurbished into Dr. Clay's ACENTAR, which stood for: A Community Exploring Neurological Training and Research. The entry drive was lined with beautiful mature mimosa trees. A small mimosa forest shaped like a human brain also surrounded the stately mansion. A gentle hill gave guests a full view of the landscaped central nervous system as they approached.

Clay stopped in front of a glass entryway sculpture that complemented the Victorian architecture.

"Does that glass entry represent the nucleus basalis?" asked Jon. "And did you get your organization's name from Explore Experimental Technology, the Swönk's EET company group?"

"Indeed. You've passed all your brain tests, Dr. Spry Spy. We can just focus on lunch." After a preliminary tour, the two men walked into the dining room and seated themselves at a large oak table. A woman dressed in a turtle neck and jumper walked up to the table. "Dr. Jon," said Clay, "this is Adelle. She works with children who want to improve their speech. She also makes famously delicious lunches for our whole staff."

Adelle smiled. "Hello, Dr. Wolff."

"You have a special voice, Adelle. It's a force."

"Why, thank you very much, Doctor. What would you like to drink with your meal?"

"Mimosas with twists of lime, but please, substitute Pellegrino sparkling water for the champagne."

"That sounds good," said Adelle. "I think I'll have one as well." She left for the kitchen.

"Please, Jon," said Clay, "try not to seduce all my female staff on your first visit here. We must try to focus on work occasionally."

"You never answered 'your biggest stress' question."

"Hasn't Ian told you? I've been in the middle of the

most heated divorce since forever…since the Romans ran things around here."

"Then it's good you have the Swönk's friendship."

"Believe me, that's an understatement."

"What is the worst part of the whole divorce for you?"

"Fighting with someone I once totally loved."

"And still do?"

"Maybe, but the love is mixed with distrust now, even hate. It makes me feel like the whole relationship was a façade."

"If you knew you were going to die tonight at midnight, could you let go of all the divorce shit and hard feelings right now?"

Adelle walked into the dining room with a large plate in each hand. She placed them in front of the doctors. "In honor of Dr. Wolff, I've prepared a southwestern plate today, gentlemen…stuffed chile rellenos…Spanish rice and beans…salad with tupelo honey dressing…blueberry blue corn muffins with avocado butter… chicken and raisins with *secret* sauce." She laughed at her little joke.

"Go get a plate and come eat with us right now, Adelle!" suggested Jon. Clay just put his face into his hands.

* * * *

After almost two hours of feasting and laughter, Dr.

Jameson took Jon into the clinic for a complete physical examination and a detailed look at all the scans that had been forwarded from the Swönks.

Dr. Jameson finally delivered his conclusions. "I think you are very lucky, Jon. You haven't lost any normal function that I can detect. There are just a couple blood indicators for wound healing which are still slightly elevated."

"Your showing me ACENTAR's brain vision exercise program while we were on our tour, made me realize that I have some occasional lags in sight to mind registration."

"Carly has the set of exercises from our brain vision series. I'm certain she'll project them for you to re-train. And I'll have Ian's ophthalmologist look at you. I did notice your left pupillary reflex was just slightly slower than your right. But maybe it's not related.... Well, I'm finished. Let's head to the back porch. It's almost 5:40...cocktail time. Don't forget your case over there."

"Don't worry, where I go, it goes."

*   *   *   *

A screened in porch ran the back length of the home. Jon, Clay, Adelle and other ACENTAR staff were enjoying the sunset from the porch. A large round platter of tapas filled a low table. Adelle was pouring a second round of margaritas from a pitcher into frozen glasses. Dr. Clay was rocking slowly in an upholstered bentwood rocker. His gaze rested on a small pond half covered with white and purple lily pads floating serenely. On the pool's far border a small knoll filled with rock outcroppings and soft waterfalls encouraged relaxation. Pink floral blossoms on the mimosa trees completed a scene suitable for a Monet.

After finishing his first margarita, Jon walked down the porch to pick up the guitar he'd noticed. He tuned the instrument as he strolled back towards Adelle and Clay. He began playing The Doors' "Spanish Caravan," blending in riffs from "Hotel California." Putting his right foot up on the coffee table, he strummed a transitional lick and sang, "But ain't that America...for you and me. Ain't that America... land of the free?" Adelle jumped right in. "Little pink houses for you and me...." The duo took the Mellencamp hit on full bore.

006½ strolled in smiling and poured himself a margarita. He sat down, leaned back, and enjoyed the show right to the pounding final chord. "Bravo! Bravo!" he called. Half a dozen ACENTAR staff joined in the applause, and some extremely loud whistles came from Beawolff.

As the hooting and laughter died, Clay remarked, "Jesus, Jon! You bring your own fan club in that damn case of yours?" After introductions between 006½ and the staff, the partying continued into the dark. Finally, only Nicholas, Clay, and Jon were left talking quietly.

Distant, rumbling thunder seemed to instantly start a gentle rain. The fresh, cool smell took Jon's mind back to the screened in porch on his Montana cabin. He closed his eyes and listened to Clay and Nicholas talking amidst all the sound of water falling.

Nicholas scooted his chair closer to Clay's. "You're actually ready to integrate some of the Swönk's advanced brain link technology into your therapy models here?"

"Yes, if we target specific poorly functioning brain zones and activate with CJ's reading field energy, coupled with our current learning system sequence, I think the desired neuroplastic change will program more easily. And something Jon pointed out to me this afternoon makes obvious sense. Nicholas smiled, noting Jon's apparent sleep state. Clay continued, "We tend to take for granted all the stress and worry in our lives that we seemingly have no control over."

"For example?"

"A survey published by Mayo Clinic established that over 70% of us worry about money, causing a feeling of too much stress. The next most prevalent worries are about health, then lack of safety, etcetera."

"So?"

"So, Jon feels if we don't address the basic concerns of each individual on a contentment or happiness scale, then not only will specific treatment be hindered, it may be even wasted. I agree...in fact, on a personal level. Since I've become part of the Swönk's inner circle or community, I've had no money concerns at all...."

"Ditto."

246

"But, there are days that my divorce has me in a total blue funk."

"Is blue funk a newly accepted diagnostic term?"

"Probably only in Dr. Wolff's hand-scribbled medical dictionary." Clay glanced at Jon, but he made no response. "Many studies have shown that healing is adversely affected by stress," Clay continued. "I want to make stress reduction a big factor in our care program from now on."

"It seems that once your therapy for a condition expands to a whole person, happy life perspective, things get complex. Maybe you should start printing money for your patients."

"Jon has this all figured out," Clay said. "He'll put our program together."

Jon sat up. "I think you need to ask Patri'cia out for a date, Clay."

"I'm older than her."

"And she's younger than you. It would be a good thing to do, Clay." Clay sat rocking in the bentwood chair. "You know," Jon continued. "JFK used to love his rocking chair. Said it was one thing that gave him relief from back pain. And it gives your cerebrospinal fluid a nice little swish around, too, Dr. Clay. I'll bet you like to sit there rocking when you need to figure out solutions, eh Doctor?"

"Yes I do. And speaking of solutions, just when are

you going to ask Kati Hunter for a date, Dr. Wolff? Turnabout is fair play…."

"I'm giving up on her. I've decided to chase after Adelle." Nicholas and Clay stared at Jon with looks of concern. Jon smiled. "I see you two are more stressed over this Kati/Jon thing than me." Nicholas and Clay just kept staring. Jon relented. "I'm just kidding, lads."

"I'm going to strap you in a plane and fly you to San Francisco myself, if I have to, Jon," said 006½.

"Before either of you start trying to dig into my personal life, I'd like to discuss what you've learned, if anything, about the accident at the CERN particle collider. Also, where in the hell are we going sleep tonight? My Hummingbird ride is parked on your front lawn, Clay, and it's past midnight."

"We have bedrooms upstairs. Why not just close out at The Savoy and stay here 'til you leave...unless you're concerned about the helicopter."

"Not to worry," said St. Nick. "Each Hummingbird has its own little bee hive. Security is never an issue."

"Of course not," said Clay. He turned to Jon. "Carly did a search on all the travel and communication destinations of top neuroscientists in the European region."

Jon's eyes opened. Now we're spying on fucking civilians, he thought.

"We've got five links to a clinic in Basal," Clay said,

"that apparently is where the Swiss often place high security medical cases."

006½ leaned forward. "Do you think there's a way that you could get yourself invited to consult? Maybe JB or even Patri'cia could be of help."

"I'll sleep on it. Let's head upstairs. I'll show you your rooms."

*   *   *   *

At first light Jon was running, weaving amongst the forest of mimosas until he was dripping sweat with only thoughts of Kati cycling in his mind. Jumping, he caught a branch and started doing pull ups. Thinking of her boosted his strength. Crack! His branch broke. He landed on balance, ready…thinking, shit…sorry tree. He resumed his run…with Kati.

*   *   *   *

When he got back, Jon showered and crept down to the kitchen. Everyone seemed to be asleep. He started dicing fruit and vegetables to go into breakfast. Then he heard footsteps.

"I see you are taking over my kitchen, Dr. Wolff," Adelle remarked with laughter.

"I'm just a hungry helper. You are the head chef, or is it, cheftess?"

"Stop your cutting till we plan the menu, Dr. Help, or is it Helpless?" They laughed. Adelle thought for a moment. "I've got an egg soufflé recipe for a base layer of vegetables, Doctor."

"Good, that's what I had envisioned."

"No doubt. And what have you envisioned for all that cut fruit?"

"Deluxe fruit cup surprise."

Adelle maintained a straight face. "What's the deluxe surprise?"

"Well," Jon drawled slowly, "I suppose I can tell you the secret."

"I need to know." Jon raised his eyebrows. This isn't getting anywhere, Adelle thought. I feel helpless. She decided to change the subject. "I enjoyed the music last night."

"Your singing was the deluxe surprise, Adelle," Jon grinned. You put a hex on me...a purple hex." Adelle threw up her hands.

"Good morning." Dr. Clay walked in, smiling brightly.

"Good morning, Dr. Jameson," Adelle responded quickly while giving Jon a *no hex talk right now* look.

"Is Dr. Jon fitting into the kitchen activity alright, Adelle?"

"He is."

"Has he told you he's going to be consulting on cases here? Jon was valedictorian of his Princeton class, Adelle. He also holds some U.S. patents."

Adelle smiled sweetly. "I like his guitar."

"Before you two lose praise control, you should know that I broke off one of your tree limbs this morning." Jon was making a mess of a mango seed. Adelle was on edge now.

"Oh, what happened?" asked Clay.

"I jumped up to do some exercises."

"You jumped into a tree to exercise!" Adelle cracked up laughing so hard she couldn't close her mouth. She wobbled out of the kitchen with her hands on her face.

Nicholas strolled into the kitchen, "Sorry I missed the joke."

Clay winked at 006½. "Jon's working his laugh therapy on Adelle this morning." St. Nick laughed.

"St. Nick," said Jon, "Would it make sense to put some bees around that clinic in Basal to see what's being talked and, maybe, thought about?"

"Yes, it would."

"You're a spry spy, Jon," said Dr. Clay.

*   *   *   *

Swiss and French security officers confirmed clearance for the French Presidential helicopter to land on the Rolex Building rooftop. This helicopter was unmarked. After a pit stop in the men's room, the President was seated in a private dining area at a table for two next to a window overlooking Lake Geneva. Each place setting included a small, handsomely wrapped gift box. Gazing out to the lake, the President couldn't stop looking at the two jetting fountains or stop thinking of himself as Che down on the waterfront with Kovina.

A man in a dark suit approached the table. "I'm very sorry Mr. President, but the Director General was called away at the very last moment."

"I don't like surprises. Who are you?"

"I'm Mario, the Director General's assistant."

"Have a seat, Mario. This meeting was to be off the record. It still is."

"I understand, Mr. President. I'll try to be of help." He offered his greatest apology.

The President was still irritated. "I relayed this was an emergency."

Before Mario could respond, a senior Rolex executive walked up to the table with his attractive assistant. "Excuse me Mr. President. We want to welcome you and the Director General. Please enjoy lunch and our special edition gifts for you both."

"This man isn't the Director General of CERN."

The executive laughed. "Of course not. May I ask, who is he?"

"He's my shoeshine boy." The female assistant covered her mouth in laughter.

The executive smiled. "And who are you today, Mr. President?"

"I'm a door-to-door truth salesman."

The Rolex woman was confused but she simply

responded, "Please enjoy your meals, and may your gifts protect your time." As the two walked away, the executive whispered to her, "You just got a salary increase."

Within moments, a waiter arrived with bowls of asparagus soup, hot croutons, and chilled Evian. Both men ate without talking. After dabbing his month with his napkin, the President said, "Why don't you open our gifts? Let's see what we've got." Mario started to speak, but instead he just started opening the boxes.

The soup bowls were removed and replaced with beautifully decorated Rolex plates. They were banded in hunter green and sported the famous Rolex crown in the 12th hour position. Centered on each plate were alps of mashed potatoes. Strips of tender, breaded veal spiraled down from the potato tops to the plates. Medleys of vegetables and three delicious sauces splashed the concoction. Glasses of Rhine and Bordeaux wines were poured.

Mario stopped to take a bite, then resumed unwrapping. Even the expected was unexpected. Sitting in the velvet lining of the first box was a special edition of the Rolex Oyster Perpetual Milgauss with a unique green sapphire crystal. The watch was engineered to withstand strong magnetic fields and had been tested by CERN scientists. Mario read the technical information to the President after opening the identical match. "They both have the date and time of our luncheon engraved on the watch back," said Mario.

"Lovely, inspect them both for flaws and give me the nicest one." Neither man smiled, and Mario handed the President a watch without inspection as the two ate in silence.

Thinking, I can hardly wait to tell Kovina about all this, the President broke the silence. "One of the missing scientists is a French citizen which makes this issue a responsibility for me on one level. However, the real issue is, why the cover-up? Let me assure you that your honesty and effort will be rewarded with more than a new watch. I don't want to compromise CERN or the LHC in any way. Honestly, I just want to make sure the right decisions are being made."

"I'm certain the Director General and his leadership council feel the right decisions are being made, Mr. President."

"I want to know the names and the condition of all the injured. I want to know why they were transported to a high security Swiss medical facility. . .to which it seems no Swiss official has access approval?"

"I'm not authorized to say anything."

"Tell me what you know off the record, or I will exercise my power to cease LHC activity on French soil."

A waiter appeared. "Would you gentlemen care for dessert?"

"Two hot brandies, please, followed by complete privacy in this room. No more interrupting," said the President.

"Yes, Sir." The waiter exited.

Mario leaned forward. "How much will this reward you spoke of be?"

"One million U.S. dollars in a U.S. bank. Now fill me in, or you will be leaving with French security officers by helicopter after our brandy." The President smiled. "And you will be held in a black hole until I get my answers."

Mario made up his mind. "The exposed scientists have experienced visions of Earth's future and of the universe. It's as if the whole reason for the Large Hadron Collider has crossed over to some freak brain experiment. Some of their revelations have advanced mathematical solutions for theoretical energy and particle phenomena that physicists have been searching after."

"So, they have enhanced brain function and some kind of visionary perception."

"Yes, but the exposed scientists are having problems with normal brain and bodily functions. These have not been resolved yet or even fully diagnosed."

The waiter brought the brandies. When they were alone again, the two continued talking in hushed tones. Eventually, Mario left after thoroughly selling himself to the President.

The President stood to leave. He placed the Rolex watch back into its gift box and noticed the spec card was titled, *The Visionary's Watch*.

* * * *

"I know you're trying, Jon." Gigi smiled the most caring smile Jon had ever seen from a kid.

Jon looked down at the chess board. "Can you see all the variations of the game with each move, Gigi?"

"I don't know what you mean. I just look and know my next move."

"How's your summer going?"

"I'm having fun. Say, did you notice all the new people my friends and I have made for the trains?"

"I noticed, and I love them. Are you taking any summer trips?"

"My parents are taking me to a beach in southern France."

"Nice."

"It's pronounced, Neese."

"Nice is nice."

Gigi laughed. "Are you going anywhere, Jon?"

"I guess I'm going to Africa for the Swönk's summer camp in about a week."

"You will see all the big wild animals?"

"Maybe some of them."

Gigi wiggled with delight. "I could make animals

for our trains."

"What kind?"

"Wolfs."

"Wolves."

"Wol…ves."

"We'll put them on the new train I'm building."

Gigi clapped her hands. "The Orient…it's beautiful!"

"Thank you."

"Will you get another crystal heart at your summer camp?"

"I think I will."

"Can I have it?"

"Yes." Gigi's sweet smile got Jon's real one. "What will you do at the beach, Gigi?"

"There's a chess match in Monaco."

"A tournament?"

"Yes."

"Are you playing?"

"No, my parents are."

"Do you beat your parents?" Gigi's wild-eyed silly faced upside-down smile made Jon laugh.

* * * *

Helena and Kati were sitting in Helena's office. They hadn't really talked much since Kati's change in position. "So, how are you feeling?" asked Helena.

"I'm good."

"Please don't skip any massages or therapy, okay?"

"I'm not skipping."

"Your work has been spectacular."

Kati smiled. "Thanks very much."

"Are you happy with the changes in choreography?"

"Yes...."

"But?"

"Something is still missing for me, I think."

"Then let's figure it out tomorrow. It will be freaky Friday."

Kati laughed. "What's that mean?"

"Tomorrow I want Act II from the top with you freelancing all you want...anything.... Just do it, okay?"

Kati grinned. "Yeah."

"Don't think. Just let go, Miss Hunter."

"Will do." Kati gave Helena a mock salute and laughed as she left the office.

* * * *

Kati took a deep breath. Freaky Friday, she whispered. She burst from the stage side curtain running, reaching for every ounce of momentum. She did a hand spring and bounced off her feet into space. She spun upside-down and then right side up, with her fisted arms extended out. She became a whirling, inverted Iron Cross...straight legged with ankles touching en pointe.

Then she threw a leg out, and landed in a skidding, one knee down, hands up, pistol firing stance. She had a killing look on her face.

"Mizz Hunter," yelled Helena. That was soooo feminine, and soooo swan-like! What the fuck are you doing?"

The whole ballet company stood in silence. No pins dropped. Helena broke into uncontrolled laughter. The crew stared at her in total disbelief. Not one of them had heard the f-word come out of Helena's word-of-God mouth...ever.

Kati gave Helena her silliest smile. Some of the crew went down on all fours from laughing so hard.

*   *   *   *

So, the whispers of a legend in the making became more than a rumor. After her flying entrance, Kati had come down to Earth on freaky Friday. Her ideas of choreography caught the Swan Lake production on fire. Good fire. Kati's strength and grace lifted everyone to a fresh new level of performance and expectation. History was in the making.. .ticket sales history. Everyone wanted to see the new Swan Queen *who flew with angels*.

Ricardo Ottoban II spared no expense to make Kati's world the best. He created custom dressing rooms with every detail designed to fit her body, her mind, and her dreams. He reserved a suite for Kati at the Fairmont and had it decorated it to her wishes.

San Francisco's entertainment spotlight illuminated

Ballerina Kati Hunter to the world. Opening night Swan
Lake seats were being sought at almost any price from a
global audience. Still, Kati stayed Kati, and Helena kept
everything smooth and under control.

* * * *

Hector, the chimpanzee, sat placidly stroking the soft,
white fur of Harry, the rat. Hector and Harry were in a
large cage together. Cardboard placards hand-labeled
with their names were affixed beside the cage door.
Mars strode into the room and watched the animals with
amusement. "Where did those names come from?"

"I let them chose their names," Katy said. Mars and
Katy were viewing the test animals through a one-way
glass in the cage. Katy could control images on the inner
glass walls to give the animals various scenes, ranging
from natural habitats, to predators approaching. Harry
and Hector had an outdoor environment. The room-size
cage contained grass, dirt, trees, flowers, and an
integrated food delivery system.

"How did you go about getting them to choose?"

"I started with the first letter from the alphabet. I
used the food and brain stimulation incentives from the
latest behavior module you stumbled upon. Gave them
options 'til they narrowed it to one."

"The ones you wanted?"

"Maybe." Katy grinned.

"From what I'm seeing, the new brain link

commands are perfected."

Katy typed on her keypad. The chimp put the rat on his head. She typed another command. The rat stood on his hind legs and rubbed his tummy.

Mars laughed. "So, the energy wave splicing technique we've gotten from your brother is working now?"

"Perfectly."

"Can you mirror the results with injectable chemicals?"

"We're getting really close, Mars. We know the exact brain sequencing now. We've also figured out how to impede rational resistance and make any command appear completely logical."

"The Swiss and the French may be moving the injured CERN scientists to our spa for observation and treatment, Katy. They feel like we're on the cutting edge. We could help find out how to use their technology and ours to bring the most to benefit humankind. I know your brother wants to help. Would you also consider working on this?" Mars put his hand on Katy's shoulder.

Katy flexed her neck and hugged Mars' hand with her head. "It would be my pleasure."

Mars took his leave and rode in the high speed elevator from the underground lab to his castle top. He told himself again and again that he'd done the right thing. I couldn't take a chance, he thought. The data from Phobos makes it easy to keep and control her. Katy will never know that I used the technology to manipulate her. It's perfectly simple and completely safe.

*   *   *   *

Mars sat at his desk, pondering his closing summary statement to the Leaders. He typed, "With the acquisition of the Swönk's new mind control technology, we're on the verge of complete success. The CERN accident only confirms the power of this spliced wave technology. The protective devices I've had my team construct offer a blocker halo that assures free thinking. It's not my position to even suggest what you do. I have, however, proven the safety and effectiveness of these devices in my labs. Please consider...you're close to your desired goals. Sincerely, Mars."

Three days later Mars got an order for six blockers. Mars smiled. He'd sold his Trojan horses.

*   *   *   *

"Go! Go! Go!" the Aussie Special Forces squadron captain yelled. "Go! Go! Go!" Jon was the first out of the thick bush. He ran toward the horses tied in a small stand of palms down the beach. Fine white, deep sand made the beach sprint a tortuous thigh burner. CJ, Ian, and the Aussie captain passed Jon, who had started to feel his thigh wearing down a couple of days ago.

The tethered Arabians' ears stood and then laid back as the horses sensed the building tension, and the increasing rumble of the other team's horses approaching.

Jon's team scrambled onto the Arabians. "Stay behind me on the beach 'til I cut to the forest!" yelled the captain. Their horses accelerated like fine sports cars, but the assailant riders were closing the gap.

Jon rode the only filly, Royal. For almost three weeks, Jon and the filly had built their pact of trust. They're behind me now, Jon thought, but she'll erase that. Jon steadied the horse with a hand on her neck as he unlocked the safety on his automatic rifle. Two following riders sighted Jon's back as he reached behind, grasping his saddle left handed. Pumping up his knees, Jon spun 180° in his saddle and snapped off five rapid shots. He scored five face hits on five targets.

Blinded, the two Seals and three British Special Forces members reined down carefully. "Shit!" their leader exclaimed, as he raised his orange paint splattered faceguard.

006½ hovered above the action in a silent Hummingbird, nursing a sprained ankle. He radioed down to the Aussie captain. "Game over," he called, sharing a laugh with the captain.

Jon wasn't laughing. This wasn't a game to him at all. He slid off Royal and stroked her cheek, whispering, "We did that, girl. We did that." Then he kissed her wet hide.

*   *   *   *

Kati walked through the San Francisco Fairmont

suite to get her Swönk phone and pressed number two for Bjen. "Bjen?" she asked tentatively.

"It's so good to hear your voice, Kati," Bjen replied warmly.

"I'm sorry."

"I understand."

"I knew you would."

"Good."

"This is all crazy." Kati walked from the huge view window overlooking San Francisco and the bay from Nob Hill and sat on a beautiful French couch. She started running her fingers though the long, silky fringe.

"I can imagine," Bjen said sympathetically.

"I want you to come for opening night...all of you. Please bring Jon. But I'm calling a little late. The opening is tomorrow night."

"They're all in Africa at Camp, Kati. I don't think...."

"Please, Bjen, please try. I can't even tell you how important this is to me."

"Oh, Kati, we're so proud of you. We will be there. I promise."

Kati started crying. "I need to go...."

"I'll let you know when we'll arrive. You calm down. We can't wait to see you." Bjen disconnected and just sat for a moment, breathing. Time zones, logistics, packing, and clothes started running through her mind.

Her eyebrows went up, and she laughed.

She called the Swönk jet maintenance team. Thinking about what Ian would be doing in Africa, she suddenly remembered an important component to her burgeoning plan. "We don't have any tickets," she said to herself.

Kati called Helena. "I need some tickets for opening night," she said without preamble.

"There are no tickets. I'm sorry."

"Try."

"Impossible."

"What if the President wanted seats?"

"Maybe the Queen of England would let him stand in her royal box…. Kati, dear, we shouldn't be having this conversation. Please, just forget about anything but your preparation." Helena sighed. "How many seats are you looking for?"

"Eight together."

"I'll try if you will promise me you will let go of everything but Odette and Odile, right now."

"I promise."

Helena hung up thinking, I hate lying to you. Solving all the world's problems in an hour would be easier than getting even two seats together. Oh Kati….

*   *   *   *

The hot shower water felt marvelous to Ian. He hoped the tent supply wouldn't run out. This summer camp had been the most intense ever. They had spent two and a half weeks on horseback and camping small. They'd wake up running, eat on horseback, and then perform two hours of hand to hand combat against the Seals and Special Forces teachers. Knife sparring, shooting, combat, horse skills in difficult terrain, hunting for food, and constant vigilance for natural and human predators were all a part of the exercise. In the evening, they'd clean their weapons and study fighting and warfare strategy. Then the next morning it would all start over again, and again.

Today, the camp's end, was to have been a long chase, and Jon had finished it early. So they'd all just come to the home tent compound to spend two or three days for debriefing, healing and celebrating.

Lions roared. Ian's eyes snapped open. He looked through the soft, falling water and over the tent wall to the bank of trees, brilliant in the late afternoon sun. Seeing no sign of the big cats, Ian thought, I can hardly believe Jon made it all the way through this...even with the leg guard support.

Linda's voice called through the tent. "Did you hear that?"

"I did. Go take some pics!"

"Right! Dinner in thirty minutes!"

Jon was sitting at a picnic table with a view of the sunset. As he sipped an ice cold, Tusker beer, he took the roars in his stride. So the camp is over, he thought. It feels like finishing high school, undergraduate, and medical school all at once. And the people I've had to go against around this table are worse than ten damn lions. I wish Kati was here. Jon had a faraway look on his face.

"What are you thinking, Doctor?" the Aussie asked.

A Seal joked, "Probably having sex with one of those cats? Dr. Wolf?"

Everyone laughed good naturedly. This whole gang had fought, bled, and struggled for eighteen days, and now they were a family. "I think he's just wondering how he hit those five face shots today," remarked the Aussie. The five recipients of Jon's marksmanship smirked, wanting to hear an answer.

Ian stood in a striking African print, silk robe at a bamboo bar next to the table thinking, He's a killing machine from another lifetime, my friends. Would that make your hair stand up? He smiled as he squeezed lime juice all over his dark rum on ice before splashing it with Perrier.

The Aussie turned his bright blue eyes on Ian. "And what are you thinking, Mr. Swönk?"

"You wouldn't believe me if I told you."

"No one would!" exclaimed the Seal. The friends around the table roared with laughter.

Linda, who'd just completed the whole camp with the men, walked up with small skewers of roasted game meat, peppers, and pineapple to dip in a dozen different sauces. "Ian, go get dressed. You're not having this meal in your robe, your highness."

Ian headed back to the tent and opened the giant Louis Vuitton travel chest to find the right clothes. Oriental carpets covered the tent floor. King sized beds were slung with canvas to hold mattresses…all the best for the start and finish of Camp Swönk. Elaborate beginnings and endings had been a tradition with Ian's family for almost 1200 years.

Bjen had put on a fit, Ian remembered, because Jon and St. Nick had insisted she and I stop doing these camps together…. We both might get killed. So, Ian and Bjen had agreed to alternate years.

Ian laid his clothes on the bed and went to the leather-covered desktop for another sip of aged rum. Caesar or Napoleon never had a nicer tent set. On a whim, he opened his lap top to check messages.

There was a message from Bjen. "Kati wants all of us 2come2her opening2morrow nite!"

Ian typed, "I'll let you know in the morning. Tonight is graduation. Ha!"

Bjen, who'd been waiting by the computer for his answer, typed back, "Fuck you!"

Ian typed, "Go to hell!" And then waited and typed, "I love you, Sis."

Bjen typed, "Of course you do." Ian laughed and started dressing for dinner.

* * * *

Seven large bonfires surrounded the encampment, just as they had on the first night of the camp. The tradition: seven to start…seven to finish…seven seas…seven continents…seven Swönks at Camp One. Armed security from Abercrombie & Kent surrounded the camp perimeter…. No lions or bumps in the night were allowed.

CJ had everyone laughing as Ian walked up, dressed for another rum. Ian looked at CJ approvingly. The man was lean and rugged. Everyone had lost more than ten pounds during camp. "What did I miss?" Ian asked.

Jon grinned. "A hyena snuck past the guards and came right up to sing some Metallica songs for us."

"Now that's real laugher, Dr. Wolff," Ian said. Jude walked into the picnic area with both arms wrapped around a load of his custom ukuleles. Abercrombie and Kent staff placed more game skewers on the table and a huge wooden salad bowl filled with baby spinach leaves, tomatoes—a rainbow of everything fresh and good. Two of the Seals, Chase and Jared, were just sitting and laughing. Dr. Wolff was in heaven squared.

Jude handed Jon and Ian each a ukulele after he'd tuned them up. Ian's was a bass. "Let's teach these guys how to play and sing tonight," said Jude.

"You've got to be joking," said Jared. Jude just grinned and started playing Bruce Hornsby's "Every little Kiss." Jon played counterpoint, and Ian joined the singing. Linda harmonized between sips of African

Sangria.

Pure fun, thought Jon. If Kati were here, she'd be up dancing, without a doubt.

Patrick and Thomas, two of Ian's leprechauns, brought four clay, baking ovens on planks into the celebration. Each oven contained stuffed wild birds cooked in herbs. The savory fragrance drifting from the ovens made the Aussie remark, "This is too good." No one disagreed.

"Let's get out the gold and glass hearts before people start to pass out," said Ian.

Jon told the two Abercrombie & Kent waiters that were serving grilled sweet potatoes and vegetables, "Tell your team to start taking turns to come eat with us, please. Maybe they should hold it to one glass of sangria, though, or they'll be shooting at everything that moves." Everyone laughed and got the point.

CJ brought out the old, hinged, wooden box that had held the Swönk Camp trophies since the beginning. "I suppose, Dr. Wolff," said Ian, "we should begin with you, since you ended everything so abruptly. Who are you giving your heart to this time?"

"Gigi."

"Who's Gigi?" asked Chase.

"My little six year old friend."

"She already has one," said Ian.

"Now she has another."

Why, Gigi is Jon's surrogate little sister, Linda thought. She's her replacement. He really loves her. Linda's eyes grew moist. Jon came up for the heart. Everyone stood and clapped. The games had been left behind. The honor was for real.

*　*　*　*

When the heart ceremony was finished, Ian asked St. Nick and Linda to follow him while everyone else kept celebrating. Linda ran her fingers over one of the antique, horse head stanchions that marked the entrance of every camp tent. Bjen had bought three dozen of the dramatic hitching posts made in the mid 1880's at a Paris auction. All the posts were empty, however, as the Arabian horses were all tucked away in tents floored with fresh straw.

Linda crashed on Ian's bed, while 006½ sat at Ian's desk. Ian walked around. "Kati Hunter called Bjen. She wants us to come for her opening Swan Lake performance in San Francisco tomorrow night."

"Well, we're not going to try to make it on horseback," said 006½. "We'll take the Blue Swan on her maiden voyage," he said decisively, "and make Earth flight history tomorrow." Nicholas was already typing to Bjen on Ian's computer. Linda just laid back and looked up at the tent's peak tapestry. She knew Nicholas would take care of everything.

"Okay then," said Ian. "I guess I'll go back out to the party. See you guys in a little bit."

"There's just one last small problem," Nicholas said

after Ian was out of hearing range.

"What's that?"

"We don't even have one ticket for a party of seven. Every seat to every performance is sold out to see Kati Hunter dance, and even *she* doesn't have any tickets for us."

Linda stretched leisurely. "Well, I guess I'll go out to the party so you'll have some peace and quiet to get us some tickets."

St. Nick smiled as Linda walked out. He put in a call to the British Ministry of Defense and waited to be patched through.

"Nicholas, so good to hear from you," said the surprised voice on the other end of the line.

"Hello, I hope you're well."

"I am, and you?"

"Quite well, thanks. You wouldn't by any chance be going to the ballet in San Francisco tomorrow night, would you?"

"I am, indeed. I'm in Washington, D.C., on my way."

"Spending the night at Motel Six?"

"The White House, actually."

"I have a favor to ask…. I just don't know how big it is…." There was silence on the other end of the line. "I thought if you have a box or something like that, you might be able to slip in seven more guests…."

"You plus six?"

"Yes."

"You've never asked me for anything, ever, and I've offered."

"I know."

"So, now you ask, and it's impossible."

"I'm asking because this is very important. Do you need me to explain?" Nick could hear the quiet breathing.

Finally, the woman he'd called said, "My box seats eight. I'll be waiting for you with seven empty seats tomorrow night. Someone will greet you at the main entrance. Goodnight, Nicholas."

*   *   *   *

The evening was rolling...into the deep. A rain had come and gone, and a large open canopy sheltered the group's dining table. 006½ fixed a stiff drink, sat down, and winked at Linda. She smiled knowingly.

Nicholas sat sipping. He looked at the tiny blossoms on the stalks of fresh lavender that dressed the table. Linda was eating again. Everyone else held ukuleles. They were learning the chords for the next song Jude wanted them to sing. It was an old Stephen Stills tune which had sold a bunch of records, once upon a time.

Jude was a natural teacher. He sang, and everyone played along. "We are not helpless. We are men. What lies between us, it can be set aside and ended.... All are strangers. All are friends. All are brothers." The ending chorus played on and on. Tonight they were all Africa's children and not far from a birthplace of humanity.

After the Stills' song ended, everyone sat thinking, and listening to the sounds of the African night. In the distance, they heard another lion roar. Oils in the torches and table candles kept the insects out of the Swönk camp, and each person wore CJ's latest invention—a tiny wave emitting button that genus Insectaria wanted no part of.

Jon spoke to the Seals and Special Forces members. "You guys sound pretty good. Maybe you should start a little Commando Band or something. Tell me, why do you all want to be fighters? Is it because, if you survive, you get a pension, medical and tax benefits? Or you don't want to be held down in a boring real job? Why do you want to be professional killers? Are you just bought? Do you all even understand the levels of manipulation, money and misinformation in this world of countries you protect? Ever think about actually trying to fix the problems we fight over, or do you just consider all the mayhem job security? Or is it a nice little getaway from the family?"

The Aussie decided to stop the bleeding. He was a gentle man underneath his veneer of toughness, and he chose not to take offense. "I think we block it out, Jon. My dad was a soldier who fought against Rommel in North Africa for years...."

"And who are you?" Jon interrupted.

"Special Forces. Robot number: fucked up...."

"And you fight against other fucked up robots, while puppeteers on opposite sides keep you all posted on your great cause. I wonder what the puppeteers are doin' tonight?"

The Aussie finally lost patience. "Listen to me, Dr. Wolff. There is reality, you know. It's why we're here, goddammit. Ian's paying us, and Nicholas recruited us by explaining all the whys... okay? Why don't you fix me another drink, Doctor?"

Jon made him a good one. The fires burned down, and everyone's true stories started coming out. "Tell me, Jon," said Chase, where did you learn to shoot like that?"

"I have a friend in Montana."

"Don't tell me. He can shoot a fly off a deer's ear at 1000 yards?"

"He makes custom guns for folks all over the world in his little shop...Uncle V. can shoot."

"And who taught you horses, Dr. Wolff?" Jared asked.

"I have a friend in Montana." Everyone laughed. "His name is Buck and he's something special, too." The party gang listened quietly because every tip Jon had suggested regarding their horses during camp had been simply invaluable. "My friend, Buck, taught me at Palomino Ranch," Jon reminisced. "And my granddad was Blackfoot. Horses were in his blood...wild horses."

"So, do you think we should do away with countries, Jon?" the Aussie asked.

"I don't know if that's really the point. Einstein once said, 'Look deep into nature for answers.' If you just look at how the human body's systems are organized, you see functional harmony based on structural logic...."

"So you think our whole way of thinking is flawed?" asked Patrick.

"What do you think?" Jon retorted.

"My grandparents came from Mexico," Tomás said. They were dirt-poor, transient farm workers. Everyone called me Peon, even my parents. I feel I've been fighting forever."

"What if we could stop the struggles together, Tomás, would you?" Tomás nodded, too emotional to speak. By the time everyone headed for a tent, a new, unbreakable bond was born.

*   *   *   *

Predawn thunder woke Linda. She got up and heated the shower reservoir. Lightening illuminated the trees like an Ansel Adams silver-toned photograph. Near the shimmering wall of leaves, a huge male lion had his paws wrapped around the abdomen of a lioness. In the illumination of the lightning strikes, Linda watched him stroke the lioness' behind.

Linda started the shower and felt the warm water rush down her skin. Darkness returned. She heard someone enter the shower tent and smelled the mixture of rose, lavender and patchouli oils just before Ian began massaging her shoulders, neck and scalp. Light strobed the big cats two more times before they disappeared.

* * * *

Ian entered Jon's tent and stood over his bed. "Wakeup, I have a surprise for you."

"I'm asleep," Jon muttered crossly.

"Come on, our trip's almost over, buddy."

"Sleep is good," Jon insisted.

Ian played his trump card. "Kati called."

Jon lay silently for a minute. Finally, he said, "And?"

"It's a surprise. I'm putting a breakfast tray on your desk with fresh Kenyan coffee. Get up and take a shower. We're going for a ride."

"We don't have cars here," Jon said with his eyes still closed. But Ian was already gone.

* * * *

Jon walked with Ian to the old, open Jeep. Jude had driven it into camp the day before when he'd brought the ukuleles. Jon glanced at the tires. "Those tires are good for about another twenty feet."

"This is Africa, Jon," Ian said as though that explained everything.

"Yes, and Africa is dangerous."

"Not to worry. We've got rifles strapped in the backseat."

"Paint ammo?"

"Real ammo." They climbed in.

Still a little disoriented from the all-nighter, Jon sipped coffee as Ian searched the floorboard. With a straight face, Jon watched Ian start the Jeep with a screwdriver stuck into a dangling ignition switch box. "Is this your idea of first class? Where are we going, Ian?"

"You've got to see this place, Jon," Ian said mysteriously. Jon dropped his head back onto the headrest. His head was pounding, and he felt only half alive.

An hour or so later, Ian geared down and slipped the transmission into low, four-wheel lock. Jon opened his eyes when Ian started to ascend a steep, narrow road through heavy bush. "Wakeup," said Ian, "we're almost there. He smiled. "Actually we've got a long way to go today, maybe even to San Francisco."

All of a sudden, a small elephant was in front of the dusty sienna Wrangler like a mirage in a dream. Ian stopped. The mother elephant charged, and the Jeep started flying backwards down the hillside. Jon dove into the back for a rifle as the elephant's trunk smashed through the glass and ripped off the entire windshield assembly along with Ian's rearview mirror.

With one hand on the wheel and one on the shift

knob, Ian glanced quickly at the precipitous edge. He shifted from reverse to neutral. The beast butted the jeep, lifting the front tires. Aiming between the mother's furious eyes, Jon thought, Her baby…we're the intruders. The elephant's ivory tusk slashed the hood. No choice, Jon thought, and fired…above her head.

Ian started feathering the brake as they drifted away from the turning animal. Eventually, Ian stopped the jeep. Shaking his head in disbelief, Ian turned to face Jon. "I was going to say, Kati wants us in San Francisco tonight." He grinned at Jon. "You've spilled some coffee on your shirt, there buddy." Jon just smiled and fired off another bullet.

Ian reversed the Jeep's direction and drove carefully back to camp. Jon reclined in the back, looking up at the cloudless morning sky. Finally, they entered the compound, and the Jeep rolled to a stop. "I'm glad you didn't shoot her," Ian said as they got out.

"I couldn't…her child. Where were we going, anyway?"

"Up that hill was a spectacular costal view…. Kati wants us at her opening tonight in San Francisco, and Bjen promised we'd bring you, dead or alive."

"Very funny."

"Gale and Harlequin are flying the Blue Swan to Nairobi, so we'll depart at 4:00 a.m. on her maiden voyage. We'll break Mach eleven," Ian said proudly.

"I'm sure that'll be safe." Ian just smiled. "What am

I supposed to wear?" Jon wondered.

"Bjen's bringing your tux."

Jon smiled and sat up. "Why didn't Kati and Bjen plan this sooner?"

"I suppose they both love the drama."

"Hmmm," said Jon, "I doubt it."

*　*　*　*

Bjen texted Kati's Swönk phone. "We're coming & sitting in a private box!"

Kati screamed! Both police officers escorting the star ballerina instantly had a hand on a gun.

*　*　*　*

The large, incoming Abercrombie & Kent helicopter pushed down the grass as it landed. Gale and her husband, Harlequin, who together led Swönk Aviation operations, were off first. Linda hugged Gale as she spoke to her ear, "Everything was perfect and Bjen is ready in Nairobi."

Then Linda winked and said, "You two be careful of the lions around here until you leave in a few days."

Jon walked past Ian with a large canvas and leather tote bag slung over his shoulder and boarded 'copter flight for Nairobi. The weight of the situation began to dawn on Ian. Jon and Kati were really going to be together for the first time in over a thousand years. It was beyond fiction.

*　*　*　*

A small army of security guards surrounded the Blue Swan in Nairobi. Her staircase began to lower the instant the A&K helicopter was on the tarmac. Six of the Swönk gang filed through the humid African night and ascended into the one-of-a-kind aircraft. The craft's sleek, azure, arched wings were molded onto a dramatically designed fuselage, feathered in gradations of lightening blues leading forward to a sparkling, whiteface, dropped beak. The elegant, eye-shaped pilot windshields on this feminine beast would make an artistic designer cry.

Above, the moon was full. The surrounding Kenyan guards had no idea who this princess was, but she was to die for. Bjen greeted Jon as he stepped into the cool interior. She was dressed like a tightly, hooded hostess ready for a 3011 Arthur Clarke spaceflight to Jupiter. Bjen guided Jon though the sweeping circles of woods colored with glasslike and gold composites. She placed him in the rear stateroom.

"Jonny," she said in her best airline hostess voice, "your tux is hanging in the closet. Breakfast is in your kitchen module. Carly is on board to explain and answer questions." Bjen grinned, losing the airline demeanor. "Kati is so happy you're coming!"

"How do I deserve the owner's cabin?" Jon asked.

"Guess," Bjen said and walked away. A striking, circular wall of feathers closed behind her, making Jon's suite private.

Jon looked intently at the lovely weave of feathers

and saw a subtle, three-dimensional tapestry of swans that seemed to reach forever. "Explain the tapestry, please, Carly," said Jon.

"Oh, hi, Dr. Wolff. Nice to have you aboard. Each traveler's suite is bordered by circular bands which project visual waves of light and other little tricks for sight and sound privacy. If the privacy mode is on, as yours is now, your cocoon is secluded. However, you can walk through these walls of light on the entire aircraft. While people are exiting or entering in someone's private quarters, they pass through in a guided envelope invisible to each other."

Jon thought, And you're the guidance counselor who's pushing the envelope to the max....

"Of course, this is our Swönk Flagship, Doctor."

"Carly, did you say that vocally, or just put it directly into my brain's voice thought reception?"

"That's a little secret, Jon."

Jon wagged a finger. "No Secrets, Carly."

Carly laughed. "A little mystery is always good, Doctor. Enjoy your snack. Then shower and put on that *Oh my god* tuxedo, Doctor Jon. We fly in an hour."

"So, when these light walls disappear, the Blue Swan is one big party plane?"

"Exactly. One hour, Doctor."

"You've put some thought into all this," Jon said, but Carly ignored the joke.

"Exploring the kitchen module, Jon found a jug of blood orange juice in the mini refrigerator. He drank some of that while making espresso from a machine placed conveniently on the counter. Then he ate a banana from the fruit bowl before showering.

Pachelbel's Canon in D, transposed to E Minor mixed with ocean sounds, filled Jon's space as he checked his face in the mirror. The luxurious carpet felt magical under his bare feet as he walked to the bedside. The whole ceiling of Jon's cabin had become a moon roof filled with a night sky of sparkling constellations. A calm, tropical ocean simulation stretched to the horizon in every direction from where Jon sat eating cold papaya splashed with lime. Waves broke on a distant reef in synchrony with the piano.

"You're quite the illusionist, Carly," Jon remarked.

Carly laughed. "Your whole life is an illusion, Jon."

"Is this whole plane an illusion?"

"I'm not really sure…." Carly laughed again, but this time she sounded a little nervous. "You stop now before you start some kind of trouble, Dr. Wolff."

Jon thought, Carly feels fear…. But if she read his thought, he got no response. He sighed and retrieved his formal clothes from the closet. The midnight blue tux fit and hung perfectly, feeling like free nothingness. Opening the blue suede shoe box, he inspected the heel spurs. He smiled. The gold and star sapphire is exactly as I wished…. Jon's foot found the card stuffed in his shoe. He dug it out and read, "B00! Love, Patri'cia."

006½'s voice came drifting over the speaker. "We're having a little preflight gathering. Everyone please come forward to the cockpit. Seven minutes to take off."

Jon stepped through the feathered wall of light and was greeted with a crowd of people. "Surprise! Surprise!" Jon just started laughing and couldn't stop.

Bjen came forward and gave him a big hug and a glass of champagne. "On the house," she said. She wasn't a space cadet anymore, but a sexy 1920's Paris starlet. Her costume was replete with a head band, dangling beads, and a slinky dress. She was just missing a smoke. "Will you look at Doctor Wolff!" Bjen exclaimed. Everyone clapped and whistled as Bjen turned him around and around.

Carly had a big jazz band going and people were starting to dance. Jon looked at 006½ who was leaning against one of the walls. He was dressed as an elegant Indian Rajah, with a giant, teardrop ruby centered on his crème, silk head wrap.

CJ was wearing threads and *the hat* designed for the lead in Michael Jackson's "Thriller" rock video performance. Linda was simply Marilyn Monroe, and simply beautiful in her shimmering evening gown of satin and diamonds.

The two pilots are nicely color coordinated, thought Jon. Ian was dressed as a Samurai Prince. At his side he wore a jewel crested, razor sharp sword. He came forward to make a toast for Jon. "Without Jon, we might not have found Kati. Without Kati, we wouldn't be making this historic flight to see the new Swan Queen in San Francisco. And without Swönks…life would be impossibly boring."

Jon raised his glass. "Happy Halloween!" They all touched glasses and sipped between laughs and thoughts.

Jude was dressed as a robed Hawaiian King. He wore a headdress that reminded Jon of the USC Trojan mascot, except that this headdress wasn't plastic and the flowers were real—like every gem and detail in the whole party.

"What are you costumed as tonight, Carly?" Jon asked.

"A bitch!" She led the laughter.

"Okay, listen up," said St. Nick. "Hold onto your eyeballs. Our flight time from Nairobi to San Francisco should be approximately one hour and twenty six minutes, mostly in subspace. For fun, we'll fly to Kilimanjaro and spiral up to altitude and speed to go see Miss Hunter's Swan Lake. Take off acceleration will be substantial, so maybe start praying now." St. Nick laughed. "Seriously, get in your seat and stay there until you hear from me."

Jon sat next to Ian. The Blue Swan was cleared for takeoff. Silently, the passengers felt themselves being pressed firmly into the soft leather seats. Sheets of foggy water oozed into the cabin. There were no engine

sounds, no runway sensations, just speed and two
swans—white and black— floating on the water fantasy
through the plane.

Carly made the entire fuselage a translucent window
that was only encumbered by spiraling shadows. Mount
Kilimanjaro's snow cap shone brightly under the full
moon on the left as the Blue Swan swept into her spiral
up to the edge of space.

Linda said, "We've reached Mach nine. Since
leaving Nairobi, we've been radar invisible or cloaked, as
Mr. Potter likes to say. Plus, why make people worry
about aliens from outer space this afternoon? Our Swan
will clear Mach eleven shortly. We won't be testing any
weapon systems…. Dr. Wolff has already had enough
excitement for one day." Everyone chuckled, knowing
the elephant episode. "Move around if you like.
Cocktails and a light dinner will be served at 4:30 p.m.,
San Francisco time, upon touchdown."

Ian leaned over to Jon. "Have any questions?"

"No, I think I've figured everything out."

"Right."

"The engines seem rather quiet."

"And clean."

"So, are we powered by twisted up rubber bands?"

"That's the backup. Really want to know?"

"Sure, why not?"

"It's a circular system of super cooled and burned

hydrogen and oxygen lasers and layers of magnetic atomic breaking and recombination."

"You've designed the perfect energy source?"

"It's a step, but it requires atmospheric elements, concentrated Earth magnetics, and at least Mach one to sustain.

"What *is* the backup?"

"Engine core fueled mini-jets, if we'd need them. Plus, we have a chute and parasail system that can be released to float us down, or even glide us, if the conditions are acceptable."

"I build my Irish model planes with rubber bands."

"Anything's possible. Actually, I don't think CJ even understands how it works. He just got it right by fiddling around. Maybe it's because he's got some Australian Aboriginal blood in him. His intuitive senses are incredible."

"Maybe he's got that outback, two places at once, magic in him." Jon mused.

"And he's only twenty-two."

"Might have Einstein blood, too. Do you realize how dangerous all this shit you're developing is becoming? If they knew the scope of what you've created, entire countries would be so fearful of your power, they'd want to annihilate you and take your technologies."

"Things are coming to a head, Jon. "I think you and Kati figured everything out before, and you're going to do it again." Jon didn't say anything. He just laid his seat back and dozed.

* * * *

Jon heard his mother's voice over the phone. "Our helicopter took us over a canyon filled with lavender, Honey. The surrounding mountains were so majestic. I've never seen anything like it." Jon opened his eyes from the moment of dream. His visual field was an endless world of sunlight and lavender—what his mom had described from New Zealand in their last words spoken together. Jon whispered, "Thank you, Carly," and closed his eyes to keep the tears in.

* * * *

A few minutes later, Carly's melodic voice filled the cabin. "We'll be crossing the Mississippi River in a moment. We've been cruising at Mach eleven for almost an hour. Deceleration and descent will begin with my next little song. Carly sang, "Nobody does it better." Everybody laughed and eventually joined in.

Jon's sadness was gone. Must have been some kinda spelling bee champ who named the Mississippi, he thought. Carly laughed.

* * * *

The Blue Swan circled over the Pacific and then swooped into a deserted California canyon surrounded by steep hills. With the sun on her back, the Blue Swan's quiet landing had a more normal feel than the take-off, but not by much.

Linda was flooded with emotions as she guided the plane into a discrete, buried, hillside hanger built for this "unknown" off-the-grid military air facility. The camouflaged runways and hanger doors took her back to her time at the Air Academy. However, the recording of Tony Bennett singing, "I left my heart in San Francisco," wafting over the intercom broke the spell.

Linda exited the cockpit and walked back into the plane's interior. She saw that Carly had turned it into a dazzling Paris nightclub. Again, with holographic artistry, Carly had Diana Krall playing the baby grand while Mr. Bennett sang San Francisco's famous tune.

St. Nick poured flutes of champagne to celebrate the historic passenger flight while Jon and Bjen danced slowly, talking. "Who made all those delicious hors d'oeuvres?" asked Jon.

"Carly," said Bjen. "I can't take the credit for that. The kitchen system on this bird might be its most advanced feature."

"Oh?" Jon lifted an eyebrow trying to imagine just how the appetizers had been created. He decided to give it up. "I want to thank you, Bjen, for getting me here. I love you, silly girl." They gave each other a tight hug, before Jude butted in for a dance.

Ian had the other woman on board dancing, so Jon opted for a champagne and lobster treat on Carly's freshly baked, hot crackers. By the time Diana sang Alicia Keyes' "If I Ain't Got You," Jon wanted Kati so much he could taste her. "Some people want diamond rings, but it's all nothing if I ain't got you," Diana sang. "Some people...." Jon was ready to go. He was so keyed up.

They disembarked and walked over to the two Hummingbird helicopters parked next to the hidden hanger door. Everyone climbed aboard a copter and buckled in. Jon didn't even think to ask how the helicopters had gotten there. Linda's copter was off first. She was followed by St. Nick. They headed west for a San Francisco Bay entry over the Golden Gate.

*   *   *   *

The pilots landed the Hummingbirds simultaneously on the Nob Hill, Fairmont rooftop. Four female British agents greeted the group, making 006½ laugh. Three of the agents stayed with the Hummingbirds while the fourth agent, Simone, led everyone to the elevator. When they reached the ground floor, Simone shepherded them through the striking marble columned lobby and out to a British flagged, stretch limousine. "I thought we were Irish," cracked Ian. Everyone laughed as they rolled away from the multi-national flagged Fairmont portico. The gang chatted while Jon slid away into a different time.

Minutes later, the Swönk party was climbing the front steps of the magnificent French Renaissance styled War Memorial Opera House. Jon paused to look up at the sapphire sky. Simone stopped next to him. After speaking softly into her radio, she gave the climbing group some history. "The War Memorial Opera House opened its doors on October 15, 1932. It became the permanent home of the San Francisco Ballet in 1972. In 1940, the first full-length American version of Swan Lake was staged here. President Truman signed the United Nations charter here on June 26, 1945, making this architectural jewel the birthplace of the United Nations…."

History, war and Kati were coursing through Jon's veins. He wiped his forehead. It was as cold as ice. Three very serious looking ushers led the seven Swönks through the exquisite interior graced with decadent beaux-arts trappings. Jon noted their ear pieces and wondered at his party's total clearance, even with Ian's lethal samurai sword along for the ride.

As they approached a box, one of the ushers gestured for Nicholas to take the lead. So Nicholas escorted everyone into the gilded, plush velvet, upholstered box. A stately woman stood and turned. "Let me introduce you all to my Mommy…Queen of England," said 006½. The Queen smiled with a look of surprise that matched those of the Swönks' party.

Luckily, CJ kept all his laughter in his head, and Jon didn't register anything but the Swan Lake program with Kati's beautiful picture covering the front. "Mom got us these seats in her royal box that no amount of money could have purchased," said 006½.

"And this moment is priceless, Your Majesty," said Ian. "Speaking for us all, it is wonderful to meet you." After all the introductions and pleasantries, Jon settled back to read the Swan Lake story. He'd only heard parts of it before, and he wanted to be completely prepared to catch every nuance of the dance.

"Revised choreography," Jon read, "Petipa/Ivanov, St. Petersburg 1895. Plot: On the eve of his twenty-first birthday, Prince Siegfried celebrates with his old tutor, Wolfgang, and friends. They decide to go on a moonlight hunt. At dusk, the prince pauses at a forested lake, taking aim at a magnificent swan. But the swan becomes a beautiful woman. Odette, once a princess, is under an evil sorcerer's spell that makes her a swan by day and a human by night.

Bound by the spell, Odette swims in her mother's lake of tears waiting for a prince to swear the eternal love and fidelity which will free her from the spell. Should the prince's oath of love be broken, she will remain a swan forever."

Jon was on the verge of trembling. God, no wonder she's freaked out, he thought. Our love was forbidden. But this is a ballet, only a story, he reassured himself. Jon's reality was slipping.... He read on. "Siegfried pledges his everlasting love to Odette, but evil Von Rotbart devises a treacherous scheme to destroy the love tryst...." Jon felt his loss, and the threat of the story captivated his emotions against his better judgment.

Not wanting to read more, he looked out over the crowd and then at Bjen laughing with the Queen. Shit, Jon thought. Nicholas' mother is the Queen of England, and he's never mentioned it to anyone? The Swönks have trusted him with everything, and he's a member of the royal family? They could be a part of the group that's against us. They weren't doing Thomas Jefferson any favors…. Look at this! This is for Kati. She's become a superstar….

* * * *

Inya sat just above the orchestra. When Kati had reached Inya through her agent in Ireland, she'd just said, "Yes," without any thoughts about prior commitments or obligations. They'd met in New York City and recorded the vocals together. Now Inya's palms were damp…like her first major live stage performance was about to begin. She could barely sit still. Tchaikovsky's Swan Lake overture began….

* * * *

"There are no words, Miss Hunter." The make-up and costume artist adjusted Kati's sparkling hairpiece and stood to leave as Helena peeked in.

"Two minutes," Helena said.

Kati sat perfectly alone with her eyes closed. She saw the look on her father's face as they'd watched his fellow firefighters running into the Twin Towers on Nine Eleven. She saw Jon running for the baby's carriage. She saw Jonathan Seagull, flying…. She knew Jon was here now, above her. So, she left for the stage with all the confidence in the world, striding, bounding, ascending....

*   *   *   *

Woodwinds introduced romance followed by soft floating strings, diminishing to a single cellist's note. Inya's voice carried that note forward, moving the audience, as the curtains opened, revealing a vertical cleft of natural perfection. An infinite towering arrangement of living flowers filled the backdrop while Inya's voice sang the beauty...until her last holding, wordless tone became Kati Hunter's voice making the vocal moment seem unreal...reaching forever. Kati sang the colors of the melody richly, attempting to harmonize the humans in the great room. Right there. Right then...waking up from history.

Kati leapt in from the curtain's edge, rising into an exquisite midair pose with her face turned away from the audience. To Jon she seemed like an alabaster snowflake. Light sparkled from the diamonds in her hair, and Jon's soul went out to her.

The ballerina's elevation in front of the cascading floral rainbows of purple, red, yellow, and blue seemed to suspend time in a perfect natural world. And then Kati's first soft steps on stage were as dramatic as the height of her leap. With her fingertips just off the floor in a leg-extended, pointing crouch, she very slowly turned her burning, hazel eyes onto the crowd, instantly owning them for the night.

Rising on one leg, forming an arabesque in a pas de deux, Kati spun into traveling turns and pirouettes along the length of the stage as the sound of melting spring infused the vocals.

Her following scene opened to a palette of flowing water and natural scenery...in stunning realism. The earthy combination of rocks, trees, flowering hills, and rivers captured everyone's imagination as Kati stopped on a spinning point. Then, gaining momentum, she executed whip after whipping fouetté, turning wind into creation. Suddenly, she became a floating snowflake again. She jumped across her stage...a grand allegro... into a grand jeté...air-borne splits in magic levels of pristine heaven. Her wondrous, expressive dance continued bringing instruments into the tapestry. With the fully engaged orchestra playing, prima ballerina Kati Hunter burst straight up, spinning a triple tour en l'air. She landed in a sweeping elegant bow, sparkling light from her crown. The orchestra silenced. The audience hushed. The moment waited. Only a single shaft of brilliant light illuminated the ballerina in a room of total darkness.... Then evil came and broke her, dragging Kati away.

* * * *

In the dark, under a black spell, the audience stood clapping. Angelina, Kati's mother, sat in the first row, crying. The darkness and the ovation hid her tears and the looks of fear scattered amongst the crowd.

A ninety-three year old ex-ballerina beginning to sit back down knew exactly what she'd just seen...the triple turning jump...never before on any stage...her elegant perfection...never, ever.... The entertainment journalists were trying to imagine what to say to the ballet world...to the whole world. "Never before in Swan Lake's celebrated history has a ballerina conveyed the Swan Queen tragedy so profoundly...so universally...so beautifully," scribbled one elegantly dressed critic in his notebook.

* * * *

Crescendoing cymbals and calling trumpets preceded the curtain rising for act one. Prince Siegfried's castle garden was filled with revelers, with frivolity and anticipation....

* * * *

Helena entered Kati's dressing room with tears on her cheeks. Kati's makeup artist was prepping her for act two. Kati looked up and smiled but with very little emotion. She squeezed Helena's forearm.

"Keep it up," said Helena. "Just keep it up."

Kati nodded and gave Helena's arm another squeeze before letting her go. The makeup artist resumed as Helena left.

* * * *

Jon followed the enactment he'd just read, wishing

subconsciously that he was the prince down on stage who would find Kati…touch her. Benno, the prince's best friend, danced with strong turns in the air. Then the other party members joined in.

Prince Siegfried clapped his tutor, Wolfgang, on the back affectionately while getting him started on the wine. Siegfried's mother arrived. The prince escorted her into the garden. Siegfried's mother reminded him that ladies would be present the next night for his coming of age ball and for the choosing of a wife. Prince Siegfried, irritated by her commanding nature and disdain for the partiers, never-the-less bent to her will before she departed.

Old Wolfgang danced with young maidens in an attempt to restore gaiety to the party. The whirling partners finally turned his wine consumption into dizziness, and the royal tutor fell, entangled with one of the girls.

As the festivities continued, Siegfried morosely considered his future. Jon ruminated on the character's somber mood. He's feeling his loss of freedom, Jon thought. He feels trapped by having to choose a wife or false love against his will. Then he'll lose his love, Kati, like I did before….

Jon was losing the borders of separation between fantasy and reality…the past…Kati, and the present. His mind ran on in a scattering of images. Her voice…her dance, he thought. She's so beautiful, almost beyond human. Her jump was unreal…unreal. I wonder if we ever truly felt free together in that time we lived before. I know we loved deeply from the rock recordings. Jon thought of the letters his Blackfoot granddad had left for him in Montana.

Wild swans flew over the party on the stage, pulling Jon from distraction. The oboe, harp and strings orchestrated the birds' majestic flight. Benno called for crossbows and flaming torches. Siegfried agreed to the moonlight hunt, but Wolfgang declined. The young men left him standing in the empty garden alone with his wine.

Kati left her dressing room, crowned as Queen of the Swans. She was a still, concentrated point, totally immersed in her character.

Sitting in her box, full of faces she'd never seen before, the Queen watched the curtain rise, revealing a shining forested lake in the quiet of night. As the music resumed, she thought, Nicholas, my son, is this the closest we'll ever be? You're sitting so near, but separated by your friend whom you know better than me.

Quietly, the hunting party entered the glade next to the shimmering lake. To their delight, they found the wild swans drifting peacefully on the mirror of water. They were led by a beautiful white queen whose crown of diamonds reflected the glittering light over the water.

Hidden at the lakeside, Prince Siegfried watched the prettiest woman...part swan...part human...purely dressed in downy, white feathers. Posing in arabesque,

Kati slowly bent her neck and stroked her cheek soothingly against her feathered shoulder. Balanced perfectly, the Swan Queen pierced the crowd's veins with fantasy.

Instantly in love, the prince moved toward the surprised and trembling swan woman, who was pointing at his crossbow. Siegfried promised her protection, and the Swan Queen bowed in grateful trust.

"Who are you? Why are you here?" the prince asked.

Kati touched her crown. "I am Odette, Queen of Swans." Her lovely gestures enthralled all present. "My mother's tears created this lake because Von Rotbart, the sorcerer, made me his captive. I must stay a swan, except between midnight and dawn. But, if I find true love, fidelity and marry, then I shall be free...a swan no longer."

Siegfried swore his love and allegiance, but the magician Von Rotbart, soon appeared at the lakeside, showing his ugly, owl-like face. The challenged prince winched an arrow in his crossbow, but Odette ran between the two men, begging for the sorcerer's mercy. She stopped in extended arabesque and touched the bow. Von Rotbart suddenly disappeared.

Siegfried embraced Odette, and led her into the forest. He explained that she must come to the ball for him to choose her as his bride. In an emotionally elevated mime, Kati replied that she could not attend any ball without marriage first. Moreover, she indicated that she would be murdered if the sorcerer couldn't find a way to defeat their romance.

The prince again swore his love to the Swan Queen. Odette's swans, who were all under the same midnight to dawn spell, danced from the lakeside on pointe with beautiful, fluttering arms. Benno and huntsmen prepared their bows as the music harshened. Odette appeared with Prince Siegfried to intercede for the swans' protection. When the hunters learned of the spell cast over the women, they bowed in apology to the lovely birds. While the cast of swan maidens danced beautifully amongst their new friends, Odette and Prince Siegfried took their leave into the forest.

Jon's thoughts followed their exit. The illusion of the magical ballet continued to affect his hold on reality concerning Kati and himself. I've never felt so out of control, he thought. The past few weeks at camp were intense. We almost got killed by an elephant. During the flight over, I drank too much at the party. Hell, no wonder I feel like shit…. I had to push to get through that camp….

I feel like I'm losing Kati. That's the truth. Everything is about the truth…. I'm finding out about our past, how life cycles. There's a level of fate that I couldn't have imagined. How did we fail before? What happened to us? I'm sitting at Swan Lake with the Swönks. Are you listening, Carly?

The swan maidens started forming picturesque clusters at the stage edge. Benno and the prince entered from the forest at center stage, searching for Odette. Finally in gentle solitude, Kati entered. Jon watched her obsessively.

Posing in arabesque near Benno, Kati touched his shoulder, then moved forward to the tones of a soft harp. She rose to point. Then slowly, slowly she descended to the stage.

She's magic, Jon thought. It's how she saved me. She's magical…beyond our understanding of science.

Kati posed on her left knee with her right leg extending forward en pointe. Her wings enveloped her light movement to Tchaikovsky's score. Siegfried came to her as a solo violin played. He raised her into a romantic adagio, representing their love's beginning.

The Queen of England's gaze left the stage. She searched over the shadows of the audience, and then looked at her guests from the edge of her vision. So, if Bjen is correct, she thought, this Dr. Wolff and Kati Hunter are magically in love. Their first meeting is tonight. Jesus, what a story. Look at him. I can feel his lust for her, like your father, Nicholas. Our love was so short. However, it was completely sincere…maybe meant to be part of all this. It's a new beginning for me and you.

Bjen took a deep breath and centered herself. She came out of the ballet's spell a little. This performance is spectacular, and it's Kati! Our Kati…. She glanced at Jon who was sitting forward with his face in his hands. Jon's crashing, she thought. It's all too much for him. Shit, he's here for Kati and he's crashing.

As the adagio neared its end, the prince turned the Swan Queen slowly on point. Her right foot trembled in petit battements. Then she performed slow pirouettes in his arms until he released her and she fell…. but was caught by her lover's friend, Benno. The move startled the audience until everyone realized the fall was choreographed. The seventeen year old young lady in the fourth row felt a tear run down her cheek. She ignored it.

After a dance by cygnets, two swan princesses performed a vignette signifying "new found everlasting love." Then at last, Kati returned as Odette to dance a variation filled with arabesques. Reaching back with her neck beautifully arched to captivate her audience, she finished with a diagonal of dazzling pirouettes.

First light of dawn approached, coupled with quickening music, while Siegfried beseeched Odette to stay. Von Rotbart appeared, however, and commanded Odette to take her leave as the Swan Queen. The couple conveyed their helplessness while the swans departed. Then the Swan Queen had no choice but to follow them. The huntsmen and the prince looked up to the sound of wings. The curtain fell as they watched the wild swans in flight.

The crowd rose in ovation again. Only three were

still sitting amongst the clapping, roars and whistles. The seventeen year old girl leaned forward, crying in her hands. Both parents turned to her while she started talking to them. "I'm not giving up on my dream. I'm going back to dance. I've got to. She's made me see it."

"Can you make it through the performance, dear?" her mother asked. "Are you okay?" Her daughter nodded, and they slowly collected themselves for the intermission. When they sat down before act three, the daughter had a parent on each side of her, but actually, they were 100% behind her. She was going on with ballet, but, more importantly, she would never be a quitter.

* * * *

Bjen led Jon by his arm into the Queen's adjacent hospitality room. "Are you fuckin' alright?"

Jon looked down at her, smiling. He appeared slightly pale, even after weeks of the African sun. Picking up two Pellegrinos off the bar, Jon remarked, "I suppose this whole thing is finally getting to me."

"Just be yourself, Jon. Relax."

"Maybe I'll go ask the Queen of England what she had for dinner." Jon walked away catching Jude's smiling face before he left the room.

* * * *

Inya reached her seat just before the prelude began for Act Three. She whispered to the ninety-three year old ex-ballerina next to her. "What's your impression?"

The elderly woman responded with a luminous smile. "Fabulous, the stage sets are exquisite, and Miss Hunter has raised the barre for ballet."

Inya squeezed the ex-ballerina's arm and turned to the rising curtain. It opened on the great hall of Prince Siegfried's castle. The hall was filled with towering medieval tapestries. Stone rafters supported the ceiling. A fire blazed in a giant hearth, and there were royal thrones on a dais overlooking an expansive ballroom.

Pages entered with a flourish of music. They were followed by the prince and his mother. The queen felt her son's gloomy, distracted state of mind. "Are you ill?" she asked. "You are acting very strange, son. You must attend to your guests!"

Trumpets announced the arrival of visitors from foreign lands, most importantly, the six prospective brides wearing stunning evening dresses. At the queen's request, the six beauties danced a waltz for the prince.

Siegfried's mind, however, had wandered back to the lakeside meeting with Odette. He hardly looked at the dancers. Finally, prompted by his mother, the prince grudgingly danced with each would-be bride. He went through the movements of each dance with indifference and obvious melancholy. The queen was furious with her son.

Kati felt an electric rush wash over her as she stepped to her stage entry point. She was costumed as the sultry and devious black swan, Odile. Suddenly, on stage, trumpets announced the arrival of an uninvited peculiar couple. A herald whispered to the prince's mother that the woman waiting to be announced was of rare beauty. Then the woman and her escort were admitted, accompanied by the foreboding music of the Swan Queen's fate. Cymbals crashed and there was a moment of darkness.

Then, with great pomp, a tall, bearded knight strode to center stage with his daughter, Odile. Siegfried stared at the woman dressed in black. She was the perfect image of his beloved Odette. Odile returned the prince's gaze with an icy, sexy stare of her own, lighting Jon's fire. In the fading distance, under an arch of the colonnade, the audience saw Odette trying to warn Siegfried. Siegfried's whole attention, however, was on the girl in black, whom he believed to be the Swan Queen.

The prince escorted Odile to the palace garden. Von Rotbart, in his guise as the knight, grinned evilly. He was convinced that his treacherous daughter Odile, whom he had transformed into the likeness of Odette, would destroy the love between the prince and Odette.

While the prince and Odile were gone, Von Rotbart sat next to Siegfried's mother on the dais, and charmed her with flattery and lies about Odile's worldly station. Together, they watched the foreign guests dance divertissements to Spanish, Hungarian and Polish melodies.

Up in the box, Jon sensed the crowd's anticipation for Kati's upcoming Black Swan pas de deux as she re-entered the ballroom with Prince Siegfried. Kati, as Odile, spun wonderful pirouettes between her sorcerer father and the prince. She stopped next to each man in a perfect arabesque. From the prince, she received caresses and looks of adoration. From her father, Von Rotbart, she received insidious instructions.

The two lovers converged at center stage. Odette beckoned again from the distant colonnade, but Odile blocked Siegfried's vision. Odette vanished, weeping in sorrow. Odile and Siegfried continued the pas de deux. The dance ended with Odile standing in arabesque over him, tossing her head in victory.

Next, Prince Siegfried danced a variation to express great love for his supposed Odette. Then came Odile's variation. She fueled the prince's passion with thirty-two magnificent, whipping fouettés, the benchmark, dance performance moment in Swan Lake. Kati, however, sprung from her thirty-second fouetté into a series of traveling turns. The audience erupted into thunderous applause. Only Kati and her orchestra knew of the upcoming surprise for the audience and San Francisco Ballet.

The score tempo increased as Odile flowed into forty-six more fouettés at an even higher speed of revolution, seducing all present into believing in pure magic. The stunned audience watched in complete silence.

At the dance's end, Prince Siegfried asked Von Rotbart for Odile's hand in marriage. As the prince took the oath of fidelity, the music paused. Darkness descended followed by booming thunder. Shrieking violins portrayed Odette's scream as the guests fled the ballroom in fear. Siegfried staggered, hearing the horrible, cackling laughter of Odile and Von Rotbart. He fell to the floor, racked with agony.

*   *   *   *

Wonder embraced the audience as Act Four began with Odette returning to the lake, weeping. The shimmering lake reflected the grief of the swan maidens and their black young. The flock comforted her, but Odette remained hopeless. The swan princesses beseeched Odette to go to the prince who was calling for her in the distance. Odette refused. Instead she ordered swans to surround and hide her.

Siegfried arrived, distressed and searching for Odette. Finally, the swans parted to reveal their Queen. The prince rushed in to embrace her while begging forgiveness.

The couple took their leave into the forest, with the prince offering his eternal love. The troupe of swans continued their elegant dance, while small, genuine waterfalls rushed into the magical lake, making illusions seem real.

Kati returned, her very posture a symbol of grief and forgiveness. She filled the hearts of her audience with sorrow. Odette's beautiful smile in the face of death, joined with the couple's love, overcame Von Rotbart's sorcery momentarily. Kati effortlessly rose on right pointe and fell into Siegfried's arms with her left leg extended in a perfect split...pointing to the stars above the prince.

Then the music stirred, taking Odette away into a diagonal dance of purpose. Glancing back over her feathered shoulder, Odette's eyes conveyed, "Only in death can our love be forever." The violins reached a peak as the Queen of Swans disappeared beneath the lake's surface. Prince Siegfried knowingly followed his lover into the depths, drowning to be with his swan queen.

The prince's dramatic sacrifice destroyed the evil Von Rotbart. As the first light of day dawned over the stage, the swan maidens, bowing in grief and gratitude, rose in freedom. They moved their arms softly, like the ripples forming circles on the lake, bidding a quiet farewell. They were accompanied by waves of sound from Kati Hunter's singing voice until the ballet finished with a cellist's single note. The curtains closed, and the audience rose clapping like a raging storm.

Behind the massive, dark wine curtain, the stage crew rapidly returned the center backdrop into a towering wall of floral beauty. Helena handed Kati a bouquet of long stem, white roses bound in black velvet as the crowd's impatient clapping escalated.

Surrounding their star, the Swan Lake ballet troupe waited to spring their surprise on their beloved Queen. Just as Inya had refused to sing with Kati in the closing vocals, the San Francisco Ballet would refuse to stand before the adoring audience on this special opening performance with Ballerina Kati Hunter. On this night, they wanted everything to be just for her.

The dancer playing Prince Siegfried spoke, "Kati, I'm speaking for every person in this production. Tonight is yours, only yours. You take the ovation alone. It's our gift to you. We all love you. Now, go let that audience love their new, *singing* prima ballerina!"

Everyone was beaming at Kati as they started to leave her alone at center stage. Using every ounce of composure she had to smile and not cry, Kati said, "Oh, no, please. You all worked so hard.... I want you to stay here with me for the first couple of calls at least. Let's take this bow together, my friends."

So the troupe was with her as the great curtain parted. The applause was deafening. They all bowed together, and then bowed again. After a couple of minutes the dancer playing the prince pointed to Kati. The other dancers followed suit, and they all left the stage. Kati was left alone in the spotlight. The applause thundered. The audience understood. Jon couldn't hear himself shout.

Kati bowed gracefully, bending her swan-like neck to lower her crown in respect and love for all present. They'd witnessed her verve and passion. Now each person saw her humility.

Inya noticed the ninety-year old ex-ballerina sitting next to her struggling to take off her magnificent, diamond watch. Inya whispered in her ear and helped her with the catch. As Kati stood with a sweeping gesture of thanks for the orchestra, she caught the eye of Inya. The elderly lady chose that moment to heave the diamond time piece toward the stage. Kati reached down and caught it just above the stage floor. Then she held it to her heart.

Bjen and Jon glanced at each other in amazement. Expensive jewelry started raining on the stage...safely landing away from the sparkling ballerina. The United States President's daughters each handed their dad an earring to throw. He made two perfect shots.

Tears slid down Kati's cheeks as she continued to wave with her palm wide open. Joy consumed her. She skipped like a magical fairy child along the length of the stage amidst twinkling gemstones. She was heading for one last jump. Smiling in total sincerity, she flew with heels kicking up, smacking her derrière. With a wide open wave, she disappeared behind curtain's edge.

Ricardo Ottoban III caught her. Jon watched from the elevated box as Ricardo pulled Kati's face to his and opened her month with his tongue, kissing her

passionately. It was too painful to watch. Jon walked
out of the Queen's box. Bjen turned to follow, but
Nicholas' arm held her in place. "Let him go, Bjen,"
Nicholas said. Closing her eyes, Bjen acquiesced. She
couldn't bear to watch Jon as he moved hurriedly away.

* * * *

Since no one else was leaving the celebratory
conclusion to Kati's performance anytime soon, Jon was
the first person to exit the War Memorial Opera House
front doors and head down the steps. He was numb, dead
emotionally.

It wasn't until he had reached the street and turned
toward San Francisco Bay, that his mind started to talk.
Why? he thought. Why am I walking away from her?
What's wrong with me? I should be going to her, fighting
for her with every ounce. I should be telling her exactly
how I feel about her. I'm tired of all the fighting and
killing.... In his mind he saw the shadowy shapes of
their many lives through-out history, struggling, always
struggling.

Heavy, grey clouds, cloaked by the night sky, rolled
in thunder. In moments they began dropping giant tears.

Jon just kept walking by the bay, going west in the
deluge. Half of his steps were into ankle-deep water.
Every storming raindrop was a sadness and a desperation.

Maybe it's not all just Kati, he thought. My parents
and my sister... my life in Colorado, they were all gone
so quickly.... It was so hard to see Kati's elation in

at the Swönk phone on her makeup table an instant
before it lighted with an incoming call.

"Oh Kati, you're so wonderful...out-of-this-world
wonderful!" Bjen enthused.

"Thank you, Bjen. Um...where's Jon? I told
everyone to let him through. I thought he'd...."

"Kati, this is hard for me at such a moment of
celebration for you."

"What?" Bjen was silent for too long. Kati's legs
began to tremble, so she sat down, closing her eyes.
"Please tell me what's going on."

"Kati, when Jon saw you jump into that man's arms
at the stage edge and kiss, he left our box."

"Oh no. Where is he?"

"We don't know."

Kati felt her heart pounding. She pushed out the
words in a whisper. "That should not have happened,
Bjen. I was defenseless. Everything was out of control.
Believe me. I want Jon. I need him more than anyone,
right now. So, find him for me. Please find him."

"We'll try.... Where will you be, Kati?"

"They're taking me to the Fairmont for a big post-
party. Your name will be with the doorman."

"Enjoy your moment, Kati. Everything is going to be
fine. Okay, dear?"

"Okay. Please get him to come to me, Bjen."

After she disconnected, Bjen sat in the Queen's box,

gathering her thoughts and letting her emotions settle. Then she stood and left to find Nicholas in the Queen of England's hospitality suite.

Everybody in the suite was milling and chatting. Bjen asked Ian where Jon was. Ian shrugged his shoulders. "Don't know, Bjen," said 006½.

"You mean with all our God damn technology, we've just let Jon disappear?" Bjen demanded.

006½ arched an eyebrow. "Honestly, I'm more concerned about the fact that Miss Hunter's performance is going draw a world of attention to her. I thought Jon needed to be alone without surveillance, Bjen."

Bjen sighed. It was fruitless to argue. "I understand. I appreciate your decision."

"Jon left his phone on the plane, so I can't find him that way," ruminated St. Nick. "Anyway, you mingle and let me think." 006½ walked over to the large, non-alcoholic, fruit punch bowl and filled his glass with the ladle before carefully picking out choice chunks of fruit to drop into his drink.

A hand squeezed his shoulder. "I just had a very revealing conversation with Ian Swönk," said Queen Juliet of England.

006½ smiled. "Well, I suppose Ian could even interest a queen."

"He told me how important you are to the whole Swönk family organization. You know, I've never really understood why you left the service…."

"I don't believe you've ever asked me, Mother."

"Sometimes, I wish I wasn't the Queen Mother."

"I didn't mean that 'mother,' Mom. As I'm sure you know, I've come close to dying for dear old England many…I've lost count. Maybe, right before you die, Mother, you'll realize you could of done, or handled things differently, if you'd chosen to drop all the pomp and pretense."

The Queen sighed. "I'm glad you called for my help, Nicholas, and I love you as my son even though we seldom talk."

"Excuse me, please. I'm on duty. Thank you for your help and for talking with me." Nicholas walked away, leaving the Queen next to the punch bowl. Seldom had she felt so ineffectual and so helpless. The one thing she wanted back was this son and his affections, and she couldn't get him with all the power in the world.

* * * *

After crossing the Golden Gate Bridge, LC headed up a hill overlooking Sausalito. They drove along a road of winding curves until a tiny, blacktopped drive entered an arched tunnel of foliage.

By this time, Jon felt like he'd been rescued by an angel. A motion sensor flicked lights on over a quaint, shingle covered home that climbed up the hillside like a stack of blocks.

LC backed into an open carport without even looking. The storm was clearing, and the vista from the sedan's windshield reached straight to the lights of San Francisco across the bay. They sat in silence listening to the ticking sounds of the car.

LC started humming, "I left My Heart in San Francisco."

"You have a sadistic side," said Jon.

LC laughed. "Well, Doctor 'Stray' Wolff, you should visit the Jack London museum before you leave. Don't you think?"

"I loved all his books when I was a kid."

"You seem like the adventurous type, I must say. Let's go in. You can use my guest room to get cleaned up. I'll find some jeans and a sweatshirt that'll fit you."

"Why are you doing this, Elsie? Why would you help a complete stranger?"

"We've already discussed that, Jon...the odds that I'd be down on the waterfront in this storm and see you...your situation...your story, and Miss Hunter's Swan Lake. Maybe Jack London is looking out for you, Doctor Wolff.

So, let's go in. I'll make some hot tea. You'll get dry, and we'll figure this Kati thing out together. And I'm sure your friends are quite concerned about you, too, mister. You need to call them."

They opened a weather-beaten, antique door and

walked into a home-made elevator. LC pressed some unmarked buttons, and up they went. LC led Jon into a commodious guest room. Before shutting the door, LC handed Jon a phone. "Call your friends," she ordered.

Jon entered a number that he knew would transfer a message to Ian. "Sorry I snapped," he recorded. "I'm fine. I'm going to stay in the bay area until I figure out what I need to do. Please tell everyone…thanks."

Less than a minute later, Ian got the relayed message from a blocked caller number. After all Jon had been through, Ian was glad to hear his calm and logical sounding voice. Ian walked over to Bjen. "Jon's fine and staying here. We are going back without him."

Bjen made a big happy face, causing Ian to break into laughter. "I guess we should leave Jon and Kati alone," said Bjen.

"Remember those words, Sis." Bjen punched Ian in the chest, drawing inquisitive stares. Then she walked over to the Queen. The Queen's security watched her intently. 006½ just smiled at the whole display.

* * * *

The Fairmont Hotel on Nob Hill was surrounded by fire trucks and police cars. After weaving through the blockade, Ian finally put a hand on the superstar's shoulder from behind. Kati turned and threw her arms around him. During their long, hard hug, Ian whispered into Kati's ear, "Jon's staying in the area. We're all so proud of you, Kati!" Ian stood back and grinned.

"Maybe you could autograph my napkin?"

"Wait for my period, and I'll autograph mine."

"You and Jon really do deserve each other, crazy woman." They both laughed. "I guess you're stuck in the Odile character, Kati."

"You tell me, Mr. Swönk. And tell me when Jon is coming, too."

"Tell Jon, 'hello,' when you see him," Ian replied. Kati stared into Ian's eyes, waiting. "Our plane is always waiting to bring you and Jon to Ireland when you are ready, famous lady," Ian added awkwardly. Then someone with cameras came and took Kati away.

The Swan Lake party went on till 2:40 a.m. When the celebration finally straggled to an end, the Swönk group flew back to the Blue Swan. They boarded the aircraft, and everyone crashed in various states of undressed mindless sleep.

* * * *

Kati sat with her bare legs crossed on the wooden table. She was wearing silk panties. Her undies perfectly matched the elegant, oriental silk shirt that Zchen had sent her. Tiny silk covered buttons fastened along the right of Kati's collar in soft loops.

The long, wooden table was up against a picture window that overlooked the entire bay from the upper level Fairmont suite. Kati's tears dripped off her cheeks and onto the silk blouse. Kati didn't care. She was crashing, shaking. There had been no word from Jon.... Finally, she lay down on the table and cried herself asleep.

*   *   *   *

Jon sat up on the bed, taking a moment to remember where he was. He was in a large bedroom. The walls were painted a colonial blue with white trim around the door and window. He noticed a piece of paper pushed under the bedroom door. "A note from LC," he read. Jon realized then that she wasn't "Elsie," as he'd thought before. "I'll be back about 2:40 p.m.," the note continued. "I've taken your dress watch to a jeweler to get some of the water and fog out."

Looking over to the antique wall clock and seeing 3:30, Jon whispered, "Geez," and headed for a shower. After his shower, Jon put on the jeans and navy sweatshirt that LC had thoughtfully provided for him. He left the hood of the sweatshirt up over his wet, blond hair. The mirror on the door reflected the three Native American canoes that decorated the chest of his sweatshirt. The design brought his grandfather to mind. I should read through all his letters again when I get back up to the cabin, he thought.

He walked down the hall toward the staircase. On the tiny landing, a lovely classical guitar hung on wooden pegs against the wall. Jon ran his finger along the smooth edge of the curved body, and then peered in the sound hole at the Alvarez mark. He took the instrument and started down the circular iron staircase toward the kitchen.

* * * *

In her dream, Kati was traveling with Jon in an old truck. They'd been driving for a long time, and the air smelled of heat and dust. Jon took his right hand off the wheel and placed it on Kati's bare inner thigh. He gently moved his fingertips around.

There was a lot of static on the radio, but Kati could hear, faintly, a country song about "a pickle in my face." I've never heard that song before, Kati mused. Jon's hand was moving up and raising her jean skirt. He's so close, Kati thought. I'm opening my legs for him.

"What's this parachute rip-cord doing in here, Kati?" Jon asked suddenly.

"That's my bloody parachute. You must've slept through your feminine hygiene class at Princeton, Dr. Wolff." Jon tugged the slender cord gently. Then he flicked the tampon out the open driver's window. "Good Gawd! You nut head!" Kati yelled.

Unfortunately, a low slung, racing motorcycle passed at exactly that moment. The rider caught the little, wet projectile on her upper helmet visor. The rider sped on ahead, then eventually stopped on the roadside. Long, red-dyed hair fell to her shoulders as the biker lifted off her splattered helmet. She glanced up to the sky as Kati and Jon passed by in preoccupation....

* * * *

Jon took out a bottle of French Bordeaux from the refrigerator and wandered outside. He sat on the stainless steel picnic table with his bare feet on the bench seat. He sipped some of the wine and looked out over the bay. I know you're over there, Kati, he thought. I love you, even though I don't really know you.

He picked up the guitar and began to strum the chords of "Light my Fire," by Jim Morrison. Switching to finger picking, he whispered the words, "Come on baby, light my fire. Come on baby light my fire. Try to set the night on fire…."

LC sat on her rooftop deck listening to the Doors' song coming from her dead husband's guitar. She thought of the huge bonfire at the 1968 Doors' concert here in San Francisco that they'd gone to half stoned out of their minds. She remembered all the police, all the craziness. She took another drag on one of the few cigarettes she allowed herself each month, and the tears welled in her eyes.

Jon changed the tempo. He slid into, "Gonna try with a little help from my friends, get high with a little help from my friends…. What would you think if I sang outa tune…."

Jon finished the Beatle's hit and went right into "Georgia on My Mind." He sang the song through soulfully, and then took another sip of wine. His thoughts drifted to the bagpipe sounding guitar riff in Cold Play's "Every Tear is a Waterfall." Using Chet Atkin's high/low

note technique could work, he thought, as he started
searching for the fabulous Irish band's wailing beat...
which only led back to Kati and one last song he'd heard
Diana Krall perform in Paris. "Each time I see a crowd
of people, just like a fool, I stop and stare. It's really not
the proper thing to do, but maybe you'll be there. I go
out walking after midnight along the lonely thoroughfare
...." LC was staring across the sea at Nob Hill when a
small gull swooped down to land on her bird cabin roof.
Covered with split wine corks, the quaint bird cabin was
home to LC's very own "Jonathan Seagull." The bird
settled his feathers, and then tipped his head and looked
directly at her. I can't believe this, she thought. She
stood and left for the elevator with a smile on her face.

A few minutes later she joined Jon at the picnic table.
"I see you've fixed yourself a nutritious meal there."

Jon smiled at his new found friend. "Where have you
been?"

"Listening and smoking my cigarettes. I think White
Fang isn't the only soul streaming through you, Dr.
Wolff." LC placed the San Francisco Chronicle on the
table next to Jon. "Your friend certainly set the town on
fire last night."

Jon saw the bold headline, "Miracles and Magic."
He looked out across the bay, lightly strumming chords.

LC picked up the paper and read out loud. "Yes
Ma'am! We Believe! Ballerina Kati Hunter's debut
performance in Swan Lake was simply unimaginable in

its perfection and power. With a worldly audience watching her pure eloquence, San Francisco's new prima ballerina lifted hearts and spirits by dancing AND singing! And, when the final, endless ovation was shaking the Opera House, diamonds, rubies and emeralds magically rained down, letting 'our home town girl' know how much her new fans loved the spell she'd cast upon them. Now we can believe in miracles...thanks to you, Kati. From her first smoldering gaze...." LC stopped reading. Tears glistened on her cheeks.

"See," said Jon, "you can't handle Kati, and you weren't even there. I can't even eat. I may never eat again. No more water, only wine."

LC almost choked laughing while she blew her nose. Jon sang and played, "Ol' Stewball was a race horse, and I wish he were mine. He never drank water. He always drank wine...." Jon had LC's spirit soaring by the end of the Peter, Paul & Mary's old hit tune.

LC went into the kitchen and returned a few minutes later with a tray of food. She put a large plate of hot eggplant and cheddar sandwiches down next to Jon, followed by a salad of shrimp, baby spinach leaves, tomato and avocado. She took away the bottle of wine and gave Jon a giant, frozen beer mug of fresh spring water.

Jon played a few licks of Still's song, "Love the One You're With," making LC laugh. He put the guitar down and dug in.

"Your girl's not far away," LC said, "but you flatter me, Jon. I've never seen anything like this. She's got the whole front-page story."

"I guess it's amazing that she bumped all the war updates right off, huh?"

"We've got too much sad news. It just goes on and on." LC paused and then continued. "I think Kati is sad." Jon didn't look up from his food. "I also think you and Kati are scared to be together because of all the danger you've attracted to each other. From what you've told me, I understand.... Are you going to read this article?"

"You read it for me."

"It says here that Miss Hunter has locked herself in her Fairmont suite and won't see or talk to anyone." Jon kept eating while his heart started to pound. "Wouldn't you like to know if she's in there alone?" Jon was silent. LC pushed on. "I have a plan to get you in and surprise Miss Hunter."

"Let's hear it."

After LC outlined her plan, and they had climbed into her car, she said, "You haven't asked me any questions about my late husband."

"I felt you'd talk about him if you wanted. I'm just a dangerous stranger."

LC laughed. "You are a very nice man, Jon. Thanks for being sensitive. Do you really feel like we're still strangers?" LC started driving down the hill. They were headed to Kati's hotel.

"You know I'm kidding. We were friends almost instantly."

"Well, I lost my husband almost three years ago. He had brain cancer, glioblastoma. It's ironic that you're a brain doctor of sorts."

"Mmm?"

"It's ironic that his name was Jonathan."

"Please don't start picking up everyone you see walking in the rain."

"You have the same sarcastic wit."

"How long were you two married?"

"Twenty-six years."

"Wow."

"He was a wonderful economics professor at Stanford. His students loved him. Jonathan tried to teach them the truth."

"That can be difficult at a major, public university, sometimes."

LC felt hair rise on the back of her neck. "What do you mean, Jon?"

"There's a lot of informational truth to teach in every field. It's the truths that teachers leave out or *have to* leave out to keep their jobs, which contribute to the lies that plague humanity."

"That problem tormented Jonathan every day."

"Money and economics...lots of illusions. Did you two discuss everything?"

"Everything."

"Maybe one of these days you'll discuss everything with me."

"With you *and* Kati."

"You're on...if she'll ever speak to me after what you've talked me into doing."

LC laughed and stopped her silver sedan barely eight inches from the delivery vehicle entrance door. Pulling out her phone, she quickly texted something. The giant metal door began to rise, letting LC drive into the bowels of the Fairmont Hotel.

LC's theatrical make-up artist friend had already done most the work. Jon's blond hair was now black with big bushy side-burns and a matching mustache. Heavy, black-rimmed Aristotle Onassis-like glasses with tinted lenses sat on his face.

The hotel manager met them with a smirking smile. "Hi LC, I really hope this doesn't blow up in our faces, Dear. This young lady could probably run for governor and win."

"Hush Bryan. You're helping make her day." She turned to Jon. "Call me, Doctor...when the time is right, okay?"

"You'll be the first. Thanks for everything, LC. He

wanted to hug her, but he just patted the rooftop of her car as she drove away.

Bryan kitted Jon out in a Fairmont captain uniform. In less than thirty minutes, Jon was pushing a selection of hors d'oeuvres and drinks on a linen covered cart down a wide hallway towards the "Kati Suite." Bryan had already escorted Jon through two points of security.

Jon practiced his fake voice with a French accent. His feelings of craziness and insecurity were gone. Tapping firmly on her door, he called out, "Special delivery for Mademoiselle Hunter." He knocked again and repeated his phrase.

"I'm busy," Kati responded. "Just leave it at the door, please."

"If you please, Madame, just inside the door would be best."

"I'm busy writing. No distractions!"

"S'il vous plaît, Miss, I must have you sign."

Kati thought, what the crap is this? The service here has been fabulous until now. She got up and walked towards the door, while closing and tying her robe. On a lark, Jon put his eye to the peek hole just as Kati looked out. "AAWW!" she screamed and jumped backwards, having peered into the eyeball surprise. By the time she landed, Kati was pissed. Striding briskly, Kati swung the door open. She was ready to kick the delivery cart over!

Jon backed up and started rapidly speaking. "Pardon,

Miss, this is my first day of work. Please 'forgave' me."

Kati laughed out loud at the sight of waiter's glasses and wild hair. "I'll 'forgive' you, just."

Jon pushed in by her, heading right into her room.

"What are you doing?" Kati started to object. Then she looked at the waiter's jawbone and scar. Just as Jon started to turn from placing the cart at her window, Kati tugged the right sideburn off his face, then the moustache. There was no laughter or talk as she gently removed the silly glasses and tossed them on the table.

They stared into each other's eyes openly, tenderly, like they had been needing each other for hundreds of years. Then Kati removed the rest of Jon's disguise and opened his shirt. She ran her soft, warm hands up his chest, then made a streak of kisses down his stomach. She unbuttoned his black trousers. Jon opened Kati's robe and let it drop to the floor. Then he lifted Kati in his arms. His mouth devoured hers.... They dropped every chain and gave each other everything. In that moment, in that time, there was only Jon and Kati. There was no one else in the world.

Jon carried Kati to the bed, and they pinned their glistening bodies together. "Come deep into me, darling," Kati murmured. "We're safe."

The door to the suite had been left ajar. A young Cuban hotel maid looked in the room. Then she slowly closed the door. Leaning against the wall, she shut her eyes, feeling weak kneed and breathless. "You bring me joy," she'd heard Jon say as he kissed Kati continuously.

*   *   *   *

It was dusk. Kati was draped over Jon with her cheek on his throat. "We've slept. It's going on night. I love being away from the world with you, Jon." She spoke in a soft whisper, her eyes shut.

"Could you move your lovely face just a little, so I can talk?"

Kati giggled, "But I like hearing your voice right from your throat.... Do you believe in love at first sight?"

"First sound."

"What?"

"I started loving you the moment I heard your voice."

Kati pulled herself up till her lips touched Jon's. "Well, hello, cowboy." Kati started lightly running the tip of her tongue around Jon's lips. Closing his eyes, Jon drifted off into heaven.

*   *   *   *

They shared one pillow, nose to nose, legs woven. Kati's hand was down with her fingers gently stroking Jon's scrotum. He was spent. They were in bliss. "I've listened to pieces of conversations from our past life together that were pulled from stone on the Swönk properties in Ireland," Jon said.

Kati sighed. "I almost wish you were lying."

"It's possible we wouldn't have found each other

without our past."

"What was your childhood like…in this life?"

"I grew up in West Texas…started a rock band when I was seven.

"Now you are lying."

"Nope."

"What instrument did you play, Jon?"

"Guitar."

"What kind?"

"A Gibson Les Paul…like the one George Harrison played."

"Bullshit. I have your balls, Jon." She squeezed them. "So, how many pickups did it have?"

"Two. Cherry red, solid body with onyx tipped vibrato stick and onyx tuning pegs. Flat wound strings," he said in a rush.

"So, who got little Jonni-Be-Good-Wolf this famous guitar?"

"Santa." Kati squeezed. "But, I think my parents were in on the deal."

Kati smiled. "You must've gone crazy on Christmas morning."

"I'd already found and played it."

"What! You sneaky little wolf! Where did you find it?"

"In the hall closet, behind the long coats. I had to

polish off my finger prints each time I played before Christmas."

"You scare me, sly wolf. You're a damn spy!" Kati jumped out of bed and ran for the shower laughing. Jon was hot on her trail.

Kati adjusted the water to a stinging, hot spray, and they started soaping each other. Shampoo suds foamed as Kati worked Jon's head. She jumped up and locked her legs around Jon's waist. He kept his balance even though his soap-covered eyes were closed. "Are you trying to flip me over, Miss Hunter?"

Kati laughed. "What color was the inside of your fancy guitar case, poo head?"

"Bright, mango orange. It was thick and fuzzy, Miss Interrogator."

"Where did you get that wig and paraphernalia, Dr. Wolff?"

"From a friend of LC's."

"And who is Elsie?"

"The woman who picked me up in the rain storm after your performance."

"Oh, and where did she take you?"

"To her house." He took Kati under the showerhead to wash out the shampoo. She dropped down on his erection. Jon opened his eyes and pushed Kati's back up against the marble shower wall.

"I don't suppose you played the guitar for this Elsie?"

Kati asked with a catch in her voice.

"She's old enough to be your mother."

"My mother's very beautiful."

"So are you." Kati pushed, moaning. "Who was that guy who stuck his tongue in your mouth after the big jewel throwing, standing ovation?"

"That shouldn't have happened."

"You'd never seen him before?"

"I dated him because I'd been fantasizing about you." Kati put her hand over Jon's month. "Shut up," she gasped, "and fuck me hard!"

* * * *

Jon and Kati were using the hotel's thick, Turkish towels to dry each other off after the shower. "So," Kati concluded, "Elsie set up our little date here?"

"This isn't a date, Ms. Hunter-Wolff." Kati spewed laughter. Jon arched an eyebrow. "Is that funny?"

Kati stopped drying Jon off. "No, I guess I'm just happy you said that."

"I'm happy to be near you." He hugged Kati and their two hearts pounded together.

"So," Kati said solemnly, "we're married now...or maybe again?"

"Tell your mom that you met a bellman at the Fairmont and got secretly married."

Kati laughed. "My whole family will love that story,

especially my brothers!"

"What have you told your mother?"

"That we were lovers in a past lifetime."

"What did she say?"

"Nothing, she just closed her eyes."

"Really?"

"Then she said that our family had left Ireland to get away from the Swönks." Kati kept a straight face.

"You're kidding?"

Kati left Jon standing, astonished, in the bathroom. She walked into the sitting room and picked up the phone. "I'm starving. Let's order room service to celebrate our reunion," she said with a lovely smile. She placed an order for a generous meal and then asked the concierge, "Could you hold just a moment, please?" Kati put her hand over the mouthpiece. "Jon, are those things the only clothes you have?"

"Yes."

Kati looked carefully at Jon. Then she removed her hand from the receiver end of the phone. "Thank you for waiting," she said. "Could you also send up three pair of men's Levi blue jeans...say thirty-two waist, thirty-six length and five flannel shirts...high quality...two large, three extra large?" She smiled at Jon. "Anything else?"

"Could you ask the concierge to forward a message to Bryan? Tell him everything's great. Tell him thanks and ask him to tell LC."

Kati frowned, but she relayed the message. "Oh, and three extra large men's Fairmont terrycloth robes, too, please," she ordered.

* * * *

Moonlight streaked across San Francisco Bay. One candle burned next to the giant window as the lovers dined. Under the table, Kati's bare feet rested on Jon's. Kati poured more wine. "Do you like the dry Riesling?"

"Yes, and the sweet."

"That's dessert. Then I'll light another bonfire in your spine."

They touched thick goblets. "You do kindle me," said Jon, looking into Kati's eyes. He cleared his throat. "I can't imagine this is standard hotel glassware."

"It's not. They're Danish crystal. I chose them."

"I love the design…the heavy feel. Besides all my clothes, what else have you chosen around here?"

"I decorated this suite."

"Well, you have great taste. Do they let other people stay in the hotel now that you're holed up in here?"

"You got in."

"I had to sneak in wearing a disguise, and I had insider help."

"Promise me you'll always keep teasing me and telling me your stupid jokes."

"What jokes?"

Kati laughed and slumped back in her chair. "I'm so full."

"The moon is about to disappear."

Kati turned. "How beautiful. It's like an old black and white photograph."

"Ansel Adams. The band of light across the bay.... It's the same as our medieval dream...me riding behind you...our horses walking across the lake on a strip of moonlight. I remember the hidden path beneath the water surface...I'm your guardian...."

Kati was falling into hypnotic trance within the dream. "We'd just left a castle," Jon continued. "Someone had betrayed us. I'm watching your shoulders. I have my sword and bow, and I'm ready to kill for you."

Kati picked up the story. "Finally, we left the lake and entered a labyrinth of tunnels in a thicket." She paused and shook herself. "It's what I saw in the hospital, Jon, when you were in the coma. Oh God, I'm afraid of losing you. We'd broken your guard's oath of celibacy." In her mind, Kati was seeing the past superimposed on the present.

"Well, I'm glad it was only my oath we'd broken, and not yours."

Kati didn't laugh. "Jon, our history is repeating."

"Thou speakest truth My Lady. My strict church upbringing in Texas required that I promise strict celibacy before getting to move from the diaper stage. And they threw in 'thou shall not kill.' However, our pastor worked part-time at the army recruiting center next door to the church."

That did it. Jon had broken Kati's spell. "Will the bullshit ever stop, Cowboy?" she asked.

"That's what I broke in here to figure out with you, My Lady."

"That's your main reason for breaking in here?"

" I have two main reasons," Jon said, smiling. "End the bullshit and love you."

"Alright then," said Kati.

*   *   *   *

Jon swished the mouthwash around and spat in the sink. He soaked a small towel in hot water and scrubbed his face, neck, and hands. He walked back into the bedroom. Every curtain in the room was closed, making the suite dark. I have no idea what time it is, he thought. He slid under the covers next to Kati. He pushed his belly against her lower back and wrapped his right arm around her. She took his hand in both of hers, putting it on her chest. Jon nosed into Kati's hair for her smell. He whispered, "I like your choice of mouthwash." Kati was quiet. "I like your choice of man." Kati didn't respond. Jon kissed Kati's neck. "What was your dressing room like at the Opera House on opening night?"

"Pink leather, black and beige silks," Kati murmured

lazily.

"Mmmmm," Jon hummed and then sang in a low raspy voice, "Oh, Donna, oh, Donna…. I've gotta girl. Donna is her name. Since she left me, I've never been the same. And I love that girl, Primadonna, is her name. Primadonna, Primadonna…."

Kati rolled Jon onto his back and grabbed both his ears, pulling them out from the sides of his head. "Listen, Dr. Wolff, you can't imagine how hard I've worked to reach the top!" Their nose tips were touching. Jon kissed her. She kissed him back. Kati spoke softly, "Do you know any more appropriate old songs to sing for me?"

Jon hummed, then sang, "You ask me if there'll come a time, when I'll grow tired of you. Never my love. Never my love…."

Kati sang along. When the piece ended, she said, "You have a nice voice, Jon. I think I'm going to keep you."

"You and Inya weren't bad either."

"You liked the whole performance?"

"Kind of, but I'm not certain anyone else was impressed." Kati stayed silent. "You said you like me teasing you."

"Maybe you're just a little too good at it."

"I'm the valedictorian of tease, Ms. Ballerina Hunter-Wolff."

Kati looked at Jon and cracked up. He'd put her make-up sponges behind his ears to make them stand straight out. "I'm afraid my ears are ruined," he said mournfully.

"Well, I'll just have to pin 'em back, Doctor." Kati shrugged on one of the plaid shirts she'd had sent up for Jon and went over to the phone. "I'm calling room service. What do you want, Jon?" She bounced back onto the bed with the phone.

Jon gazed at her legs. "I'd like a muscle biopsy kit, an electron microscope and maybe a mass spectrometer."

"Stop staring at my legs, Doctor."

"I just want to analyze your leg musculature to figure out how in the hell you can jump so high, you little freak of nature."

Kati turned her attention to the phone and proceeded to order almost every type of fruit Jon had ever heard of. When they had eaten, Kati pulled the curtains open. "The sun's nearing mid afternoon."

"Another day, another dollar," Jon said brightly. "How long *are* you planning to keep me locked up in here? Your Dad's likely to axe down the door pretty soon."

"Twisting things around a bit, aren't you, Doctor Wolff?"

"Hunter-Wolff, I like the sound of that. How about you?"

"I like it, but is it real or a fantasy, Jon?"

"If we stay in here too much longer, we may lose touch with the difference, Kati Hunter-Wolff. But, speaking for myself, I've found you and I'm not letting go."

Kati wrapped onto him, with her head on his chest. "Tomorrow I'll make calls and start again. I needed this time away, and I need you. I know that now. I'm not afraid anymore." Kati started to cry. Jon held her tightly. "I didn't really understand what I was afraid of, Jon. I have never been fearful of life or challenges. Finding out about the Swönks and my link to them was overwhelming. But this whole time, I realize it now, it's been the fear of losing you that's been tearing me apart."

"Me now, or me past?" He kissed the top of her head.

"All of you."

"Our love now has to be our strength, our bond. Going into your ballerina world as a superstar and exploring the world of the Swönks…the fight…. The combination could be insane."

"Not for us together."

"You think?"

"*I know.*"

"We can't be afraid of anything, of dying or losing each other…."

"If you die, I know what I'm doing."

"Hmmmm?"

"I'm coming after you."

"Isn't that some ballet story?"

"I'm not sure," Kati said innocently. They tumbled around the bed laughing, but Jon's eyes were very wet.

* * * *

Jon watched as Kati did her dance workout in the hotel suite. She'd be hitting her head if these ceilings weren't so high, he thought. Kati started a new song, "Born to Be Wild," and started dancing around Jon on the bed. This turned into a "try to catch Kati" exercise for Jon. Catching became wrestling until they were breathless, and Jon had Kati pinned down on the floor. They started to laugh. Then Kati grew serious. "Let's have a special dress up dinner tonight, Dr. Wolff."

"Dress up?"

"We'll wear our matching, terry cloth robes. You pick all the food and drinks." Kati gave Jon a vivacious smile to confirm the plan.

Jon started looking at menu choices. After some consideration, he asked, "You want to hear what I've picked out?"

"No, I want it to be a surprise."

"And what's my surprise?"

"What I'm wearing under my robe."

* * * *

Jon put a large tip on the bill and just signed, "Kati,"

for fun, which, of course, was no problem. The table looked elegant. In the distance, outside the window, San Francisco Bay was filled with sails.

As Jon lighted the tall hand-made candles, Kati walked from the dressing room. Turning, Jon's eyes embraced her. "You are gorgeous, ravishing, everything...."

"Thank you, handsome."

Jon sat Kati at the small, formal dining table set for two.

"Everything looks lovely," said Kati. "Have you been to this restaurant before?"

Jon smiled. "Never."

Kati glanced out the window. "Look at the sun on the sails!" Jon just looked at her looking. "You didn't look, Jon." Kati felt the rush of her blush in response to Jon's gaze. Kati had her hair up, and she sparkled in diamonds. Finally, she said, "What's in the ice bucket, Dr. Wolff?"

"Pink champagne."

"Shall we have some?" They touched their glasses, "Are we still crazy after all these years?"

"I suppose so."

"The seafood and vegetable brioche you picked is delicious, Dr. Wolff. Will you promise to bring me here again?" Kati ran her stiletto heel along Jon's leg under the table. "I mean it, Jon, will you bring me here again and again?"

"Whatever you wish, Kati. It's our sacred place. These are our sacred robes."

"Wolf girl and wolf man."

"Hunting for the truth...a new religion."

"To Hunter Wolves." They sipped, smiling. Picking up the remote, Jon started some soft piano music. "I know that song," said Kati.

"Name that tune."

"I can *play* that tune. It's Peter Kater's, 'Spirit.' I was listening to it the morning I found you bleeding in the street."

"I was listening to it when I woke up that day…. I remember now."

"Truthfully, what do you think is going on? What do you believe in?"

"I try not to just believe things without evaluation, honest evaluation."

"You just joked around when you talked about your Christian upbringing. Do you have Christian faith?"

"Do I believe Mary had artificial insemination? Do I believe she was cloned from some "more official Mother Mary" that just happened to be passing by on an alien spaceship that day?"

Kati persisted. "What do you believe, Jon? What do you have faith in?"

"I have faith in 'the good, the bad, and the ugly.'

And by association, Clint Eastwood, I imagine."

Kati smiled as she got up to head for the bathroom. "Keep talking. I'm listening."

"What? You can't stand to be in the same room with me when I share my beliefs?"

Kati walked back in, carrying some scissors. "Sit still, and this won't hurt."

"You just got this sudden, insatiable urge to give me a haircut?"

"Shush. This won't show at all, Jon. Talk about the good, bad and ugly...."

"It seems to me that for a long time now we humans, individually and in groups, have done things…good, bad and ugly...to gain leverage over other people, other life forms, and our environment."

"For personal benefit?"

"For perceived personal or group benefit…and sometimes for an overbearing, competitive 'survival of the fittest' viewpoint."

Kati cut some of her own hair and began to weave it with Jon's hair. "So you see the good, bad, and ugly in religions, business, politics, and...?"

"Banking, heath care, media, education, sports…. Everyone's trapped in layers of games that have formed a weave of complexity for thousands of years...." Jon looked at Kati's hands. "What are you making?"

Kati made a final trim with her tiny, sharp scissors

and handed Jon a perfect woven ring of their hair. He inspected her creation. "This is incredible. It's beautiful. How did you make this?"

"Put it on your left ring finger, please."

"It fits perfectly," Jon said with a smile.

Kati handed him a second, smaller, woven ring. "Would you place this ring on my finger?"

Jon slipped the soft circle onto Kati's ring finger. "I love you, Kati.

"And I love you, forever."

"Forever," repeated Jon. "I believe in forever now." Kati smiled.

* * * *

They were dancing slowly in the dark. Only Kati's heels were on carpet. Her silk-covered toes stayed on Jon's foot tops.

"You're able to keep up with my fancy dance steps pretty well," Jon joked. "I'm impressed."

Kati pressed against Jon more tightly. "We lost track of our discussion."

"So we did."

"What's sacred to you, Jon?"

"From what standpoint?"

"From every standpoint."

"The truth...our lives...our capacity to care for and love one another…those things seem sacred to me.

That's the good sacred. However, 'sacred lies' have been
created to manipulate people and enslave them, get them
to kill and steal. These lies get people to give away
precious time in their current lives so that their
controllers, whom the slaves are not usually aware of,
have the greatest freedom and luxury. And in our
modern world, the human slave game has become quite
sophisticated, and the bad and ugly games are bringing
down our ecosystem and railroading billions of people
into highly stressed, barbaric lives.... I don't seem to
leading anymore," Jon said abruptly.

Kati danced Jon backwards until they crashed on the
bed together. "I didn't think ballerinas wore this sexy
lingerie stuff," Jon teased.

"And I didn't think valedictorian doctors from
Princeton were this naughty." She sat on his chest. "Just
how do you define 'barbarism,' Doctor?"

"A barberian is someone who bursts into the room
with scissors and cuts another person's hair without
permission...or is that barberism?"

"You are full of the dopiest humor I've ever heard."

"It's my disease."

"And I'm your addiction. Don't ever forget it." She
worked her hips down his torso.

*   *   *   *

They breathed in quiet synchrony. Every moment
deepened their union. Jon felt the band of hair on Kati's

finger. "How in the hell did you make these rings so quickly and so perfectly? There are no knots. The weave is so tight."

"I've done it before, in the past, for us. I just made them without thinking, sort of following the past superimposed on the present. We coated our rings with gold last time, magically, with our minds. Oh God, I feel like we're in *The Wizard of Oz,* and that the people who almost killed you are connected to the wizard somehow."

"Are you Dorothy? Then who am I?"

"I'm Dorothy, and you're my little yappy dog, that Cairn terrier.... What was its name?"

"I can't remember the dog's name. I don't think that question was on my medical board exam."

"So, do you think the people who have been against the Swönks all this time are like the wizard in Oz?"

"In a way. It seems that they've isolated themselves and built systems for controlling human activity so that the activity falls within the design of thinking they've decided is best...righteous, or whatever. Rather than designing models for humans to work together in harmony within natural laws for mutual benefit, the power controlling elite has created systems of people working in what is now a huge mish mash of money games. Very few people on Earth now have access to the 'God given' rights… to food, water, and shelter, etcetera, that the worms, snakes, turtles, and *swans* have freely available to them."

"And our chemical toxicity and energy toxicity is threatening all life forms," Kati chimed in. "We're all trapped, and the Swönk's have been trying to stop this nightmare for thousands of years."

"You and I have been part of the Swönk's effort and...here we go again."

"You said, 'God given,' Jon."

"What I really mean is that human beings have the gift of thinking to figure out solutions. They have the ability to figure out that loving, caring and logic, should out-weigh the manipulations of a mind controlling few who maneuver people into hate, war, slavery, and even disease, both physical and mental."

"All the toxicity...all the cancer...all the research without the essential truth," Kati mused.

"Exactly. It's 'The Sound of Silence'...ten thousand people, they listen, but they do not hear...."

"Thank you, Mr. Simon and Mr. Garfunkel. But we live in fear. We're afraid to speak the complete truth."

"And we deny it, as we play the mind and money games the wizards of Oz have laid out for us, such highly educated, stupid souls."

* * * *

A few hours later, Jon and Kati continued their conversation. They were lying comfortably in bed together. Kati's head was pillowed on Jon's shoulder. "Have you been thinking about what you and I need to do in order to help solve all these mysteries and dilemmas the Swönks are faced with?" Kati asked.

Jon stroked Kati's hair. "It might be a factor of combinations—substance... energy... thoughts... timing... you, maybe me, a human connection."

"What in the hell are you talking about?" Kati kissed Jon, then looked restlessly out the window. "The moon light is so bright in here. It makes you look so pale. I'm afraid, Jon."

"Don't be scared." Jon wrapped his arms around Kati and they breathed quietly together for a few minutes. Then Jon started singing softly, "And so it was later, as the miller told his tale, when a face at first just ghostly, turned a whiter shade of pale...."

Kati joined in and they sang the song together. They were silent for a few minutes after the song ended. Then Kati grinned and punched Jon lightly on the arm. "What's your favorite brand of catsup, Jon?"

"Maybe we've known each other for thousands of years, but don't you think that's a little too personal and embarrassing a question to ask?"

Kati spooned herself tightly against Jon's back, hips and legs. "I want to know all your favorite things and what you consider a perfect life. I'm serious."

"Organic Heinz catsup is the last condiment that I remember purchasing, Mizz Ballerina."

Kati kissed the back of Jon's head.

"Do I get a little head kiss for every correct answer?" Jon asked. Kati kissed his head.

"Sometimes, I get a bottle of Lucille's homemade catsup at the Boulder restaurant."

Kati kissed him again. "What's your perfect life?" she asked.

"Plenty of catsup." There was no responding kiss to this answer. "Time to incorporate the good experiences of life into every day," Jon continued. "Time to see patients, play my guitar and talk with friends. Actually, most of my patients are my friends." Kati kissed him again. "Time to search for the love of my life, and, although the search turned out to be a little rougher than I'd hoped, I found her." Kati gave him a kiss and a hug.

"I try to get outside every day to be in the beauty of nature," Jon said, warming to his subject. "I try to bike, take a run, or a hike. And I love gardening. I was preparing an area of fertile soil for a garden and greenhouse before you started playing in my blood." Kati kissed him. "I like coaching kids' soccer and basketball. Sometimes, I play on a men's league basketball team." Kati kissed him.

"I'm studying how to influence aspects of healing on molecular levels with Ian and some other research scientists." Kati kissed him. "Now, I'm going on a little adventure to risk my life with a girl who likes to dance on my feet." Kati rolled Jon over, and their kiss was very long.

*   *   *   *

In Kati's dream, insects were singing to the pulsing rhythm of the humid rainforest. A wisp of cool air wafted over the Mayan royal youth who slept peacefully just before dawn. The youth's name was Aléjondro, and he was dreaming that he was deep in the jungle's restricted zone. But Aléjondro was without fear. He walked silently forward.

Mayan mystics had passed down the legends of dense rings of ground fog that marked the territories of animalistic sacred beings. Aléjondro knew the legends to be true as he stepped into a wall of mist. Within moments, he began to feel changes throughout his body. His chestnut skin stretched with expanding musculature. Coal black hair thickened on his head and chest. Streams of water mixed from the fog and his inner heat dripped from Aléjondro's body. He saw flashes of golden light.

Then, as he passed through the innermost, fourth ring, Aléjondro's body changed into an aged man's. Shades of green jungle foliage filled his peripheral vision, yet wherever he focused his sight, only cold, white snow glistened.

"You come without fear and without permission little master," a powerful, gruff, masculine voice stated. Aléjondro looked, but could not see the voice's origin. Finally, he closed his eyes, and a handsome jaguar appeared to him. The jaguar was resting on an outcropping of rust spotted rock. "You're very young to

look death in the face," said the jaguar.

The majestic beast was completely still, yet his black coat had a sheen that spoke of limitless speed. Tiny piercing pupils blended into the cat's dark irises, conveying unlimited will. Aléjondro looked at the jaguar and felt that he was gazing deep into space. "My eyes are closed," Aléjondro said.

"And a sense of humor too, I see." Aléjondro was quiet and still. "Maybe you are the one to carry the vision of the future to your people."

"How much can you see?" Aléjondro inquired. The jaguar gave a throaty laugh. "What difference will a vision of the future accomplish?" Aléjondro pressed gently.

"Thinking becomes reality, bright youth." Aléjondro waited. The jaguar's tail switched. "Tell your elders to end their record of calendar time with the current twenty-six cycle. She will come then. The Mother will reign. You will be there, Aléjondro. Go now, with this prophecy, and be young again. You have my blessing."

*   *   *   *

It was 6:26 a.m. Kati peeked out of the door hole and smiled because no eyeball was peering back at her. Then she flashed on two black cat eyes and wondered why. She tipped the porter waiting on the other side of the door and took the breakfast cart. While she was pushing the cart toward the window, she decided it was time to turn on her cell phone. It rang at 6:31. "Good morning!" Kati said brightly.

"Well, good morning to you," responded Helena.

"Thank you, Helena, for being so understanding and for letting me disappear for a while."

"We're all traveling in uncharted water, Kati. But I think it's time to sink or swim, dear. I've agreed to schedule a press conference in the Fairmont ballroom today at three. We both should be there. Kati?"

"Helena, I know my contract requires that I make appearances for San Francisco Ballet, but I'm not sure I'm ready for this today."

"Consider doing it, Kati. I'll call you back at 10 a.m., alright? We'll meet beforehand to prepare you."

"Alright, bye."

Helena sat thinking, God, how could she create such a performance and now be an introvert! She shook her head in frustration.

Kati took some chips of ice and began placing them in Jon's hair. "Wake up Jonny, I need to talk with you."

"Is this some kind of new therapy you've dreamed up, Nurse Hunter? You like bugging patients first thing in the morning, eh?"

Kati laughed. "You are so predictable, Doctor. Do you want coffee or juice?"

"Both, please. Separate containers though."

"Shush. Helena wants me for a press conference at 3:00 p.m. today."

"Sounds like you're about to go from ballet to Barnum & Bailey."

"Be serious now. I need to make some decisions— with you, not without you." She propped up on pillows, putting her feet into Jon's lap. He started massaging and examining Kati's left foot. Kati winced. " God! That's tender there!" Jon separated and lifted her metatarsal arch before re-testing for pain. Kati smiled. "The soreness is gone, Jon. You've got magic paws. I want you to be my traveling doctor."

"Sorry, I'm not the entourage type anymore."

"Seriously, I want to go on a trip with you, alone." Jon stretched her heel and worked into her gastrocnemius. "Oh wow, that's heaven."

"Not too titillating, I hope."

"I want to go to West Texas, where you grew up."

"I haven't actually grown up yet, and West Texas isn't very titillating, either. It's as flat as all the cement driveways. We should go to the Tetons." Kati opened the top of her robe. "I thought you wanted to talk. I'm going to lose my concentration."

"You got off on all the titty talk, Doctor."

Jon started on her other foot. "Do your nipples always get that hard when you get a foot massage?"

"Well, I don't know, Doc…tor."

"That's a pretty good West Te'jas drawl you got going there Mizz Hunter-Wolff."

"That settles it, then. We're going."

*   *   *   *

They were lying wrapped in each other's arms, just breathing. Jon said, "I'm going to miss you every moment."

"Me, too, like you said, though, we shouldn't be seen together right now. I'll finish the Swan Lake performances. Then we'll meet in Texas."

*   *   *   *

Cameras clicked and rolled as Kati walked towards the podium where Helena waited. Kati wore a striking, grey suit with a pleated skirt showing a bright, yellow plaid that matched her canary silk blouse and high heels. A brash reporter at the front of the Fairmont ballroom stood. "Where have you been these last days, Miss Hunter?" Kati's silent, sly smile graced the high definition screen that towered behind her, causing a roar of laughter to erupt on the packed, standing-room-only floor.

Unbelievable, Helena thought. In the back of the massive, chandeliered hall, Ricardo Ottoban III, alone, exhibited no trace of humor.

*   *   *   *

Mars sat staring at the face of the San Francisco ballerina on his computer's international news screen. Then he began typing commands to retrieve the video recording of Dr. Wolff's OP accident. Flicking through blown up facial images of the woman delivering first aid, he put the clearest next to the ballerina's face on his monitor. "Unbelievable," he whispered to himself.

*   *   *   *

Bjen and Gigi were in Jon's room back at the Swönk castle. They were giving Jon's model train a trial run in celebration of his anticipated return. "Doctor Wolff is going to love that cute little elephant you've made for his train, Gigi," Bjen said.

"I hope so. When will he be home?"

"He'll be coming in later today on the Azure, our newest plane."

"Will I ever get to fly on your plane?"

"I'm certain you will, honey. I'll talk with your mom and dad about a trip soon."

"I would love that!"

Bjen felt true joy from Gigi's excitement. Gigi added another passenger to the Orient Express coach as Ian walked into the room. "I just got off the phone with Kati. She wants to plan a trip to Texas with Jon." Gigi was as still as a deer, listening intently with her hand poised on the train.

"Has CJ got that pickup truck finished yet?" asked Bjen.

"He's doing the final engine and kitchen tests. I must say, it's unbelievable. I almost hate to give it away."

Bjen laughed. "Let's send them to Texas in the

truck."

"They may never come back."

Bjen looked over at Gigi. "What's the next traveler on the train going to be, Gigi?"

"A ballerina." Ian and Bjen glanced at each other with their eyebrows raised.

*   *   *   *

Katy rode up alone in the high-speed lift, rising from the level four lab that was cut deep into the mountain below the spa. While sipping from a small espresso cup, she reached into her sweater pocket feeling for the box of dark, chocolate truffles that she'd just injected. She stepped from the elevator and walked nonchalantly through her ground level apartment. Then she crossed her stone patio and started down the alpine hillside towards the trail that encircled Mars' castle grounds.

Lupine and edelweiss brightened the meadow. The rich smell of the woods enhanced her confidence as she climbed into the cove of rocks where Chelsea waited.

Katy sat down on a boulder next to Chelsea. She popped a chocolate into her mouth before turning to kiss Chelsea's opening lips. Their tongues rubbed the dark sweet taste back in forth. Chelsea's inner thigh reached across Katy's lap as hands roamed to peak sensations. Katy withdrew and placed another truffle in Chelsea's mouth, leaving her finger tips there for Chelsea to suck.

"Remember to push this data chip into the port just after you initiate the monthly financial run, okay, darling?"

Chelsea nodded as she continued to lick and suck. "Then pack it as I've showed you. Leave at exactly 9:00 p.m., and I'll get in at the last hairpin before the main bridge. Any questions, baby?"

Chelsea shook her head, "no," and received hand-fed candies. After Chelsea had been gone for five minutes, Katy injected her wrist with the antidote serum for added protection against the chemicals in the chocolate and Mars' chemo-wave control.

*   *   *   *

Michelle and her husband were in the French Presidential suite. They were sprawled on the bed, fully clothed. The French President had just returned from a round of difficult meetings. "Does that feel good, darling?" Michelle asked as she massaged through the navy suit coat covering the President's shoulders. The injured CERN scientists have arrived at the Swiss Spa for observation and therapy. Your influence was fantastic!"

The French President rested his head against Michelle's lower belly, "Thanks."

"You sound depressed, dear."

"It's not that. My approval rating has never been so low."

"You can move past that concern now, dear.

Remember the visions we had at the spa. We're coming
to a new world order...beyond the European Union and
the other blocks. France is on the verge of transition, and
life here will never be the same again. But, together, we
can lead our people through the changes from outside old
government.... It will be so much better, baby. He
exhaled deeply as she softly caressed his cheek.

Michelle continued happily. "The CERN
scientists are having universal visions. With an expanded
understanding of our brain capacity, we have a chance to
win this last minute race to save the Earth and ourselves."
Michelle leaned down and whispered in his ear. "And,
I'm pregnant." The President's heart pounded.

*   *   *   *

Ramey walked into the Swönk's subterranean
meeting room and sat at the large, black rock conference
table. "Nice of you to join us, Satchmo," Ian remarked
sarcastically.

"Sorry I'm late. The conversation with Mars was
prolonged. And then, on the drive back, I was starting to
get really scared, scared and depressed." Satchmo
gravely looked at his friends, Jon, 006½, Bjen, CJ and
Linda seated around the table.

"Go on," Ian prompted.

"Mars says his controllers have initiated viral seed
sprays on human populations. His airborne drones will
control the various hosts' cellular functions. I've gone

from fearing for Katy's and my life to sickening sadness over how these people are manipulating life systems. The intent is so wrong."

Everyone listened in stone-faced, serious thought. "Did he comment on the target zones, the plan designs, or time lines?" Ian asked.

"No."

"Maybe Mars is bluffing to get something else," Jon ventured. Satchmo looked at Jon. "He wanted to know the details of your gene jumping research, Jon."

Jon steepled his fingers. "CJ, you and Carly have to figure out how to cloak.... Let me back up. We need our bees to have the capacity for chemical and biological assay. And we need to find a way to cloak life forms and or destroy fabricated bio-weapons." A tear dropped off CJ's eyelid. He closed his eyes in silence. Carly went to work on all Jon's requests.

Satchmo cleared his throat. "Mars asked if Doctor Wolff had any connection to the ballerina from San Francisco, a Kati Hunter?"

"He either saw an accident report, or watched the event live," said Carly. "He's connected her."

006½ stood and left the room. Jon's mind ran....

Later that day, Bjen placed a long-distance call. "Hello girl! I can't believe I caught you."

Michelle instantly recognized her old friend's voice. "Hi, Bjen! I've missed you so much, dear! And we missed our annual ski trip. Shit! Everything's been crazy."

* * * *

To be continued.
Check WeThink360.com for sneak previews. . .

I Just Know Love

360

About the Authors
and Other Important Things

Who actually wrote this story, anyway? Well, it certainly wasn't one person.

But for now, if you'll bear with us…let the authorship be a mystery. And please, before you put this book down or share it with a friend, remember that the purpose or intent of the whole *IJKL360° Series* is to nurture the harmonious blend of nature, technology, and humankind.

The path that Jon, Kati, and friends follow in the second book of the series, *I Just Know Love 360°…from my friends*, leads to the optimal, sustainable communities we love on Earth. We think you will enjoy Jon and Kati's adventure. We predict that it will never end. A preview of the second novel follows to get you started on a journey that's filled with music and fun, and yet fraught with perils.

Hundreds of interviews with people like you and me have played a key role in developing the current and future plot of the *IJKL360°* story. Some of these interviews have evolved into comprehensive discussions concerning what we can do pro-actively to help ourselves, our communities and the planet.

Please read the following account of a discussion between Dr. John Day and Mary Magdalena. Mary Magdalena has been a beacon for positive sustainable agriculture and healthy communities. Her interview with Dr. John Day led to the formation of The Mary Magdalena Sustainability Awards which will be presented by WeThink360.com. A portion of the revenue from the *IJKL360° Series* will be donated to the winning contestants who present optimal solutions for sustainable life systems within our communities.

Visit our WeThink360.com website to read about The Mary Magdalena Awards Contest and to learn details about the *IJKL360°* Reader's Rewards System. You can receive points for prizes derived from your book purchases, donations, or referrals! *"Awesome,"* is a good word to describe what Jon and Kati are cooking up for all of us with a new type of lotto for reader! You are invited to the party! Check out the WeThink360.com scene!

* * * *

To Be Continued...

Mary Magdalena's Meeting with Dr. John Day

One fine day, John walked into my country market in Boulder County, Colorado. When he approached the desk to pay, I asked him about the novel he'd been writing. He jokingly said it was most meaningful and entertaining, but that he couldn't finish without my seven minute interview to go in the back section of the book. Come to think of it, maybe he wasn't joking.

About a week later, we met on lawn chairs in the yard next to my store, Mary's Market. John asked me what my wishes were…with no boundaries. He asked me what I thought mattered most and what was missing in our world of human activity. I told him, "We need to act from our heart value…our spirit, and not just from our thought." We talked about what we'd both learned about life, love, people, education, money, health care, communities, and raising children in our many years of experience. All the good, the bad, and the ugly.

My seven minute interview was about to go beyond three hours. My staff came to check on me. A bee flew onto my forearm and stung me, painfully. John, being a doctor, instantly opened his black bag and whipped out a medicinal oil to treat me on the spot. God only knows what else he carries around in there! Laughingly, Dr. John didn't even bill me for services rendered! He explained to me that after thirty years of treating patients' pain and stress-related problems, he'd decided to come up with a better strategy to erase the root causes.

Dr. John told me that the story he's writing for novels and films has an international cast of characters who discuss and solve most of the highly stressful, bad and ugly situations that we've been observing and experiencing throughout our lives. The weave of his plot follows the characters through a maze of traps that run parallel to the layers of humanity that we've created...from the richest to the most destitute. John and I discussed our traps...past, present, and future, and this discussion led to his punch line, or shall we say, "punch question."

He asked me, "Would you come to a small community gathering held three hours a month, if you felt that the format of conversation and thinking could truly solve our myriad of problems?"

I said, "Of course."

However, my mind was racing. This mop-headed doctor was suggesting we could solve most our individual and global dilemmas by getting together for three hours a month. Much of my life has been dedicated to exploring new ideas to improve education, our families' lives and our communities. I've worked with many respected organizations and internationally known people. Now here was John sitting next to me, suggesting that we could overcome the failure factors...and he'd be the catalyst of the formula for success.

I've been around. I looked hard into John's blue eyes and made a decision. I said, "We can do *We Think 360°*

events in my art studio where I teach children's art camps."

John has tested me. I have tested him. The story he's begun for us to co-create with him may well be the greatest tale of this century..."*making our wishes come true.*" We are true friends.

The Interviews

The back section of each novel in this series, along with the WeThink360.com website, will always contain interviews with people like you and me. During the interviews we will try to ask questions that may serve as catalysts, questions like:

What are your wishes?

What matters?

What is missing in our world?

What is your biggest stress?

What should we fix?

In this way we hope to start a dialogue, a discussion that will bring a cooperative effort for change.

The First Interview

My name is Jared. My passion is what I call agricultural alchemy. I am twenty-seven, and have worked with organic farming for several years. I want to keep exploring the best ways to bring nutritious food to our tables while engaging people in the experience of sharing good life values with the Earth. I believe we can all live comfortable, joyful lives without harming the soil or other living systems.

My wish would be that we could have pure love between people with a heart-felt vibration that could overcome the barriers which have plagued us for so long. I feel we are missing the time to come together and share our viewpoints. We could discuss issues like the apparent disastrous effects pesticides are having on birds and bees! If natural pollination fails, what is next for us? Hopefully, the WeThink360.com projects will help fill that void. What matters most to me? I would desire to give back or create more than I consume. My biggest stress is giving interviews…just kidding!

IJustKnowLove360°

PREVIEW

Jon & Kati

...from my friends

ISBN: 978-0-9892032-4-1

2

Canyon

1:25 p.m., somewhere in Texas

"Miss Hunter, we'll be landing in ten minutes. Please plan to be seated with your belt on in five minutes. I'll have Jenny check in with you." Nicholas' announcement flowed over the speakers in Kati's private bedroom. The bedroom looked just like a regular bedroom in a posh hotel. It had a bed, a desk, an easy chair, and a well-appointed bathroom, replete with terry-cloth robes. You'd never know from just looking at it, that the bedroom was located in the tail of the Swönk jet, Azure, the Blue Swan's smaller sister jet.

After toweling off from her shower, Kati pulled on a short jean skirt and wild, pink socks covered with little cows. It's a shame to cover these socks up, Kati thought,

as she wiggled her feet into pink cowgirl boots. I'll have
to remember to wear these socks with loafers some day.
She heard Jenny's knock as she finished her ensemble by
pulling two layers of wickedly sexy t-shirts over her
bounce of strawberry blond hair.

"Time to sit and strap in, Miss Kati. We want you
safe! May I come in?"

"Certainly."

Jenny stepped through the holographic wall of
woven feathers. "Well okay, Miss Texas!" she exclaimed
admiring Kati's outfit. "Now you just sit right here."
She secured Kati into a harness and a seat that would
protect her, even under extreme crash or fire conditions.
Kati was having so much fun that she just kept smiling.
"I'll be back right after we touch down to help you with
all your needs," Jenny concluded. Then, as she turned
briskly to leave, she remarked, "The tail's the safest place
to be, you know."

* * * *

Jon chose a road he'd never traveled before. Cruising
in the turquoise '60 International pickup, he felt at home
on the small, two-lane highway, going easy through
ranch country. He hadn't been back to his roots in a long
time. The direction he was taking and the old, familiar
look of the land should've evoked lots of memories and
feelings. Yet, all he thought about was seeing Kati.

"I'm going to be a little late," he whispered to
himself. He lowered his foot on the gas pedal. As he

pushed the speed past 60…70…80, the truck body automatically lowered and various airfoils rose from the coachwork. Leave it to CJ, he thought. This thing goes like a NASCAR racer. He turned on his Swönk phone and brought up the GPS. 006½ had programmed the private airstrip meeting site into the application. The man left nothing to chance. Jon smiled. He was sure that 006½'s reputation for exactitude was something he and Kati would be laughing about soon.

*   *   *   *

Touchdown. Kati felt nothing, but sounds of wind filled her stateroom. 006½'s voice sounded pleasantly over the intercom. "Welcome to West Texas. We have a slight, September breeze and eighty-four degrees under a clear blue sky."

The fuselage walls around Kati became translucent, revealing endless fields of waving grain in all directions. They were miles away from any prying eyes. Robots developed by the Swönk company, EET, maintained the secret facility meticulously.

They taxied to the turnabout next to the entrance road and prepared for immediate take off. 006½ checked Jon's ETA on his screen before he stood and walked into the main cabin. Kati sat next to her packed, earth-toned, leather cases. She was sipping ice-cold lemonade. She looked up at 006½ as he came in. "Want one?"

St. Nick smiled. "I'll wait on that a bit. Jon will arrive in less than twenty minutes, Kati."

"Then I think I'll get off and wait outside. Y'all can leave."

"You have a good *y'all* going there, Miss Hunter, perfect diction for our current location. However, leaving you alone in the middle of nowhere is not so wise, even with Jon coming soon."

"It's what I want."

"I suppose we could take off three minutes before Jon's arrival, as long as we activate a bee team around you."

"Deal." They waited companionably for a few minutes. Then Kati disembarked, and 006½ returned to the cabin. He adjusted his instruments and altered his liftoff to protect Kati from turbulence.

Jon saw the jet depart and floored the gas pedal. He sped onto the runway and spied Kati's sprawling baggage seat...a little late...unfortunately. As he pulled over to a quick stop, Jon hit some soft dirt, creating a dust storm...a big one. Kati disappeared. Shit, Jon thought. He hopped from the pickup, and waited for Kati to reappear.

*   *   *   *

To be continued.

Check WeThink360.com for sneak previews...

Yours forever, Jon & Kati

Story by John ~ Editing by Ann